MURDER AT THE TOWER OF LONDON

THE KITTY WORTHINGTON MYSTERIES, BOOK 4

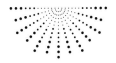

MAGDA ALEXANDER

HEARTS AFIRE PUBLISHING

ISBN-13: (eBook) 978-1-943321-16-2

ISBN 13: (Paperback) 978-1-943321-20-9

Hearts Afire Publishing First Edition: October 2022

CAST OF CHARACTERS

Kitty Worthington - Our amateur sleuth

The Family

Mildred Worthington - Kitty's mother

Edward Worthington - Kitty's father

Ned Worthington - Kitty's oldest brother

Richard Worthington - Kitty's next older brother, in Egypt

Margaret Worthington - Kitty's older sister, engaged to the Duke of Wynchcombe, and away at Oxford

The Worthington Household

Betsy - Kitty's maid

Carlton - the family butler

Mrs. Simpson - the family housekeeper

Cook – the family chef and Betsy's aunt

Cummings - Mrs. Worthington's maid

Sir Winston - the family's beloved basset hound

The Andover Royal Family and Staff

The Queen of Andover
The Prince of Andover - her son
The Princess of Andover - the prince's wife
The Duke of Andover - the prince and princess's son
The Count of Andover - cousin to the prince
The Countess of Andover - the count's wife
Colonel Bouchard - Equerry to the prince

The Wynchcombe Family

Sebastian Dalrymple - the Duke of Wynchcombe and Margaret's fiancé

Lady Lily Dalrymple - Sebastian's sister

Other Notable Characters

Robert Crawford - Chief Detective Inspector and Kitty's fiancé

Lord Hollingsworth - a marquis, friends with CDI Robert Crawford

Lady Melissande - Lord Hollingsworth's sister

Lord Marlowe - an earl

Lady Emma Carlyle - co-owner of the Ladies of Distinction Detective Agency

Mister Clapham - former Scotland Yard detective inspector, currently helping with investigations

CHAPTER ONE

WORTHINGTON HOUSE, MAYFAIR, LONDON

OCTOBER 1923

*W*ITH THE SEASON OVER, one might think things would have settled down at Worthington House. After all, we no longer had evening balls, afternoon teas, scavenger hunts, or pig races to attend. But quite the opposite was true. You see, we had Margaret's December wedding to Sebastian Dalrymple, the Duke of Wynchcombe, to organize.

And what a mammoth project that was turning out to be. We had all known the previous Duke of Wynchcombe had been a miserly sort who didn't spend a pence unless he benefited from it. As a result, the castle was in dire need of everything that made modern life worth living.

While Sebastian had taken on the monumental task of installing new plumbing, making castle repairs, and arranging for new kitchen equipment, his sister, Lady Lily, and Mother were buying furnishings in London. The list of rooms that needed refurbishments was long and varied. Everything, from the chambers to be occupied by the wedding guests to the formal rooms used to entertain, needed something. One would think Margaret would be in charge of this duty since she would soon be the new duchess. But she was away at Oxford studying for her degree and was more than glad to delegate the undertaking to Mother and her future sister-in-law. Since they both loved to shop and redecorate, they relished the challenge. So, everyone was happy with the arrangement.

And as for me, after my engagement to Robert Crawford, now promoted to Chief Detective Inspector at Scotland Yard, my life had taken quite a turn. Whenever Scotland Yard did not claim his time, which frankly happened more often than I'd liked, he escorted me to the theater and restaurants where we would enjoy intimate suppers. Once, he'd taken me to a jazz club where I'd finally had the chance to drink fizzy cocktails and dance the night away. I'd come home with very sore feet, but it had been totally worth it.

The changes did not stop there for I'd also become a full-fledged detective. Together with Lady Emma Carlyle, we'd created the Ladies of Distinction Detective Agency. We'd thrown open our doors expecting a deluge of inquiries. Unfortunately, the anticipated business did not materialize. We'd failed to consider that the vast majority of our prospective clientele would flee town to enjoy hunting, horse races, and house parties at their country estates. But neither Emma nor I were ready to throw in the proverbial towel. After all, the business had existed for barely a month.

I'd spent the weekend planning a new strategy for drumming up business, so I was eager to share my views with Lady Emma. But first, I needed food to break my fast. As everyone knows, you can't set the world on fire on an empty stomach.

I walked into the dining room to find Mother and Father enjoying a spirited discussion while Lady Lily, who'd temporarily moved in with us while Sebastian attended to matters at the castle, listened with silent amusement. While listening to their repartee, which they thoroughly enjoyed, I approached the sideboard and filled my plate.

"Why would an English castle be decorated with Asian motifs?" Father asked, a confused look on his face.

"It is all the rage, Edward," Mother said. "In any case, it's not the entire castle, only the duchess's chambers, which, of course, Margaret will occupy once she marries Sebastian." A proud smile rolled across her lips. To say she was pleased about Margaret's marriage to Sebastian was an understatement. It was not every day a lady with no claim to nobility married a duke. And not just any duke, mind you, but a handsome, rich, and intelligent one who simply adored Margaret.

Father quirked a brow. "And she's agreed to this?" Not an odd question for Mother who, if given a decorating inch, had been known to paper over every wall and replace every stick of furniture.

"Yes, she has, Edward. Other bedchambers will have similar themes. The ones that face the garden will be decorated with Japanese-inspired cherry blossoms in pinks and reds. It will be truly lovely. Don't you think, Lady Lily?"

"Absolutely, Mrs. Worthington. Margaret will be in alt." Lady Lily knew better than to contradict Mother when it came to decorating matters, especially when the results tended to be absolutely charming.

But Father was not so easily convinced. "Rather feminine, don't you think?"

"Those chambers will be for female guests, of course.

Lady Carlyle will be assigned to the Cherry Blossom room while her daughter, Lady Emma, will be situated next to her in the Cherry Orchard chamber."

Clearly, cherries were a theme.

"The gentlemen's chambers," Mother continued, "will adopt more somber shades—brown, black, and grey with splashes of blues." She glanced askance at Father. "Edward, I do wish you'd allow me to refurbish your study. The cushion in that leather chair of yours is horribly cracked."

He put down his fork with a clatter. "My study is not to be touched, Mildred."

"It cannot be comfortable for you, dear."

Total silence met her.

Not one to give up, Mother tried once more. "It could be easily repaired."

He peered at her over his half-moon spectacles. "I've been hoodwinked by that remark before, Mildred. I allow you to repair one chair and next thing I know all my furniture has been replaced, and a parrot is spouting salty language from a cage. Do you know how difficult it was to explain to a client on a transatlantic telephone call that it was a bird, not me, who insulted him?"

"I admit the parrot was a mistake. But I did find him a new home," Mother finished in a breezy tone.

"To a tavern by the docks, I hope, where its pirate vocabulary would be appreciated."

Mother trilled out a laugh. "To Lady Cargyll. She gets a thrill out of guests' reactions when it spouts some totally inappropriate remark. For a parrot, he has quite an extensive stock of words, I must say."

"Good morning," I said, approaching them.

"Morning, my dear," Mother said offhandedly before she noticed my attire. "What on earth are you wearing?"

"The latest fashion." After resting my plate on the table, I twirled to show off my outfit.

"You intend to wear pajamas in public?"

"They're not pajamas, Mother. They're palazzo pants, and they're all the rage in Milan."

"We're in London where that sort of scandalous fashion is simply not worn." She turned to Father who'd resumed reading *The Financial Times*. "Edward, tell her she's not allowed to wear that outfit in public."

Father folded the newspaper and studied me over his half-moon lenses. "I imagine they're quite comfortable."

"They are," I said. "I simply adore them." Hoping that would be the last word on the subject, I addressed my plate of tomatoes, eggs, beans, and rashers of bacon.

But, of course, Mother would not allow the subject to drop. "And what, pray tell, do you have on your schedule today that you need to wear such scandalous clothes?"

"I'm meeting with Lady Emma to discuss our future plans." I reached for a piece of toast and proceeded to thoroughly butter it.

Mother pursed her lips, but she didn't say anything else. She hadn't approved my starting the agency. Just the opposite. She heartily disapproved. But she gave in when Father agreed it was a good thing to do as long as precautions were taken. Since he didn't spell out what he meant, Lady Emma and I proceeded with our plans. Our first order of business, of course, was to find a locale. So we approached my brother Ned who'd located a townhouse in a respectable neighborhood that catered to a commercial clientele.

"How is the agency progressing, Kitty?" Father asked.

"It's early days, Father. I suspect business will pick up once our adverts are noticed."

"You're advertising?" Mother said in a horrified tone.

"In several newspapers." I said spreading some orange

marmalade on my toast. 'Ladies of Distinction Detective Agency. No Matter Too Trivial.' That's our motto. 'Inquire at our Hanover Square address.'"

"Referrals will be your best advertisement, Kitty," Father said.

"Yes, Sir." We'd need to have actual clients before we could have that, but I wasn't about to inform him of that fact.

After a quick knock on the door, a footman entered carrying a box and leading Sir Winston, our basset hound, on a leash. "Forgive my interruption, Mr. Worthington, but you did say you wanted to be notified as soon as the special delivery package you were expecting arrived."

"Has it?" Father rushed to his feet as the footman approached and handed the box to him.

"Edward," Mother said, "I thought we'd agreed that dog was not to join us during mealtimes."

Poor Sir Winston had been banished when he'd suffered an unfortunate accident on our priceless Aubusson rug. Mother had been so outraged she'd had the poor thing burned. The rug, not Sir Winston.

"This will only take a minute, Mildred." After our butler, Carlton, handed him a utility knife, Father cut open the package. The beaming smile that spread over his face was something to behold. "It's perfect. Absolutely perfect." As if it was something precious, he lifted the object from the box and held it up for all to see.

A medal made of silver and plated in 18k gold with a red, white, and blue ribbon, the colors of the British flag, affixed to its ring.

"What's engraved on it, Father?"

"To Sir Winston, for his meritorious service to Britain." A suspicious moisture shown in Father's eyes.

In one of our previous investigations, Sir Winston had been instrumental in the apprehension of a criminal. So much so, the British Customs Office had promised him a medal. Of course, they couldn't publicize that a dog had discovered something they'd failed to do. But, miracle of miracles, they'd come through with their promise.

Father's chest puffed up. "Did you hear that, boy? Meritorious service. No other dog in England has ever received such a thing." Bending down, he tied the ribbon around Sir Winston's neck who acknowledged it with a bark.

"Mister Carlton?" Father asked.

"Yes, Mr. Worthington."

"Make sure he gets extra sausages today. He's earned them."

"Yes, sir. Come, Sir Winston." Carlton led Sir Winston out of the dining room, his medal dragging on the floor.

After resuming his seat, Father hid behind the newspaper as he needed a moment to regain his composure. No one said a word, least of all Mother. She knew how much Father adored Sir Winston.

Done with breakfast, I came to my feet. "Sorry to dash, but Lady Emma is waiting for me."

"You will take Betsy with you?" Mother asked.

"Of course." Officially, Betsy was my maid and, unofficially, my chaperone. In reality, she was so much more. Not only had she been of great help during my earlier investigations, but she was my trusted confidante. I felt far freer discussing delicate topics with her than with anyone in my family. In fact, I trusted her so much, I had great plans for her.

When we set up the agency, Lady Emma and I anticipated the need for office staff. We'd determined Betsy would be the perfect person to take on that role. She was bright, eager, and had no trouble winning people over. If she could chat up a Scotland Yard front desk sergeant, surely a prospective client would be a breeze. All she needed was training.

After discussing the matter with Betsy, she was speechless for more than a minute. A strange occurrence, for normally she was a chatterbox. Of course, she said yes for it would mean not only a raise in salary but a higher status in life. Subsequently, I'd signed her up to secretarial school where she would learn how to work a typewriter, greet clients, and manage the front desk of the detective agency.

Since someone would need to handle my lady's maid duties, we'd decided on Grace. She'd happily agreed to our suggestion since it would be a promotion for her as well. The next order of business was to convince our housekeeper to keep the news from Mother until after Margaret's wedding. It had been difficult, but she'd finally agreed when I argued Mother had enough on her plate.

"Don't forget, dear," Mother said. "We have supper at Lord Rutledge's tonight. Don't be late."

"I won't." Waggling my fingers, I made my exit before she could remind me of something else.

CHAPTER TWO

LADIES OF DISTINCTION DETECTIVE AGENCY

*L*OCATED AS IT WAS in an impressive townhouse off Hanover Square, our detective agency couldn't have asked for a better address. Not only that, but I doubted the most discerning of clients would find something to criticize about the interior. The furnishings certainly did not lack style. Mother made certain of that. She'd parsed through furniture she'd tucked away in the attic and donated the best pieces—one sofa, a settee, two chairs, and a smattering of small tables. She may not have approved of our enterprise, but she would never allow my business to appear less than stellar.

Nor did the family's contributions stop there. Sebastian, Margaret's fiancé and a noted botanist, had provided potted plants from his conservatory which brightened up the space to no end. The result was both charming and cheery.

In addition to the reception area, the ground floor

contained two offices, one each for Lady Emma and me, a small area for tea and such, and, of course, a WC. While the first floor held a conference room and a library, the second one held Lady Emma's private rooms.

Mother had invited her to reside with us, but Lady Emma had declined. I wasn't surprised. She had a fierce independent streak that demanded the privacy her quarters provided. Her decision to live in the townhouse by herself became a sore point with her family. So much so, they'd cut ties with her before leaving town.

I walked into the townhouse to find her pouring over some papers in her office, a frown on her face. Putting on my brightest smile, I strolled over to her. "Good morning. The daily's been in already?" I'd insisted on a charwoman for our business since we couldn't afford to be shirking in that respect.

"Yes, not that there was much to clean. She offered to make tea, but I declined."

Whether it was the worry about the detective agency failing or something else, Lady Emma had taken to skipping meals. I was afraid she'd taken it too far. Granted the weight loss made her more slender, but she might sicken if she didn't eat. There was no call to remind her of it, however. It would only make things worse.

"Have we received any calls?"

"The phone has not rung all morning, nor has anyone come to our door," she said in a despondent tone. It would be a sad day if the agency failed, and she had to return home to a family which neither understood nor appreciated Lady Emma's talents. For her sake as much as my own, we needed to make the detective agency a success.

"Lord Marlowe is scheduled to visit this morning to retrieve his tiepin," she said in a cheerier tone.

"Glad we were able to find it for him." Lord Marlowe had hired us to locate a family heirloom, an item he'd lost while visiting his gentleman's club. We'd found it in the unlikeliest of places.

"Once he settles his account, we'll be able to meet our expenses this month." She pointed to the papers she held. Bills from the look of them.

"Our financial situation is not as dire as all that, Emma."

"Well, your fees for finding that lost poodle went toward the lease. But if we want to continue to function, we need to take on new clients."

"Do you think we should pay for more adverts?"

She scrunched her mouth. "What good would that do? Nobody is in town. Unless our fortunes change, we'll be forced to close our doors."

"Emma, dear." Sitting across from her, I reached for her hands. "It won't come to that. I have more than enough money to keep the business going."

"I'd just as soon not be a burden to you."

"You will never be a burden. Ever," I said in a harsher tone than I intended. "Things will turn around. You'll see."

The phone rang, interrupting us. "See?"

"Hello," I said in my cheeriest voice.

A nasal female voice said, "I have a caller on the line."

"Thank you, operator." When I heard the connection click, I said, "Ladies of Distinction Detective Agency. How may I help you?"

"By agreeing to go to the theatre with me," a beloved deep voice said.

"Robert! How nice of you to telephone."

Emma rolled her eyes at me from her office.

"Are you inviting me to see a play?" We'd been engaged a month now and he'd danced attendance on me with regular insistence, sometimes supper, other times the theatre. One night he'd taken me to a jazz club. I'd come home with sore feet from dancing the night away.

"I am. The D'Oyly Carte Opera Company is performing *The Mikado* at the Prince's Theatre, and I managed to obtain some tickets."

"How wonderful. When?"

"Saturday. Hope you haven't made other plans."

"I haven't." With the season ended, unless we held a supper or one of the few friends still in town invited us to one of their own, our evenings out were few and far between.

"I'll pick you up at eight then. We can have a late supper afterward."

"Marvelous. Will I see you at Lord Rutledge's tonight?" Several years ago, Lord Rutledge had been attacked by a gang of ruffians in St. Giles, one of the worst parts of London. Robert, who'd been a policeman at the time, had saved his life, but he'd been hurt in doing so. His injuries had been so grievous, it'd taken him over six months to recuperate. Lord Rutledge had been so appreciative of Robert's efforts, he'd paid for his education at Oxford. Subsequently, he'd not only become Robert's mentor, but a dear friend.

"I'll be there."

"Until then."

No sooner had I said goodbye than the doorbell rang. Since Emma's door was closed, I attended to it and found our client on the other side.

"Lord Marlowe. How pleasant to see you."

"Miss Worthington." He duffed his Homburg hat. "Lady Emma tells me she's located my tiepin."

"She has indeed." The piece of jewelry had been handed down for generations from father to son. When I discovered where it'd been, I suspected he'd put it there himself, either so he could call on Lady Emma or bring business our way. More than likely the former weighed more heavily with him as he was interested in her, and she in him.

For whatever reason, he had never escorted her anywhere, depending on running into her at one social function or another. Since currently there were few on the horizon, he'd apparently resorted to 'losing' a tiepin so he could spend some time with her. I had no idea what the problem was, other than being a stubborn male who wanted to sow his wild oats, rather than settle down with a woman who was his perfect match. Knowing he had her best interests at heart, I dared to make a suggestion. "Lord Marlowe, I know this might be indelicate to mention this. But I fear Lady Emma is not eating as she should."

His brow furrowed. "Why not?"

"Worries about the agency would be my guess. Last thing she wants is to see it fail. She does not want to rejoin her family, you see."

"I don't blame her. They've treated her quite shabbily. When she didn't come up to snuff in the marriage market, they washed their hands of her."

"I know. But it's the here and now I'm worried about. Are you planning on remaining in town for the near future?"

"Ehhh . . ."

I didn't give him a chance to say no. "Marvelous. Would you mind terribly inviting her to supper or the theatre. Or really anywhere else you think she might enjoy?"

"Well, I . . ." He ran a finger under his collar.

Honestly, the man was a hopeless cause. "Oh, thank you. You're a true gentleman, Lord Marlowe. I knew I could count on you. Would you like to step into her office? She's waiting for you."

After a brief knock, I opened Emma's door. Her eyes were red. Clearly, she'd been crying. But neither Lord Marlowe nor I commented on it. While softly closing the door, I vowed to find more clients. Maybe bigger adverts would bring in more business. It certainly couldn't hurt to try. As it turned out, we needed to do neither for our fortunes changed almost overnight.

CHAPTER THREE

SUPPER AT LORD RUTLEDGE'S

*L*ORD RUTLEDGE'S SUPPER PARTY turned out to be a surprise, not only for its main topic of conversation but the number of guests present. When the season ended, anyone who had a country estate fled London, so town company had been rather thin. But tonight found fourteen gathered around the table, lords and ladies all. Well, except for us Worthingtons and Robert. We possessed not a drop of blue blood amongst us.

The reason for the sudden return of so many to London soon became quite clear.

"Oh, my dear, it's everything anyone can talk about." Lady Stonefeather's deep voice boomed across the expanse of the drawing room where the women had retired after supper leaving the men to enjoy their port and cigars.

"What are they discussing?" I normally was in the know about topics that interested the upper crust. But between the absence of the nobility and my efforts toward establishing the detective agency, I hadn't kept apprised.

"The prince, of course," Lady Stonefeather replied.

"Of Wales?"

"Of Andover. The entire royal family has been invited to London, sans the king. He's quite dotty, you know. So sad he had to be left behind." For a moment, her voice took on a lugubrious tone, only to perk right up with her next breath. "But every other royal will be here. The prince, his wife, their son, and the queen herself."

"Any special reason why an invitation was issued?"

"Andover has a cache of some mineral that is necessary to build armor, bullets, and such. The English government and our armament manufacturers would very much like to get their hands on it. For a fair price, of course. So they're rolling out the red carpet for the prince and his entourage hoping they can get him to lease the rights to mine the mineral to England. They arrive tomorrow. Everybody is flocking back to town hoping to be included in some of the festivities which are being scheduled as we speak."

"Ahh." That certainly explained the rush back to town by the English aristocracy. If there was something they loved, it was celebrations. Amazing that Mother hadn't mentioned it. Maybe she'd been so busy with wedding preparations, she wasn't aware of such notable news. I doubted it, though. When it came to the social calendar, she was always well-informed. So there had to be another reason.

"I heard they're to hold the Prince's Ball at Buckingham Palace. Can you imagine?"

"Indeed." It wasn't often such an event was held at the royal residence which only added to the mystique.

Before too long, the gentlemen joined the women in the drawing room. Eager for private conversation, Robert and I excused ourselves and headed toward Lord Rutledge's terrace. As an engaged couple, we were now allowed that luxury as long as we didn't abuse the privilege. Needless to say, we took advantage of it at every opportunity.

"Anything new on the Chief Detective Inspector front?" With his new promotion came added responsibilities. I had no doubt he was up to the task.

"I now have five inspectors who report to me. Some more seasoned than others. The challenge is to help them manage their investigations without me trodding on their toes."

"Are you so busy you won't be handling investigations on your own?" It would be a sad day for Scotland Yard given Robert's wealth of knowledge and extensive experience.

"No. I'll be involved in the more complex investigations while they handle the mundane matters. It's a way for them to learn the ropes, if you will. There's a rather bright lad among them." A small grin played fast and loose with his lips. "Reminds me of me, actually. With a little more seasoning, he'll make a fine investigator someday." He gazed down at me. "What about your detective agency? Any new cases?"

I'd told him about the lost poodle and Marlowe's misplaced tiepin. "No. And frankly, I'm getting worried. Lady Emma and I failed to consider the lack of people in town."

"Maybe now that they're flocking back, business will pick up."

"One can only hope. Enough shoptalk." I wrapped my arms around his waist.

His mouth quivered with mirth. "Miss Worthington, you make it awfully difficult to keep a respectable distance."

"I certainly hope so, Inspector."

Taking me up on my invitation, he bent down, and for a few moments, we got lost in a kiss.

I would have loved to continue what we'd started, but it'd grown cold on the terrace, and I hadn't brought my wrap. More importantly, if we didn't return soon, there would be talk. Something I did not wish to occur. Not only because it would affect my reputation but Robert's as well. He had a thriving career at Scotland Yard. The last thing I wanted was for him to be seen as a licentious cad.

On the way back, I stopped by a mirror to check my coiffure.

"You're perfect. I didn't muss you up."

"What a shame." I tossed him a saucy smile.

When we entered the drawing room, some of the ladies sent us suspect looks. My first instinct was to ignore them, but soon I reconsidered that thought. One never knew where a client might be found. So rather than keep my distance, I approached two gentlewomen who were deep in a whispered conversation—Ladies Cargyll and Molesley.

"May I join you?"

Lady Cargyll's lips pruned up, but Lady Molesley welcomed me with an open smile. "Of course."

A manservant approached with coffee, something I truly appreciated. I played mother and served it for the three of us.

After taking a sip, Lady Cargyll asked, "I noticed you left in the company of a gentleman. Inspector Crawford, was it not?"

"Robert." I laughed. "Yes, we're engaged."

Her coffee must have gone down the wrong way because she had a coughing fit.

"Are you all right?" I asked once she caught her breath.

Lady Cargyll cleared her throat. "Yes. I must have drunk the coffee too fast." Another cough. "When did you become engaged?" She wheezed out.

"Last month. He gave me the most beautiful ring." I showed them the square cut emerald, my birthstone, surrounded by a whole host of diamonds.

"Congratulations, Miss Worthington. It's a beautiful piece of jewelry," Lady Molesley said.

Lady Cargyll neither congratulated me nor admired it. She continued her interrogation instead. "How long have you known each other?"

"Four months. No, five now." I glanced over to where he stood talking to Lord Rutledge, his back to me. "He's the sweetest man."

Lady Cargyll said something that sounded like "Wait 'til Marina finds out," while I was gazing at Robert.

I turned back to her. "I beg your pardon."

"Nothing. So have you set a wedding date?"

"We haven't decided. You see, I've established a detective agency with Lady Emma Carlyle, and that is taking up most of my time."

"Lady Emma? Lord Carlyle's daughter?" Lady Cargyll's eyes practically popped from her head.

"The very one." I sipped from my cup.

"And her parents approved?" Lady Cargyll asked.

"No. But then she doesn't need their approval, does she? She is of age. We call it The Ladies of Distinction Detective Agency. No Inquiry Too Trivial. That's our motto. Isn't it divine?"

"It is," Lady Molesley agreed. "Where are you situated?"

"We found a smashing location off Hanover Square. We're quite busy, if I do say so myself." A small lie. Surely, it couldn't hurt. "But never too busy to take on a new client. We can provide references. Lord Marlowe and others." Marlowe hadn't given permission to bandy his name about. But I knew he wouldn't mind. At least I hoped so.

"Lord Marlowe?" Lady Cargyll screeched. "Why would he have need of your services?"

I assumed a serious mien. "I'm sorry, but that's confidential. We don't divulge information about our inquiries."

"Kitty." A voice over my shoulder called out.

"Mother. I was just telling Lady Cargyll and Lady Molesley about the detective agency."

"How very nice." Mother offered a smile. She might not approve of the agency, but she was not about to air our dirty laundry in public. "My apologies for interrupting, but I've suddenly developed a headache. It'd be best if we departed."

"No apologies needed Mrs. Worthington. We understand," Lady Molesley said.

After I curtsied and took my leave of them, Mother and I approached Lord Rutledge and Robert to say our goodbyes.

"See you on Saturday?" Robert asked.

"Can't wait. Good night."

"Good night, Catherine."

I sighed softly when he kissed my hand.

Once Mother and I had settled into our Rolls, I turned to her. "How's the headache? Is it unbearable?" She didn't suffer often from them. But they tended to be bilious when she did. Margaret had the same affliction. So much so, she couldn't be in the same room where people smoked.

"I am a tad nauseous. The nuts and cheese were a mistake. I know what they do to me. Lady Cargyll's perfume did not help."

"She rather reeked of gardenias. Close your eyes and rest your head. We'll be home soon."

She did as I suggested, but in another minute or so, she said, "Remind me to tell you what I overheard about Robert."

What? I wanted to ask. But the poor dear's brow was furrowed with pain. Tomorrow would be soon enough to learn what she knew.

CHAPTER FOUR

LADY CLINTON'S AFTERNOON TEA

*T*HE FOLLOWING DAY Mother was still suffering, so I didn't feel comfortable approaching her about what she overheard. In any case, I had Lady Clinton's afternoon tea to attend. With people flocking back to town, she'd resumed her weekly rituals. Lady Emma and I had both received an invitation. So, of course, we attended in the hopes of letting everyone know we were available for discrete inquiries.

Sadly, most of the guests were intent on gossiping about the prince's visit. So it appeared as if our attendance would not bear fruit.

"His wife, don't you know, a rather mousy-looking thing, barely speaks a word in his presence." Lady Golightly, a noted gossip, said. "Their son, the Duke of Andover, is a walking scandal—gambling, women, alcohol. There isn't a vice he doesn't aspire to. His father can't moderate his behavior, and the mother doesn't even try. Apparently, the queen is the only one who can curb his wilder ways."

"I heard the prince is having an affair with the wife of his cousin, the Count of Andover," another lady spouted. "He brought her along as he apparently cannot exist without her. Can you imagine how the princess must feel?"

"Isn't the cousin an Andover attaché?" A rather level-headed matron asked.

"Well, yes," Lady Golightly responded.

"Stands to reason his wife would accompany him to England then since he must attend to matters of state."

"Maybe so," Lady Golightly screeched, "but they have a child who's the spitting image of the prince. Rumor has it, he's the father."

"Oh, my," another lady exclaimed.

Lady Emma, who'd been making her way around the room, ostensibly to greet ladies, was walking back toward me.

Despondent about the scandal-ridden flow of conversation, I said once she reached me, "With all this talk about the prince, we'll never be able to share the news about our agency."

"You'd be wrong. Kitty. I got a nibble!" Her tone was low, but her elation peeked through.

"Really? Who?" In my excitement, I'd raised my voice and heads turned.

"Shhh. Not so loud." She sent a smile across the space to quiet the curious crowd before urging me to a secluded alcove where we would not be overheard. We'd no sooner sat on a settee than a servant appeared seemingly out of nowhere with a grand pastry spread and the ubiquitous pot of tea.

After we'd availed ourselves of the refreshments, I turned to Lady Emma, "Do tell."

Lady Emma did not disappoint. Speaking barely beyond a whisper, she explained, "Lady Forsythe is worried about her daughter. Apparently, a suitor has become quite interested in her. He has a title, but Lady Forsythe believes him a rake and totally unsuitable for her daughter. Unfortunately, the daughter's smitten with him. Understandably. He's not only handsome, but quite a charmer. She would like us to investigate. I promised to call on her tomorrow to finalize the details. I'll make sure to get a retainer."

"Twenty pounds?" That's the sum she'd asked of Lord Marlowe.

"I think thirty in this case. We will have to hire others to look into the gentleman's background."

"Splendid." I was more glad for her sake than the agency's for it would keep her too busy to worry about our income.

Seemingly out of nowhere, she got a pensive look in her eyes. "I think I'll ask Marlowe to help with Lady Forsythe's matter."

"Really?" Well, that was a surprise.

"Yesterday, when he fetched his tie clip, he offered to help the agency in any way he could."

The agency, not Lady Emma. How very curious. But then maybe not. By offering to assist the agency, rather than her, he avoided revealing where his main interest lay. But then, Marlowe found it difficult to discuss his true feelings when it came to Lady Emma. Whether it stemmed from his need to sow his wild oats before he settled into a staid marriage or some other reason I had yet to divine.

Her attention turned back to me. "He also invited me to supper this Saturday. Do you know anything about that?"

I dodged the question by asking one of my own. "Why would you think I had anything to do with it?" Of course, I'd had something with it. I'd asked him flat out. But I was not about to share that nugget of information with her. There was no knowing how she would take it.

She fought back a smile. "No particular reason."

"What will you wear? You have lost a fair amount of weight." Which meant her old clothes no longer fit as they should.

She bit down on her lip. "Yes, well. There's bound to be something in my wardrobe."

"Margaret is just about the size you are now. She had several gowns for her debut season that Mother intended to donate to a Magdalen House fundraiser. But she found another way. They're tucked away in a wardrobe and not being put to good use. I'm sure you'll find a frock among them you'll like. If it needs alterations, Betsy can do that for you. She's a whiz with a needle."

"Between secretarial school and her other duties, Betsy has enough on her plate."

"Well," I shrugged, "the only other choice is Angelique's." Lady Emma would balk at that suggestion. Angelique's services were rather dear, and something she could ill afford.

She gave in with good grace and a smile. "Betsy it is then."

"If you come home with us after the tea, you can decide which gowns you'd like," I suggested.

Her arched brow seemed to find an objection. "Gowns? I just need the one."

"Margaret won't mind if you choose more, and neither will Mother. You can stay for supper as well."

A bemused expression took hold of her face. "I know what you're doing, Kitty."

"Oh?"

"Marlowe asking me to supper. You offering me your sister's gowns."

My face heated up. "I worry about you, Emma. You're not eating right. And Marlowe just needed a nudge. It's not right for you to be entombed in that townhouse day and night."

"Need I remind you, I'm here at a social event."

"Only because you saw it as an opportunity to spread the word about our new endeavor."

"I take afternoon walks in the park."

"By yourself." I huffed out a frustrated breath. "You're such a lovely person, Emma. You deserve all the happiness the world has to offer."

She pressed my hand. "Dear Kitty. I appreciate your concern. I really do. Very well. I promise to do a better job of eating. Does that satisfy you?"

"It's a start."

She smiled in return.

We both ignored the Marlowe part of that equation. She'd never shared her feelings for the earl with me. I wasn't sure she even admitted them to herself. But maybe the supper would lead to more invitations. And then there was the investigation into the suitor of Lady Forsythe's daughter. That was also bound to draw her and Marlowe closer.

Thinking it best to change the subject, I asked, "Do you know where Hollingsworth has gone off to? He wasn't at Lord Rutledge's supper." Which was a strange because he was a regular guest of the marquis. Even though there'd been sufficient company for supper, he would have been invited as he was an excellent raconteur. His amusing tales of his explorer adventures were always enjoyed by all.

"He's gone to France to fetch his sister home. I'm sorry. I should have told you." Her complexion tinged with pink. "But with everything that's been happening, I forgot."

"No need to apologize." I offered a smile to show I meant it. "I didn't know he had a sister. He's never spoken of her."

"There's a large age difference between them, so they were never close."

"How old is she?"

"Eighteen or so."

"How long has she been in France?"

"Since she was six. It was their mother's wish she be educated at the same institution she attended."

"Such a young age to be separated from her parents." Mother couldn't bear to part with my sisters and me, so she'd hired governesses and tutors to educate us. "There's a story there, right?" And Lady Emma would be bound to know it. Her mother, Lady Carlyle, was an inveterate gossip who kept tabs on everyone. If somebody sneezed two streets over, she learned about it. That's why Lady Emma knew everything there was to know about the nobility.

"Lady Hollingsworth came from an illustrious French family, but not well-to-do. They lost most of their property and wealth during the French Revolution. Somehow, they managed to survive. When it came time for their daughter to marry—her name was Eloise by the way—they came to England in search of a husband. The Hollingsworth matriarch, who was determined to find a proper wife for her libertine son, found the perfect candidate in Eloise. She was modest, educated, and beautiful. Her parents, ecstatic their daughter would be a marchioness, wasted no time arranging a marriage. But once Hollingsworth was born, his father abandoned Eloise and returned to his mistress."

"So, not a love match."

"Far from it. As you can imagine, there were no more children. But about sixteen or so years ago, Hollingsworth became quite ill, and his father feared the title would go to his nephew so . . ."

"He returned to his wife's bed."

"Yes. Hollingsworth, as we know, recuperated. A good thing because Lady Hollingsworth gave birth to a girl. So there would have been no son to inherit the title. From all accounts, she found joy in Melissande. That's what she named the child. But her health deteriorated; and six years later, she passed. By that time, Hollingsworth's father had gone on to his glory, and Hollingsworth had inherited the title. Knowing of her son's zest for adventure, she feared Melissande would be abandoned, much as she was. Before she died, Lady Hollingsworth made him promise to take her daughter to France to be educated at the same convent she was."

"There was no need to send the little girl to France. Hollingsworth would have made arrangements for his sister's welfare and education."

"But she would have been all alone with no family to call her own. Her mother believed she would fare better at the school she attended. Hollingsworth, of course, complied with her wishes. Since Lady Melissande has now reached a marriageable age, he's bringing her home to be presented at court. A distant cousin will become her chaperone."

A thought suddenly occurred to me. "She can make her debut along with Lady Lily in the spring."

Lady Emma laughed. "You just can't help yourself, can you?"

"What do you mean?"

"Arranging everyone's life. What if she doesn't wish to be presented at court?"

"But you just said—"

"That's Hollingsworth's plan. Introduce her at court, find her a husband, and then he'll be free to sail the seven seas. But what if that's not what she wishes?"

"Then she won't be. We'll just have to wait and see."

CHAPTER FIVE

THE PRINCE'S THEATRE

*A*FTER I BECAME ENGAGED, I'd visited Angelique, our modiste, and commissioned a new wardrobe to reflect my newly affianced status. The styles were a bit more daring than I'd worn while a debutante, but still within the bounds of propriety. Since tonight it would not do to call attention to myself with a risqué frock, I'd chosen a midnight blue sequined gown with a conservative neckline. A slightly more alluring one I was reserving for an intimate supper with Robert.

To add a bit of splendor, I'd chosen the pearl necklace Lord Rutledge had gifted me on my twenty-first birthday, and, of course, my engagement ring. After all, it wasn't every day one attended the theatre on the same day the Prince of Wales and the Prince of Andover were in attendance.

Robert joined us for supper at Worthington House before our evening out. After enjoying the meal, we fetched his coat and my fur-edged wrap and climbed into his Rolls Royce

Phantom. The motoring robe in the automobile would have been sufficient to keep me warm. But I took the opportunity to snuggle up to him with the excuse I was cold. He obliged by curling his arm around me and pulling me close.

We'd planned to arrive early at the theatre to avoid a mob, but it seemed every attendee had the same thought. So, it ended up a bit of a crush. Robert's commanding presence, though, kept anyone from bumping into me as we made our way into the vestibule.

As we reached the entrance to the seating area, there was a bit of a tussle at the door. A trio of gentlemen—and I use that word lightly—all of whom appeared to be three sheets to the wind, were insisting on bringing bottles of champagne into the performance. The usher reminded the gentlemen this was not a rowdy music hall but a royal command performance in front of the Prince of Wales and his honored guests. As such, no food or drink were allowed. The rowdies refusing to give up their bounty were soon escorted off to the side, and hopefully out the door, for no one wanted such a display of incivility in front of the prince. But once that contretemps was settled, the rest of the audience proceeded into the auditorium without another disruption.

We didn't have to wait long for the contingent of royal persons to arrive. And what a sight they were. Our very own Prince of Wales was the first to enter the royal box. We all stood and cheered as he waved to the crowd. After acknowledging the accolade, he pointed to the back of the box and a very tall gentleman, seemingly in his fifties, sporting an enormous mustache and dressed in formal evening wear, stepped forward. A rather timid woman, who barely came to his shoulder, stood by his side. An elderly lady, wearing a tiara that sparkled with diamonds, was the next to make her entrance. Had to be his mother, the Queen of Andover. The son was the next to appear. As tall as his father, but bare of any facial adornment, he seemed to be no older than twenty-five. In contrast to his father who'd smiled while he was being presented, he wore a rather unpleasant expression, as if this was the last place he wished to be. The thunderous applause for one and all continued until the Prince of Wales quieted the crowd. Once everyone took their seats, the curtain was raised.

The Mikado had long been a favorite of mine and the D'Oyly Carte Opera Company could always be counted upon to put on a fine performance, but tonight they outdid themselves. The audience responded accordingly, laughing at the right moments and applauding at the appropriate times.

But it wasn't until the intermission that the real performance began. Raised voices erupted from the prince's box. Seemingly, an argument had broken out between the Prince of Andover and his son. The words spoken in French echoed through the theatre with the son exclaiming his father could not keep him from doing what he wished now that he was a grown man. The audience watched in shock at this unseemly display until the son stormed out in a huff.

For a few moments silence reigned over the theatre. But then in heavily accented English, the Prince of Andover made a joke out of it, and everyone dutifully laughed. But the damage had been done.

The next day, after returning from Sunday service, Mother and I were enjoying a brief respite in her parlor before luncheon was served when Carlton entered with this morning's papers. The front story of every one of them featured the argument between the Prince of Andover and his son. The more scandalous ones, like *The Tell All*, were not content to simply publish the facts but included extensive reports on the son's gambling, womanizing, and spendthrift ways.

"How very sad to read such things about your offspring,"

Mother said shaking her head. "His parents must be beside themselves."

"Do you think the reports are true?" I asked.

"Maybe. Maybe not. The London rags are not known to be truth tellers. Remember what they said about Ned and us."

My brother Ned had been caught up in a murder investigation. Many of London's newspapers had spread lies about him to one and all. My debut season had also suffered as a result. I hadn't cared for my own sake but Mother's, who depended on the upper crust's benevolence to fund her Ladies Benevolent Society's good works. It'd turned out to be a storm in a teacup, but it was something I'd never forget. The reports about the Duke of Andover's wastrel ways might also be lies. Only time would tell.

"Did you know about the prince's visit, Mother?"

"Of course, dear. It was in all the papers." And Mother read all of them every morning and afternoon. No tidbit was too small to catch her notice. And the prince's visit was no tidbit.

"And yet, you said nothing about it."

"I'm much too busy with your sister's wedding preparations to attend to something that is bound to be a nine-day wonder while the negotiations are conducted. As I understand it, their royal majesties will be holding a ball in the prince's honor at Buckingham Palace. Since only the nobility will be invited, it's nothing we need to worry about."

Although we enjoyed wealth, thanks to Father's thriving investment firm, Worthington & Son, we didn't hold a title. And the *crème de la crème* did.

"He'll either sign an agreement with the English government, or he will not. Although in my opinion, I don't believe he will."

"Why not?"

"Andover is situated to the west of France, the north of Italy, and the east of Switzerland. During the Great War, it maintained its neutrality by not taking sides. The fact that it's largely a mountainous country also worked to its advantage. No general in his right mind would want to fight in such a topography. The troops would have been exhausted by the climb. It's to Andover's advantage to maintain its nonpartisanship."

"But the fighting is over," I pointed out.

She gazed at me with sad eyes. "For now."

"You think there will be another war?"

"Not at the moment. But in a decade or two, who knows? An agreement with England would be seen as favoring us. If the prince is wise, he'll keep his country from taking sides."

"But the mountain topography would prevent troops from attacking their country, wouldn't it?"

"Mountains won't stop aircraft or dirigible airships from dropping bombs. We already saw what devastation they caused to parts of London. Such aircraft are bound to be improved upon in the coming decades. More advanced flying machines, and probably deadlier, than exist now."

I shuddered at the thought. "That's awful."

"That's nothing for you to worry about at the moment, dear."

"If you say so." I did not agree with her on this matter. We should all worry. If another war was on the horizon, we should be cognizant of that fact so we could best prepare for it. "Mother, there's something I've been meaning to ask."

"Yes, dear."

"The night of Lord Rutledge's supper. On the way home, you said there was something you needed to tell me. About Robert. For the last couple of days, you were feeling a bit under the weather, so I thought I would wait. But since you're back to your normal self, I thought I'd ask. Do you recall what you said?"

She sighed. "Yes."

I waited for her to continue. When she did not, I prompted her. "What did you hear, Mother?" Her reticence had me worried to say the least.

"Robert was once . . . engaged."

Well, that was a facer. He hadn't said anything about it. "When? Do you know?"

"When he was at Oxford, apparently."

"Did you hear anything more than that?"

"You remember I had a headache that night?"

"Yes."

"It was starting to make itself known, so I walked to one of the windows where it was cooler. Sometimes that helps. Lord Rutledge and Robert were standing in the drawing room alcove."

"I know it well." It was a place where guests could hold a private conversation but still be within sight of those present.

"They were so involved in their discussion they didn't see me."

"What was said?"

"First of all, I didn't mean to listen. I was standing in the wrong place at the wrong time."

Or the right place at the right time. "Point taken. Please go on."

"Lord Rutledge asked Robert if he'd told you about Ellen. Well, that got my attention."

Robert said, "*Not yet.*"

Lord Rutledge countered with, "*You realize you must do it. It wouldn't be fair to Kitty, otherwise. What if her sister Margaret heard about it at Oxford?*"

Robert brushed a hand across his brow, as if he were struggling with something. "*It happened such a long time ago.*"

"Maybe so," Lord Rutledge said. *"But that institution has a long memory."*

"I'll think about it," Robert responded before walking away.

"My head was thoroughly pounding by then," Mother said. "That's when I approached you and asked if we could leave."

"Ellen. Who could she be?"

"He was a student at Oxford, was he not?"

"Yes, before the Great War. About ten, twelve years ago. He would have been in his early twenties."

"Old enough to fall in love."

"But why hasn't he told me?" I asked, feeling a trifle sick.

Wearing a concerned expression, Mother joined me in the rose settee and gently held my hands. "Kitty, dear. By nature, you are a curious person. That's why you excel at discovering murderers. Robert is your fiancé. The man you will marry one day. He has a secret."

"Actually, he has more than one."

She raised an inquiring brow.

"Where his money comes from. He said it's not his secret to tell. That he would share it with me when he could."

"Then you must wait for him to share this one as well. You have a wonderful understanding with Robert. He's kind, loving, honorable. This prior engagement is in the past. It has nothing to do with you. Don't allow your curiosity to make you do something rash. You might damage your relationship. Or worse, you might lose him altogether."

"He wouldn't do such a thing. He loves me," I insisted.

Mother cradled my cheek. "Yes, he does, sweet child of mine. Don't give him a reason to break your heart."

"Very well. I won't." I glanced up at her. "But it will be hard to wait until he tells me."

A soft smile blossomed across her lips. "And thus, the

sweeter when he shares his secrets with you. It will mean he trusts you enough to tell you the truth."

I blinked away my tears. "What made you so wise?"

"Life, I suppose. And your father. Yes, I've made my mistakes with him. But he's always forgiven me."

"That's because he loves you."

"Yes, he does."

Almost as if he'd heard us, Father burst into the parlor. He'd gone to his study to make a telephone call. "Luncheon is ready. Carlton just informed me. I love Sunday roast. Beef, potatoes, Yorkshire pudding, stuffing, and gravy," he said rubbing his hands. He must have noticed the emotion in the room because he asked, "Anything wrong?"

"Nothing that can't be fixed with a serving of Sunday roast," I said, braving a smile.

"And Spotted Dick for dessert." Looking around the room, he asked, "Where's Lady Lily?"

"Ned invited her to a luncheon at The Savoy," Mother said. "Don't worry. She's being properly chaperoned."

"By whom?"

"Lady Nesbitt."

"Lady Nesbitt? She's eighty if a day."

"But sharp as a tack. And with her in full presence, nobody can claim Lady Lily lacked a chaperone."

"If you say so, dear. Shall we proceed to the dining room?"

Linking arms, the three of us made our way out.

CHAPTER SIX

A BOON FOR THE DETECTIVE AGENCY

*M*ONDAY MORNING, I arrived at our
detective agency to find a heavily veiled lady
in widow's weeds sitting in our reception area. Lady Emma
was nowhere in sight. That mystery was soon solved when I
spotted a bow hanging from her office's doorknob, our pre-
agreed signal she was occupied with a client.

"Good morning. I'm Catherine Worthington," I said to the
veiled lady. "May I be of assistance?"

"How you do, Miss Worthington," the lady's breathy voice
replied, "I'm Lady Watkins, and I have a very delicate matter
I'd like to discuss with you."

"Of course. Would you care to step into my office?" I
pointed toward my open door. Once we entered, I grabbed
my bow and tied it to the knob to let Lady Emma know I was
also occupied.

After she declined my offer of tea, I retrieved the note-

36

book where I kept track of the details surrounding an investigation. "Now, what is it that concerns you?"

She slung back her veil and gazed directly at me. "I'm a widow, Miss Worthington. Lord Watkins passed on to his glory six months ago."

"I'm so sorry for your loss." I bowed my head.

She did as well. "Thank you. But no sooner did we bury poor Wendell than the troubles started." She sniffed back a sob.

"Are you sure you do not wish for some tea? It will take no time at all to fix it."

She squared her shoulders and sat upright. "Quite sure, Miss Worthington."

Obviously, she was made of pure iron. "Very well. Do go on."

"To put it succinctly, I believe my husband's man of business is stealing from me."

"How perfectly dreadful."

"Yes, he thinks I'm unknowledgeable about business matters. But I'm the one who oversaw the expenditures in our accounts, not my husband. And he's been charging outlandish amounts for food and household expenses. Not only that, I went to the bank to get the accounts transferred to me, but they wouldn't do so without a man's signature. Can you imagine that?"

Unfortunately, such was the law. A woman could not hold a bank account in her own name without a man's signature. "Outrageous."

"Can you help me, Miss Worthington?" Her voice became rather strident. No wonder she was outraged. I would be as well.

"Absolutely. We have an ace team including a rather clever financial investigator. But in order to look into this matter, I will need your approval to get to the bottom of this." I retrieved the standard documents we had on hand, one of which provided her personal details and the other gave us permission to investigate financial transactions. After she read it over, I explained our fee schedule and the necessity of a retainer. She neither questioned the amount nor caviled at it. Once I answered her questions as to how we would proceed with the investigation, she signed it.

"I will need his name and address so we can look into this matter for you."

"Yes, of course. I came ready to do just that." She fetched a piece of paper from her handbag and handed it to me. "How soon will I hear from you, Miss Worthington?"

"I will report in three days' time with the details of our progress."

"Very well. I look forward to hearing from you." She rearranged the veil until her face was fully covered once more and walked out of my office, head held high, shoulders no longer slumped.

Lady Emma's client had already left, so we grabbed cups of tea and biscuits and compared notes.

"My client misplaced a brooch," Lady Emma said. "Or so she said. But she hinted it was stolen by someone inside the house. What about yours?"

"The household accounts don't tally up. She suspects her man of business of skimming funds. I'll need to get Ned involved."

"Ned? Isn't he too busy with his regular duties to attend to this?"

She had a point. Along with Father, my brother Ned managed Worthington & Son, a thriving investment firm situated in the City of London.

"He certainly is that. But he offered to help if a matter came up which would benefit from his expertise."

"Really?"

I grinned. "I think he likes investigating crimes. His work tends to be rather dry."

"That's three matters we're contracted to investigate, including Lady Forsythe's."

"How's that coming along?"

"Well, according to Marlowe—"

"You got him involved in that as well?"

"He did say he wanted to help," she said with a grin. "By his account, the man is a cad through and through. Apparently, Lady Forsythe's daughter is not the first young woman he's tried to enthrall. Marlowe will bring me the details tomorrow morning. I'll write a report, submit it to Lady Forsythe, and collect the rest of our fee."

"You and Marlowe work well together."

"We do, don't we? Funny when you think about it."

"How so?"

"The rest of the time, we fight like cats and dogs. In case you haven't noticed."

I burst out laughing. "Oh, I've noticed. What about your new matter? How do you intend to investigate?" She always had an interesting approach to the cases we'd taken on.

"My client doesn't want to alert the other members of the household that she suspects one of theft. So, I will be interviewing them for a piece in *The Women's Gazette*."

"I've never heard of such a journal."

"That's because it doesn't exist. I think I'll call the article, 'A Woman's Plight.' That should get them to open up."

"You are so clever, Lady Emma."

"I do try, dear Kitty. And who knows? If I gain enough of an insight into the subject, I may write an actual article and submit it to a journal. A real one."

"I hope you do."

After a full day which included putting Lady Watkins's

matter in Ned's capable hands and placing additional adverts in the papers, I returned home to find Lord Hollingsworth talking to Mother in our drawing room.

"Miss Worthington." As soon as he spotted me, he came to his feet and sketched an elegant bow, but his usual care-free air was nowhere in sight.

I curtsied in return before joining Mother at the settee. "Lord Hollingsworth. You've returned from France."

"Yes," he said resuming his seat. "And I'm here to beg a boon from Mrs. Worthington and, indeed, your entire family."

My gaze bounced to Mother who wasted no time in answering, "Whatever you need, Lord Hollingsworth. If it's within our power, we will be more than glad to grant it."

He drew a hand across his brow. "It's my sister, Melissande."

"You traveled to France to bring her home, I hear," I said.

"Yes." A sheepish grin curled across his lips. "Lady Emma told you?"

"She wasn't meant to keep it confidential, was she?" I doubted it. If he intended such a thing, Lady Emma wouldn't have told me.

"No. It was not meant to be a secret. That's why I stopped by your agency to inform you about my travel plans. I did not wish you to worry about my absence. You weren't there that day, so I left it with Lady Emma to share the news with you." Made sense he would want us to know. Since we'd opened the agency, he'd been a regular visitor, bringing us much needed conversation and blooms. If he'd suddenly disappeared, we would have noticed and worried.

Rather than dwell on the subject, I gently inquired, "Were you successful in your quest?"

"Yes. Melissande, that's her name. Lady Melissande I should say."

As the daughter of a marquis, she would be addressed in such a fashion, much as Lady Emma as the daughter of an earl, and Lady Lily, the granddaughter of a duke, were.

"We'd love to meet her," Mother said. "I'll send her and you, of course, an invitation to our next supper. Tuesday next."

"Well, actually." Another look of chagrin, "I would like to ask more than that of you."

Mother and I both waited with bated breath for an explanation. When it didn't come forth, Mother said, "When faced with a thorny request, Lord Hollingsworth, I find it best to lay it out as quickly as possible."

He took a breath, let it out. "I need a place for my sister to stay, and I was wondering if you could . . . accommodate her."

Mother did not have to think twice. "Of course, Lord Hollingsworth. We will be more than glad to welcome her. Heaven knows we have more than enough space." Worthington House had a dozen bedrooms. Right now, the only occupied ones were Mother and Father's, mine, Margaret's, who would keep it until her wedding day when she moved to Wynchcombe House, and the one Lady Lily currently inhabited, the very same one she'd stayed in before.

"She has a maid. Sadie is her name."

"It will be no problem, milord," Mother said, "to house her as well."

He leaned back and relaxed into the seat as if a weight had been lifted from his shoulders. Did he really believe we would turn down his request?

"If I may ask, Lord Hollingsworth," Mother said, "had you made plans for her arrival?"

"Yes. I intended to have my aunt, Lady Cornelia Harbot, act as her chaperone. Unfortunately, while I was in France, she fell down the stairs and broke her hip."

"How horrible. Hopefully, she will recuperate."

"Her doctor tells me she will regain mobility but will be quite unable to keep up with a hectic social schedule."

The social season, with its myriad of events scheduled throughout the months, was busy to say the least. Between clothes fittings, court presentations, balls, suppers, never mind at-homes to welcome potential suitors, a debutante, and her chaperone, needed the stamina of a Boadicea to keep up with it all. I'd been ecstatic to see the end of my season so I could finally get a good night's sleep.

"I was depending on her to watch over Melissande," Hollingsworth continued, "when I sailed on my next expedition. Now, I'll need to find someone else. If you have any recommendations, I'm all ears."

"I'll have a think on that," Mother said. "There's bound to be someone. In the meantime, you can leave your sister with us. Between Lady Lily and Kitty, she'll certainly have plenty of young company."

"Thank you, Mrs. Worthington. I can't tell you how grateful I am."

"You are most welcome, milord. When can we look forward to meeting Lady Melissande?"

"Tomorrow, if that's possible."

"Absolutely. I'll ask our housekeeper to prepare a room for her. I think the Oriental one in the back of the house would be an excellent choice. It has a lovely view of the garden." Mother had gotten a jump on her Asian decorating scheme by refurbishing that bedroom. And she was right. It was beautiful indeed.

"Thank you, Mrs. Worthington, Miss Worthington, for your kindness. I know Melissande will be safe here. I'll take my leave now so I can share the good news with her. Until tomorrow? Let's say eleven?"

"That will be fine, Lord Hollingsworth. Until then," Mother said.

He'd used the word safe. What did that mean? Was Lady Melissande in danger? Is that why he'd placed her with us? No. That couldn't be it. He wouldn't do such a thing without warning us. Or would he?

CHAPTER SEVEN

LADY MELISSANDE

*C*OME THE NEXT MORNING, Mother, Lady Lily, and I happily situated ourselves in the drawing room to await the arrival of Lady Melissande. Hollingsworth did not keep us waiting. A few minutes after eleven, Carlton announced them.

As Hollingsworth had not provided his sister's description, I hadn't known what to expect, but I wouldn't have imagined the stunning beauty who walked into the room. Her hair, the color of a bright burning flame, had been arranged seemingly haphazardly, but I knew enough about coiffures to know it had taken a skilled stylist to create such a thing. Her eyes, the shade of an ocean, were the brightest blue I'd ever seen, and her figure? Well, let's just say I envied it. Mine was straight as a stick. She, on the other hand, had curves upon curves bound to draw a man's eye without halfway trying. Her cerulean frock was stunning, clearly the work of a master. Since she'd traveled through Paris, it could only have come from the House of Worth.

"Mrs. Worthington, Miss Worthington, Lady Lily," Lord Hollingsworth said, "may I introduce my sister Lady Melissande."

All three of us rose and curtsied. "How do you do, Lady Melissande? It's a pleasure to welcome you to Worthington House," Mother said.

"The pleasure is mine." Lady Melissande's curtsy was so unbelievably graceful, I very much felt like the ugly duckling to her gorgeous swan. I could take lessons from her.

"Should we take a seat while we get acquainted?" Mother asked. "I've rung for tea."

Mother believed every situation could only be improved upon with that refreshment. And she was right. A sip of the comforting brew tended to smooth over any awkward moments.

Lady Melissande offered a tight smile but gracefully dropped into a settee.

Hollingsworth, on the other hand, remained standing by one of the windows. It conveyed the message he was merely an observer at the present time.

In the next instance, a knock on the door preceded the entrance of two footmen carrying the tea service and porcelain cups. After we took a few moments to refresh ourselves, Lady Melissande said, "Thank you for making room for me, Mrs. Worthington. I hope it's not an imposition."

Although she spoke perfect English, there was a French accent to her words.

"Of course not, my dear. We love to have you. Lord Hollingsworth is a very dear friend of ours." Mother tossed a glance his way which he acknowledged with a slight bow of his head. "I hope your journey from Paris was uneventful."

"It was." Lady Melissande answered. "Hollingsworth

insisted we stop in Paris so I could obtain new clothes. My school ones would not suit my new role in society." There was a bite to her words. I couldn't tell if it was directed at her brother, or the role that she was expected to play.

The atmosphere had turned rather taut. To lighten the mood, I said, "Your gown is lovely, Lady Melissande. Is it a Worth?"

She responded with a simple, "Yes."

Determined to be sociable, I pushed on. "Lady Lily and I adore fashionable clothes. I just had my debut season, and Lily will have hers next spring."

Lady Melissande glanced at Lady Lily. "You haven't had your season yet?"

"I had to postpone my debut until next year due to my grandfather's passing," Lady Lily explained, "so I've been filling the time arranging for a new wardrobe and redecorating Wynchcombe House."

"But you're living here?"

"Only temporarily. My brother Sebastian, the Duke of Wychcombe, and Kitty's sister Margaret are getting married in December. He's away at Wynchcombe Castle while I remain in town to buy furnishings for it. Thankfully, Mrs. Worthington has guided my endeavors. Otherwise, I'd be totally lost." She tossed a grateful glance toward Mother.

"So nice to have family, or nearly family, you can depend on," Lady Melissande said.

A choked sound from Hollingsworth, but other than that, he didn't say a word.

"And you, Miss Worthington? You've had your season?"

"Yes." Since Lady Melissande seemed curious about the subject, we soon entered into a conversation about what she could expect. We only stopped when Carlton announced luncheon was served.

"Cook has prepared a very special meal in your honor. All

French dishes," Mother offered by way of explanation as we proceeded to the dining room.

"How very lovely. You are very kind," Lady Melissande said.

During luncheon we learned Lady Melissande arrived at the Sainte-Marie Convent when she was six years old. Located as it was in a sparsely populated region in the north-west of France, she'd grown up with barely any friends. The nuns had done the best they could to keep her entertained, but it'd been a rather lonely upbringing.

"So very young," Mother said.

"I was heartsick for a long time, mostly for my mother. But in time I came to accept my fate."

"I'm sorry you suffered, Mellie," Hollingsworth explained. "It's what Mother wished for you."

"I know. She explained it to me before we said goodbye."

Maybe so, but the look she sent her brother could not in any way be considered loving, resentful more like. I could see why. She'd been sent to a faraway place with no family no friends, while he went on adventures. If that had happened to me, I would have felt the same way.

"You and I have that in common, Lady Melissande," Lady Lily said. "When I was three, my parents died. They fell from a cliff during a raging snowstorm. After their tragic accident, I was sent to live at Wynchcombe Castle."

"But at least you had your brother—Sebastian, was it not—for company?"

"No, I didn't. My grandfather took a rather hard line. He promised to house, feed, and educate me, but only if Sebastian stayed away."

"*Mon Dieu.* That's abominable."

"It was rather." For a moment, her usually bright demeanor darkened, but then she cheered right up. "But now everything is so different, and I have the Worthingtons to thank. You see, they took me in as well when I needed a refuge from the storm."

"And you've been a joy since the day we first met you, Lady Lily," Mother said.

"Thank you, Mrs. Worthington." Lady Lily turned back to Lady Melissande. "So, I know from personal experience you're in the best place you could possibly be."

"Are you looking forward to the social season, Lady Melissande?" I asked. "It's only a few months away." She seemed to be from all the questions she'd asked.

"We'll see. I'm not sure it'd be right for me."

She was most definitely sad. Could she be missing the convent? Or was it something else? Whatever it was that was causing her suffering, we would need to find out, so we could help her manage her melancholy.

After luncheon, Hollingsworth excused himself. After a two-week absence, there were matters that needed his attention. He promised to return in two days' time and show Lady Melissande the London sights.

Lady Lily and I took Lady Melissande in hand by giving her a grand tour of the house. Once we had done that, we proceeded to her bedroom. She loved the view of the garden. Turned out she adored flowers.

"Is there anything special you require, Lady Melissande?" I asked. "We would like you to be as comfortable as you possibly can."

"Thank you, Kitty. I appreciate you asking that question. There is one thing. I noticed you have a music room. Might I play the piano?"

"Yes, of course." It hadn't been played since my sister Emily passed away from the Spanish flu. She was the only one who enjoyed the instrument.

She was flagging. I could tell. Well, no wonder. A day's travel from Paris to London was exhausting, as I very well knew. And a night's stay at a hotel wouldn't have provided her with enough rest. So I said, "It's been a busy few days for you. You should have a lie in. Shall I send for your maid?"

"Yes, please."

"We eat supper at eight but gather a few minutes before in the drawing room. If you need anything before then, send your maid for me." I'd already shown her where my room was located.

"Thank you." She curtsied, and we quietly left the room.

Her arrival reminded me so much of Lady Lily's when she'd sought shelter in our home from the untenable situation she'd found herself in. Lady Melissande's situation, however, was entirely different. She was in no need of refuge, only a temporary stay. But where Lady Lily had been quite joyful once her initial shyness had given way, there was a well of sadness within Lady Melissande that didn't appear likely to fade. What had caused it, I had no idea. But I intended to find out.

CHAPTER EIGHT

THE PRINCE'S BALL

*D*AYS AFTER MY CONVERSATION with Mother about the Prince's Ball, we received an invitation to the event. I don't know who was more surprised, Mother or me, as we had no idea why we'd been honored with such a thing. We did not have long to wait for an explanation for that same day Sebastian telephoned.

He'd been summoned to the ball by the Prince of Andover himself who wished to speak with Sebastian about his vertical farming efforts. As an agriculture research fellow at Oxford, Sebastian had conducted several experiments for growing crops, one of them being vertical farming. Since Andover was a mountainous country, it stood to reason that the prince would be interested in such a project. Its arable land, which amounted to thirty percent, barely grew enough crops to feed half of its population. If vertical farming could be adopted, yields would be greater, and they could reduce their dependence on other countries for food.

"Margaret cannot attend due to her studies," Sebastian further explained, "and Lily is still in mourning."

So was he for that matter. But he could not turn down an invitation issued by the palace, not when Sebastian was a duke.

"When the Lord Chamberlain's office asked if anyone else should be invited, I immediately thought of you Mrs. W." He'd addressed Mother as such from the time we'd taken him under our wing. Even though she hid her pleasure, she'd always been secretly charmed by it.

"Of course, Sebastian, we would be more than happy to attend. Thank you for thinking of us."

Although she'd been calm throughout the telephone discussion, she was in a tizzy when the conversation ended. "A royal ball, Kitty. What will I wear?" Since the festivity was to take place in three days, there simply was not enough time for our modiste to fashion a new gown.

"Mother, you have so many lovely frocks. Surely, one of them would suit."

"But everyone's seen them!"

"Surely, not everybody. The king and queen haven't—for they hadn't attended last season's balls—and neither have the Prince and Princess of Andover. Your burgundy gown with the bell sleeves and flowing short cape would be your best choice." Not only would she sparkle under the massive chandeliers of Buckingham Palace, but with her dark hair and fair skin, the color suited her to no end.

"What about you, dear?"

"I think I'll wear the gold beaded gown."

"You don't think it's a little . . . daring for Buckingham Palace."

I could see her objection as the frock had a v neckline, nothing too revealing but a definite change from a more modest square cut. Our modiste, however, claimed it the new fashion. "Angelique tells me it's all the rage in Paris. You wouldn't want me to be seen in something that's not *au courant*, not with the Prince and Princess of Andover in attendance."

"I suppose it would be fine then. I better alert Cummings. She'll want to have my gown cleaned and pressed. Oh, and shoes, Kitty! I must shop for a new pair." And with that, she rushed all atwitter up the stairs.

Sebastian arrived the following day as he had matters to attend in town before the Prince's Ball. Since his sister, Lily, was staying with us, he made Worthington House his first stop. It was not time wasted as Mother and Lily filled him in on all the furnishings they'd bought, and he shared the progress being made at Wynchcombe Castle. A mammoth task as the castle had many bedchambers, all apparently in need of repair.

"The plumbing is proceeding smoothly, but we hit a snag in the kitchen. Cook absolutely refuses to use the new AGA gas stove I purchased. She'd rather prepare meals on the old iron monstrosity she's used for ages. Thing is the food comes out either half scorched or half raw."

"Well, dear, you can't have that for your wedding." Sebastian and Margaret had decided a weeklong celebration would be held prior to the wedding ceremony on Christmas Eve. As the wedding guests would be arriving seven days before the event and remain until Boxing Day, Cook would need to prepare several meals a day for twenty-five or so guests. It was imperative that the kitchen staff and equipment were in working order. "If I may enquire," Mother asked, "wouldn't it be better to pension her off and hire a new cook?"

"I can't do that, Mrs. W. It would break her heart if she didn't prepare our wedding feast."

I admired his kind heart, but something needed to be

done. "Hire an assistant, then," I suggested. "I'm sure Mother and Lily would be more than glad to interview likely candidates."

"I suppose that's the only solution. It's bound to upset her, though."

"Staffing matters are difficult to deal with, Sebastian," Mother said. "But it's needed if you're to have a joyous wedding celebration."

"I agree," Lady Lily said. "Mrs. Sweetwater, that's our cook, is old and set in her ways. You can explain you don't want her to overexert herself. The new assistant will be there to help with the wedding preparations. And then have the assistant quietly handle most of it."

"We'll have to be careful who we hire," Sebastian said, "as we don't want to ruffle her feathers any more than we have to."

"Don't worry Sebastian, dear. We'll explain matters to the candidates we select. Once we've picked the ones best suited, we'll send on our recommendations. You and Margaret can make the final decision."

"Thanks, Mrs. W. Don't know what we would do without your help. You're an angel sent from heaven."

"Oh, pshaw," Mother said, blushing. "Now, about the Prince's Ball. It's white tie for the gentlemen. I trust your new valet is aware of what that entails."

If left to his own devices, Sebastian would have gone without a valet. But Mother prevailed upon him to hire one as he was now a duke and needed someone who knew how to dress him. Sebastian had laughed at her suggestion for he'd been dressing himself all his life; but recognizing the wisdom of her words, he gave in with grace.

"He is. He assures me everything will be ready the day of the ball. As he'd anticipated this very thing happening, he'd taken the liberty of ordering a rig."

"Splendid," Mother said. "We'll have supper here, of course, before we depart for the ball. Neville can drive us to Buckingham Palace in the Rolls."

"Sounds like a plan, ma'am. Now I really must leave for I have an appointment with my man of business."

And then he was gone.

On the night of the Prince's Ball, he appeared in black trousers featuring two lines of braids down the outside leg, black patent lace-up shoes, a white bow tie, white plain stiff shirt, a white low-cut waistcoat and a black jacket with evening tailcoat.

"Oh, my, Sebastian, you do clean up nicely," I said.

"Wish Margaret were here to see you," Lady Lily said.

"So do I, not so she could see me, but so we could be together. I miss her."

Mother squeezed his hand. "You won't have to wait long. The wedding is in two months."

"An eternity."

His introduction to Lady Melissande did not take long, as she was rather shy about meeting him. After supper, we gathered our fur wraps, for it was a cold night, piled into the Rolls, and set off for Buckingham Palace, with Neville, our chauffeur, at the wheel.

I couldn't help but be impressed by the royal residence splendidly illuminated as it was, both outside and within. The ballroom, grand entrance, marble hall, grand staircase, vestibules and galleries, decorated in the Belle Époque cream and gold color scheme, took my breath away. After slowly making our way to the receiving line, we were graciously greeted by their royal majesties, the King and Queen of England, as well as the Prince and Princess of Andover. The king, with his stiff white evening shirt, single faded cuffs and wing collar, white tie, waistcoat, and black evening tailcoat, matched Sebastian's outfit. But he also wore a row of medals and the insignia of the Order of the Garter pinned to his coat.

His Queen Consort was splendidly dressed in a heavily beaded gold gown more than likely designed by Reville, the court dressmaker. Every bit of her was decorated in jewels from the top of her crown right down to her fingers. A tiara glistened on her head. Two necklaces—one pearl one diamond—adorned her tall, shapely neck while bracelets glimmered on both arms and rings sparkled on her fingers. The Order of the Garter was pinned to her dress. There was nothing about her that did not dazzle.

The heavily mustached Prince of Andover matched our king in elegance. The only difference was the color of his sash. While the king's was blue, the prince's was gold to reflect one of the colors in the Andoverian flag. An Order of the Wolf, an honor bestowed upon him by his father, the King of Andover, was pinned to his chest. He was dark-haired and blue-eyed, but I could not detect anything more than that, as a quite impressive mustache covered the lower half of his face. The Queen of Andover, who appeared to be in her seventies, stood next to him. Although not as splendidly bejeweled as our queen, she held her own as a diamond necklace dripped over a satin and tulle dress. Bright black button eyes glittered in a cragged face. Full of wrinkles she might be, but there was nothing dull about her wit.

Her daughter-in-law was another thing altogether. While the Queen of Andover resembled a bird of paradise, the princess seemed as dull as a sparrow. From her hair to her gown to her eyes, everything about her was brown. There wasn't one bit of sparkle to her. Seemingly, the Andover crown jewels had been reserved for the queen.

The prince's son, the Duke of Andover, was a carbon copy of his father, sans the bushy mustache and his attitude. While the prince was all smiles, the duke's eyes sparked with rebellion. Much as in the theatre, this was the last place he wished to be. He was polite enough, though, when we were introduced. "Miss Worthington, I do hope you'll save a dance for me."

"Of course, Your Highness. I'd be honored." I made sure he noticed my engagement ring when he kissed my hand.

"Aah, you're taken, I see."

I arched a brow. "Not taken, Your Highness. Engaged. There is a difference."

He bit back a smile. "You're a wit. A welcome change from those who spout nothing but platitudes. I'll come fetch you at the first waltz."

"Fetch. What a noble way of putting it." I curtsied and moved on before my unruly tongue made another insolent remark.

Once the receiving line disbanded, an officer wearing a military uniform in the red and gold Andover colors found Sebastian. Except for a missing mustache, he bore a remarkable resemblance to the Prince of Andover, down to the brilliant blue of his eyes.

He bowed to Sebastian. "Your Grace, his royal highness, the Prince of Andover, wishes to hold a private conversation with you."

"Yes, of course."

"If you will follow me."

Sebastian nodded before following the officer down the length of the ballroom and disappearing from sight.

I, of course, couldn't allow the resemblance to go unremarked. "Mother, did you notice—"

But she didn't allow me to finish. "Later, dear, when we're alone."

"Yes, of course." Whatever the tale was regarding the officer, Mother knew.

We were standing happily sipping champagne when the

orchestra struck up a waltz. So, it was no surprise when the Duke of Andover found me and bowed. "If you would do me the honor of dancing with me, Miss Worthington?"

I curtsied. "It will be my pleasure, Your Highness." He was a very good dancer which didn't surprise me. It must have been part of his training growing up. More importantly, his hands did not roam where they shouldn't. Maybe what I'd heard about him had been a rumor, or maybe he'd been cautioned to be on his best behavior.

"How do you find London, sir?"

"Crowded."

"You don't have large cities in Andover?"

"We do, but not as populated as yours. And the air is immeasurably cleaner."

"Coal burning does fog up London. Some people find it difficult to breathe. That's why those who have country estates flee there during the fall and winter."

"But not your family."

"We don't have a country estate. We live in London year-round."

He tilted his head but didn't question me.

I provided the answer, nonetheless. "Mother does not want to live apart from Father, and he can't leave his business for months at a time."

"What business is your father involved in?"

"He's an investment manager. People entrust him with their funds. He's made many of them very rich."

"Maybe I should entrust him with mine."

"Maybe you should. Worthington & Son is in the City of London's financial district. I'm sure he'd make himself available for such a discussion if that's what you truly wished."

"He employs his son?"

"Ned is a full partner of the firm. He's a whiz at finances."

"Your father trusts him that much?"

57

"He does." It was clear from the argument at the theatre his father didn't trust him to manage his life as he should. Whether that stemmed from irresponsible behavior on his part, or some other reason, remained to be seen. But after only a few minutes' acquaintance, I couldn't very well delve into their relationship. Best move on to a safer topic. "Your father is a worthwhile gentleman to care for his country so much he wants to institute vertical farming."

The duke's brow wrinkled. "How do you know this?"

"He requested an audience with my future brother-in-law, the Duke of Wynchcombe, who's a noted botanist. They're meeting right now. Didn't you know?"

"My father and I disagree about this, so he doesn't keep me apprised of any efforts he makes toward that goal."

"You don't approve?"

"It's bound to fail. The Andoverian farmers have no interest in such a thing. Not only that, but it would take too long to establish. Our need is urgent, Miss Worthington. We need to arrange for funds now so we can arrange for food for our population before winter sets in. This pet project of my father's is bound to end in disaster."

The waltz came to a close ending our conversation. He escorted me back to Mother, bowed, and walked away to ask another young lady to dance. I was sincerely sorry for I would have loved to continue our discussion. Clearly, he was not the wastrel he was rumored to be but had a solid head on his shoulders. If the situation in Andover was as dire as he said, the obvious solution was for the prince to sign an agreement with England so he could obtain the funds his country desperately needed. Whether that would happen was anybody's guess.

CHAPTER NINE

MURDER MOST FOUL

*T*WO DAYS LATER, Mother and I had gathered early for supper in the drawing room when after a swift knock on the door, Carlton entered.

Walking straight to Mother, he presented a newspaper on a tray. "My apologies, ma'am, for interrupting. A special edition of *The Tell-All* has arrived, and it contains some rather alarming news. I thought you'd want to see it right away." Having done his duty, he bowed and left.

One look at the gossip rag and Mother's face paled. "The Prince of Andover is dead."

"What? How can that be?" I rushed over from my perch on the sofa to glance over her shoulder. The body of the Prince of Andover, the newspaper stated, had been found early this morning in the Tower of London, sans head. "He was decapitated!"

"Not only that, but whoever killed him walked off with

his head. How on earth does something like that happen with all the guards stationed at the Tower?"

I had no idea. Eager to learn more, I read on. "Scotland Yard has been called to investigate. Chief Detective Inspector Rutherford, a twenty-year member of the force, will lead the inquiry." The other articles on the front page had no more to say on the murder. They'd filled the space with reports about the Andover royal family.

Mother glanced at me. "Do you know the inspector, Kitty? Has Robert mentioned him?"

"No. He rarely talks about matters involving Scotland Yard when we're together. He prefers to leave it all behind."

"A murder of a royal prince at the Tower of London. How could this have happened?"

"I don't know." With all the security around the Tower, no unauthorized person should have been able to break in.

"Inspector Rutherford should be up to the task, given how much experience he has," Mother said.

One could only hope.

We were soon joined by Father, and Ladies Lily and Melissande, as well as my brother Ned, who often dined with us. They were just as shocked as Mother and I about the murder. But with so little to go on, we couldn't even begin to speculate about the whys and wherefores.

That didn't stop the London newspapers from offering their opinions in the coming days. Since no report, official or otherwise, was issued by Scotland Yard, the scandal sheets resorted to wild speculations, including a story about a madman on the loose. Emotions among the populace rose sky-high as everyone was in a frenzy for the murderer to be caught. When the inquest was held three days later, it was no surprise a large crowd gathered at the Coroner's Court. So many in fact, a battalion of police officers had to be called in to control the crowds.

As I was eager to attend the inquest, I'd asked Robert to secure permission for me to do so. He'd not only obtained it, but reserved space for us in the gallery from which we could watch the proceedings. Getting inside the courtroom was a challenge, as we had to battle our way through the throng, especially after some ruffians engaged in a round of fisticuffs. But with the help of a few police officers, who assiduously applied their cudgels, and Robert who swung a mean right hook at one, we made it inside.

"Goodness," I said straightening my cloche hat which had been knocked askew during the melee. "That was more than I expected."

"They're scared, Kitty. The newspapers did us no favors when they printed such lurid accounts," he said, flexing his bruised hand.

"You're hurt!"

"Nothing I haven't experienced before." He flashed one of his patented smiles guaranteed to make me melt. "Don't worry. It will heal soon enough." A gentle reminder that the minor injury came along with the job he loved.

Still, I couldn't help but be irked by it. "Scotland Yard should have issued a report. It left a vacuum which the newspapers were more than happy to fill."

"We couldn't. We were ordered by the highest levels of government to keep silent."

"Why?"

"Let's just say there's more to this situation than meets the eye."

Situation, not murder. "Are you involved in the investigation?"

"Only peripherally. Inspector Rutherford is in charge."

Even though I wanted to ask more questions, I didn't. He wouldn't answer them if Scotland Yard had been ordered to keep mum.

A hush fell over the crowd as members of the Andover royal family were escorted, one by one, to their seats. The princess, dressed from head to toe in unrelenting black, her veil so thick I wondered how she could see, was the first one led into the courtroom. Her son, the Duke of Andover, dressed in a sober black suit that possessed none of the flash he'd sported at the Prince's Ball, followed behind her. The Queen of Andover made the strongest impression of all. She marched in, head thrown back, face uncovered, eyes flashing with anger. The mild-mannered cousin and his stunning wife walked in last. Attired in a haute couture gown that showcased her stunning figure, she made funereal black a fashion statement. Same as the queen, she'd left her face bare, so her feelings were there for all to see. A hint of resentment flashed through when her husband led her to the seat behind the royal family. Maybe she objected to her second-class status.

The courtroom was not as crowded as other inquests I'd attended. I recognized but a few high-ranking members of the government. Those I did not had to be part of Andover's diplomatic corps since every one wore a black armband. No surprise officials had limited attendance at the inquest. More than likely, they were trying to keep the details of the gruesome murder from leaking out. A useless endeavor if you asked me, as they were bound to find their way to the press. Someone always talked. But at least the English government could claim it'd done its best to provide what dignity it could to the proceedings.

The presiding officer was the Senior Coroner of the City of London. Traditionally, an inquest was held in the borough where a murder had taken place, but the City of London Coroner's Court had been determined a more proper venue than the borough where the Tower of London was located. Ravaged as it had been by bombing during the Great War, the East End was no place to conduct the inquest of a royal prince.

It took no time for him to call the first witness—the cousin whose duty it had been to escort the prince back to the royal suite at the Majestic Hotel.

"What time did you arrive at the Tower of London?" The coroner asked.

"At eight. The prince had an important appointment later that morning with Andoverian government representatives to discuss the lease negotiations. So he needed to return to his suite to prepare himself."

"What happened when you arrived?"

"I was escorted by one of the Tower of London guards to the chamber where his royal highness resided overnight—the room Anne Boleyn occupied the night before she was, er, executed. He'd developed an avid interest in her."

"I . . . see." The coroner noted something into a journal he kept by his side. "Please proceed."

"Well, the guard knocked on the door. There was no answer, so he knocked again. Louder this time. But his highness did not make an appearance. At that point, I grew quite concerned and insisted the guard break down the door. But there was no need. He had a key." The count's face flushed, probably with embarrassment.

"Stands to reason," the coroner said. "What did you find when you entered the room?"

The count's face lost all color. "It was rather dark as the curtains hadn't been opened, so I couldn't see very well. As I moved into the space, my vision grew used to the darkness. That's when I saw," he swallowed hard. "His highness on the floor. Blood everywhere. And his head, dear Lord, his head was not there." He retrieved a handkerchief and put it to his mouth. "It was horrible. Horrible."

"Just so. What happened next?"

"The guard pulled me out of the room and locked the door. And then he went off to fetch his superiors. I left at that point. I felt it my duty to tell the princess and the queen what had occurred. They wouldn't want to hear it from someone else."

The coroner seemed to question the count's behavior by a rise of his brow. I had to agree. At the very least, the count should have remained until the medical examiner arrived to provide an official identification. But rather than comment, he dismissed the count. "Thank you, sir. You may step down but please remain in the courtroom. I may have more questions."

"Of course." He kept the handkerchief to his face as if it could somehow erase the horror he'd seen. When he retook his seat, his wife didn't offer one word of compassion.

The next witness, the Tower of London guard, echoed what the count said, so he was quickly dispatched. And then the Chief Medical Examiner was called to the stand. Made sense he'd been assigned the postmortem as the Prince of Andover had been an important figure. He testified the decapitation had been performed with an axe. Not a wild speculation; the weapon had been left conveniently behind. The murder took place between one and three the morning the body had been discovered. To my surprise, he contributed no additional information. But then he'd probably been ordered to provide only enough details to obtain a verdict of unlawful killing by person or persons unknown.

The next to testify, Chief Detective Inspector Rutherford, proved to be a much more interesting witness. He was a large man, taller than Robert who was six three, and barrel-chested. His dark hair was streaked with sufficient gray to make him appear distinguished. He wore no spectacles. As his gaze roamed over the courtroom, his grey eyes seemed not to miss a thing, especially the royal family.

"Can you tell us about the morning of October 19?"

Inspector Rutherford retrieved a notebook from the depths of his houndstooth jacket and flipped it open. "At approximately 9:12 a.m. the superintendent stepped into my office and informed me that the Prince of Andover had apparently been murdered at the Tower of London, and he asked me to investigate. I arrived at the Tower at 9:38. I gave the guards at the front gate my name and title. Told them I'd been placed in charge of the investigation into the Prince of Andover's death. At that point, the master of the guards himself met me and led me to the chamber where the body lay. The Chief Medical Examiner was standing outside the door which was locked. The master of the guards had assigned two officers to guard the room, and they were stationed outside. After I ascertained no one but the count and the guard who originally opened the door had entered the room, I asked for the door to be unlocked and, together with the chief medical examiner, stepped inside." He flipped to the next page.

You could have heard a pin drop, so quiet was the courtroom.

"The cause of death was clear." He suddenly glanced up and steely-eyed declared in a doom like voice. "Decapitation."

Someone in the front of the courtroom whimpered. I couldn't tell who. Not totally unaffected by the dramatic telling, I searched for and found Robert's hand. He held it tight within his, lending me his strength and warmth.

"A bloodied axe lay approximately two feet from the body," Inspector Rutherford continued. "There was a great deal of blood which I took care to avoid. By necessity, the medical examiner approached the body and pronounced him dead. Not that there was any question."

Another whimper from a member of the royal family. I had no idea who.

"My apologies," Inspector Rutherford said.

The princess nodded in acknowledgement. The queen remained ramrod straight.

"During the next half hour, I examined the room very carefully. The curtains were closed. But one of the windows had been forced open, so I surmised the murderer came in that way. The forensic team arrived shortly after we did. They went over the room thoroughly and carefully. No fingerprints were found."

"Not even the prince's?" The coroner asked.

"The room had been wiped clean."

"What about the weapon?"

"It had been wiped as well."

"Do you have any theories, Inspector?" The coroner asked.

"The murderer broke into the Tower of London, and in the early hours of October 19, made his way into the chamber. There was an empty bottle of wine in the room. According to the manservant who brought his meal, it was not delivered by him. We analyzed the remnants and discovered a substance strong enough to make him unconscious. It's our considered opinion, he would have been too inebriated to struggle."

The coroner cleared his throat. "How was the death carried out?"

Sobs filled the space. By now, it was clear the princess was the one affected.

"There's a scaffold in the room, your honor. Apparently, the prince insisted on it. In the state he was in, it would have been a relatively easy thing for a man to drag him to the scaffold and execute him."

"A man, you say?"

"Had to be. The prince was a large man. No woman could have performed the deed."

"And the prince's head was nowhere to be found?"

"No, sir. The murderer must have taken it with him."

"For what purpose?"

"I don't know, but I aim to find out." His hawk-eyed gaze roamed the space. Clearly, he believed the murderer was in the courtroom.

CHAPTER TEN

THE AFTERMATH

*T*HE AFTERMATH OF THE INQUEST was to be expected. The newspapers continued to expound the theory that a madman was on the loose. Why relinquish a good story when it sold so many papers? Most of the aristocracy, wanting no part of it, fled back to the safety of their country estates. But Lords Hollingsworth, Rutledge, and Marlowe remained in London. It made sense for Rutledge and Marlowe since they were bachelors with no families to worry about. And Hollingsworth couldn't very well flee and leave his sister behind. Not that he would have done such a thing. Lady Clinton also refused to leave. She wanted to be in the thick of things when the murderer was caught. Given her love of scandal, that decision did not surprise me.

Unfortunately, with the departure of the well-heeled, our agency business dried up again. But there was one ray of sunshine. After arguing about the danger of living alone in the townhouse with a murderer on the loose, I'd convinced Lady Emma to move to Worthington Manor. I was hopeful she'd make her stay permanent, so I could stop worrying about her welfare.

With business as slow as it was, Lady Emma and I decided to curtail our days and hours of operation. We were now open on Mondays, Wednesdays, and Fridays, from ten to four, with only one of us present on any given day. An appropriate notice had been posted on the townhouse door providing the information and the telephone number of a service we'd retained to take messages in case we were needed outside business hours.

While the aristocracy had the means to flee town, most of the London population did not. They had jobs and lives that revolved around the city. But that didn't mean they didn't take precautions. People took to walking around London armed to the teeth with cudgels, knives, and other lethal instruments so they could defend themselves if they encountered the madman. As it was to be expected, that led to altercations on the streets of the city, in public houses, and anywhere that people congregated. Soon the police had their hands full carting people off to jail.

Since it wasn't safe to wander outside our home, Mother decided to throw a dinner party. Mother liked to seat fourteen at dinner. But with most acquaintances having deserted town, eleven was the best she could do. Because of the odd numbers, a hostess's curse, Mother debated whether to invite Lady Clinton to make up the numbers. But in the end, she decided against it. Lady Clinton would gossip nonstop.

Everyone invited accepted, which wasn't saying much, as Ladies Emma, Lily, and Melissande were already in residence at Worthington Manor. Father, of course, lived here, Ned popped in often enough, and Robert and I were engaged. So,

Lords Rutledge, Marlowe, and Hollingsworth were the only ones who were neither family, or almost family, nor living with us. But they all were good friends and happy enough to attend.

The day before the dinner party, I'd joined Mother in her parlor to review the dinner menu and wine selections with the able assistance of Cook. She assured us the butcher and produce man would be happy enough to deliver our orders. With everyone having left town, their businesses were suffering. They'd only just finalized their selections when Carlton stepped into the parlor with the afternoon's edition of *The Tell-All*.

What now? was my only thought.

"There's been an interesting development in the prince's murder investigation, ma'am." He presented the paper to Mother on a tray as he always did.

I rushed over to glance over her shoulder. The headline did not disappoint. "Prince's Murderer Caught!"

"Well, thank goodness," Mother said. "Maybe now things will return to normal."

The man arrested had tried to pawn a pocket watch that clearly belonged to the prince as it was engraved with the Andover crest. Since the prince always carried it on him, Scotland Yard claimed the man had killed the prince.

That conclusion did not sit right with me. "That seems rather odd. Don't you think, Mother?"

"What do you mean, dear?"

"Well, first of all, he seems to be a common thief. How did he break into the Tower of London? The article doesn't say."

"Scotland Yard is probably keeping those details confidential until the trial. Or maybe they haven't found out."

But that wasn't the only thing bothering me. "If the prince was asleep, there was no need to kill him, much less hack off his head, to steal the watch. He could have grabbed it and sneaked back out." Next to the article, there was a picture of a man being led away in handcuffs. He had a large build and a flabby stomach. "Look at the size of him! How could he have squeezed his way through that small window?" I'd visited the Tower of London and had seen the Queen's House. Built in the Tudor era, its windows were hardly big enough for a woman to slip through, much less a man of the thief's size.

"Didn't Inspector Rutherford say at the inquest that a large man murdered the prince?"

"No. He said it had to have been a man. Strong yes, but not large. This man couldn't have done it."

"Well, dear, I imagine the inspector must think so. Otherwise, he wouldn't have arrested him."

I was beginning to think Inspector Rutherford was an idiot.

The supper party was a resounding success. After everyone enjoyed the beef Wellington and *charlotte russe*, we retired to the drawing room where the main topic, of course, was the murder and the arrest. I was not the only who thought the wrong person had been apprehended. Lord Rutledge had his doubts as well. Knowing Robert would never make his opinion known in public, I made some nonsensical excuse about showing him something in the library and led him away. Given this was October, our usual rendezvous place would not do. It was much too cold to enjoy a tête-à-tête in the terrace.

"So what do you wish to show me, Miss Worthington?" he asked, a slice of a grin making an appearance.

"You know very well why I needed privacy."

He sketched a small bow. "I don't. Pray tell."

Contrary man! I huffed out a frustrated breath. "Rutherford arrested the wrong man."

He turned serious in a heartbeat.

"Now, Catherine."

"Don't. You feel the same way I do."

"You know I can't discuss the case."

"It's not what you didn't say in the dining room. It's how you didn't say it."

He folded his arms across his broad chest and gazed down at me. "Enlighten me, please."

"You nodded when Lord Rutledge asserted Scotland Yard arrested the wrong man. And when Hollingsworth asked a general question, you barely stopped yourself from answering him. Face it, Inspector Rutherford made a mistake. You have to fix this. That man is innocent."

"The last thing Billy 'the Pincher' Murrow is is innocent. He's been nicked for stealing more times than I can count."

I propped my hands on my hips. "Answer me this, how did he get into that room? The man has to be at least fifteen stone. I've seen the Queen's House. He wouldn't have fit through those windows."

"He came through the front door. He's a master at picking locks."

"But the window was broken."

"He broke it while he was there. One point Rutherford did not make at the inquest was that there was no glass in the room, but there was outside. The window was broken from the inside."

"How did Billy the Pincher know the prince would be there?"

"Easily. He picked up a newspaper. It was all over the news."

"And how did he break into the Tower of London as heavily guarded as it is?"

"Rutherford hasn't worked that out, but he will." He paused for a moment. "There is one thing, however, that doesn't track."

"What?"

"He's a thief. They've taken to calling him a cat burglar because he breaks into houses in the middle of the night. But he's never hurt anyone, much less killed them."

"Aha! So you agree with me."

"No, I don't Catherine. There must be an answer as to why he acted differently this time. We just have to find out what it is."

"We?"

He pinched my chin. "Scotland Yard. That we."

When I scrunched my nose, his mirth disappeared. "You will not involve yourself with this murder, Catherine."

Heavens! He was serious. "Did I say I would?"

"You don't have to. I know how your mind works. There's a puzzle here that needs to be solved, and your very inquisitive mind can't help but be attracted to it."

"But—"

"I'm not telling you this to clip your wings. There are matters of national security involved. Matters I can't discuss. The British government will not allow any civilian to interfere with this investigation. If you do, there will be consequences."

"I've already been jailed twice. By you. How much worse could it be?" I grinned, hoping to lighten his mood.

But he was having none of it. "You were temporarily detained. If you inject yourself into the investigation, those in power will not treat you so leniently. You might end up in a prison cell. Permanently."

I took in a breath, let it out. It was one thing to investigate murders when someone near and dear had been suspected of a crime. But as interesting as this case was bound to be, I had no reason to get involved. And if national security was an issue, that gave me even less of an excuse to concern myself with this matter. "Very well. I'll do as you ask."

"Good." He glanced toward the door. "We should return. We've been gone long enough."

"Do we have to?" I asked drawing near.

"Well, maybe a few minutes more won't hurt. How shall we spend the time?"

"I have an idea," I said, wrapping my arms around him.

CHAPTER ELEVEN

THE QUEEN OF ANDOVER MAKES A REQUEST

*B*Y THE TIME ROBERT BID ME GOODNIGHT, I was wondering why I refused to name our wedding date. While tossing and turning in bed, I reminded myself of the many reasons why. There was so much I wanted to do. No matter how much Robert insisted he wouldn't object to my forging my own path, marriage would curtail my freedom. And then there was the issue of children. Plain and simple I had no wish for one at this time. Even though we'd take precautions, there was no guarantee I wouldn't get pregnant. Unfortunately, none of those reasons held a candle to my desire for him.

I hadn't solved my dilemma by the time Betsy walked into my room the next day. Because of the alleged madman on the loose, her secretarial classes had temporarily ceased, and she'd resumed her maid responsibilities full-time. Something she probably appreciated as the double duties were bound to demand too much of her. "Good morning, Miss. I brought your coffee."

Sitting up on my bed, I stretched my arms. "Have I ever told you you're an angel sent from heaven, Betsy?"

"Yes, Miss," she said setting the service on a round table. "Would you like to wear the burgundy frock with the pleated skirt today? It looks ever so nice on you."

"I guess that will be fine."

"Anything wrong, Miss?" She must have picked up on my less than enthusiastic response.

"Betsy, may I ask you a rather personal question?"

"Of course."

"Do you ever. . . have you ever longed for Neville and you to be together?"

She scrunched her brow. "But we are, Miss. We're promised to each other."

"I meant . . . intimately."

Before she commented, she poured a cup of coffee and handed it to me. Folding her hands in front of her, she said, "You want to be . . . intimate with the inspector?"

"I do, but I can't. Not until we're married."

"Well, Miss. I do wish it, and so does Neville. But we won't. The consequences would be too great."

"Babies, you mean?"

"Yes, you remember Rachel?"

I nodded. "One of the downstairs maids."

"She got herself in the family way. Had to leave her position, she did."

"Mother found her a place that caters to unwed mothers."

"Mrs. Worthington was very generous. But now Rachel is living by herself in a home with several other unwed mothers with no hope for a future. Her man left her to bear the babe on her own."

"Neville wouldn't do that."

"No, he wouldn't. But why put that burden on our lives. Someday I'll have a career as a receptionist at your agency, Miss. And Neville wants to open a motorcar repair shop. Even though he's saving most of his salary, we're still several years from making his dream come true. Why ruin those dreams for the thrill of a few minutes?"

"Is that how long it lasts?" I asked, wide-eyed. "Goodness. I thought it took longer than that."

"It depends on your man." A naughty grin rolled across her lips. "I'm sure Inspector Crawford will make it last a good long while."

Laughter burst out of me. "Oh, Betsy, you are a star."

"Yes, Miss. Now, shall I lay out your frock and run your bath?"

"Please." Somehow our conversation lightened my mood and vanished my doubts. I was on the right path. I just had to stick to it. Of course, that was easier said than done.

After breakfast, Lady Emma and I proceeded to the library to review our plans for the agency. We'd been at it for half an hour when Carlton appeared. "Begging your pardon, Miss Worthington, but your mother requires your presence in the drawing room."

It had to be something important for Mother to interrupt our planning session. "Of course." I turned to Lady Emma. "I shall be back as soon as I can."

"No need to hurry. I'll spend the time writing a summary of what we discussed."

I walked into the drawing room to find we had a guest. And not any guest, but her Royal Majesty, the Queen of Andover, seated on one of our midnight blue settees. Ramrod straight, as in the inquest, she was wearing unrelenting black. Only the veil was missing. Her gaze pinned me so hard I felt like a butterfly.

"Your Highness," I offered her my deepest curtsy, easy to

do in my palazzo pants, but not as graceful as if I'd been wearing a skirt.

"Is that what passes for fashion these days?" she asked with a gimlet gaze.

"Yes, your majesty."

"They do appear quite comfortable."

"They are."

"Sit down, child, before I get a crick in my neck, an affliction of old age."

When I did, she turned her sight on Mother. "We require privacy."

"Of course, Your Highness." Mother came to her feet. "You'll ring, Kitty, if you require anything."

Before I could answer, the queen said, "We won't."

Once Mother stepped out of the room, the queen didn't waste any time. "Now, we can get down to business."

"Yes, ma'am."

"You must know why I'm here."

Hadn't the foggiest. "I'm afraid I don't."

"I want you to investigate my son's murder."

"Scotland Yard has caught the man responsible."

"They apprehended the wrong man."

Exactly what I'd thought, but I was curious to hear her reasoning. "Why do you think that?"

"The man is a common criminal, a thief. My son's murder was planned with a high level of sophistication. He had to gain entrance into the Tower of London and the Queen's House with no one the wiser. Not only that, he would have had to make his way into the bedroom chamber without my son raising an alarm."

"The window was broken."

"From the inside."

She knew that, did she? "He could have broken in through the front door."

"But he didn't. I questioned Rutherford extensively. There was no sign of forced entry through that portal. Whoever broke in either had a key, or my son allowed him or her entrance."

"It had to be a man. Your son—the prince was a large man. No woman would have been able to carry him from his bed to the . . . place of execution."

"Come, Miss Worthington, use your imagination. A woman intimately connected with the prince could have easily gained entry. Maybe she'd made arrangements with him to spend the night. She could have closed the front door but kept it unlatched so that the henchman she hired for the occasion could make his way into the Queen's House. Then after she seduced my son and drugged him, it would have been an easy feat for the man she hired to make his way up the stairs, drag my son to that block, and murder him." She shuddered. It was the first time I'd seen her react with horror to her son's murder.

I felt for her. I really did. But I had to bring up the obvious. "There was no evidence that anyone else was there."

"Obviously, they cleaned up after themselves."

"They would have been seen. The Tower is well guarded."

"And yet someone managed to slip in and murder my son. That fact is irrefutable."

"Why do you wish me, in particular, to investigate?"

"I've learned about your previous inquiries. In at least one of them, you managed to discover the murderer before Scotland Yard did." She took a deep breath, let it out. "Given the circumstances, I don't trust Rutherford to find my son's killer."

"What circumstances?"

"Your government wants the rights to mine the antimony mineral. As long as my son's murderer remains free, the negotiations won't proceed. So, they've pressured Scotland

Yard to solve the murder quickly. Rutherford has done that by apprehending a suspect. One with whom I'm not satisfied. I will not allow the rights to that mineral to be signed away until the true killer is caught."

There were more issues at play here than a simple murder. Best thing I could do was politely decline her offer. "I've been warned off from investigating the prince's death. A matter of national importance I've been told."

She pinned me with that glare of hers. "If anyone has a problem with your investigation, Miss Worthington, tell them to come to me."

I doubted a government representative would bring up the matter with her. England wanted that mineral. The last thing they would do was upset the grieving mother of an assassinated prince. "Very well. I'll pass on that information if I'm ever approached." There was one thing I was eager to learn. "Who do you think murdered your son?"

"I have an idea, but I do not want to cloud your judgment."

I folded my hands on my lap. "If I accept this charge, I will need to interview members of the royal family."

She banged her walking stick on the carpet. "You will have their full cooperation. I will make certain of that."

"I don't conduct investigations on my own. I will need to consult family and friends to see if they want to assist."

She leaned forward and gave me a full smile that seemed more fearsome than anything else. "I'm counting on it, Miss Worthington. I know how you work. Now about your fee. Will three thousand pounds be enough? Or will you require more than that?"

"Three thousand?" I asked, aghast at the vast sum.

"Let's make it five. You'll have expenses, of course. I shall have our bank issue a draft as soon as you agree." She came to her feet. "I'll expect to hear from you by tomorrow at two that you have accepted this assignment."

"Yes, ma'am." I curtsied.

A bare minute after she sailed out of the room, Mother, and Ladies Lily and Emma rushed in.

"Well?" Mother asked.

"She wants me, us," I gave a pointed look to all three of them, "to investigate her son's murder."

"Oh, Kitty," Mother said.

"Heavens," Lily said.

"What did you say?" From Lady Emma.

"That I would need to consult my family and friends. I can't possibly take on such a monumental task by myself. And then there's the fact that Scotland Yard has already named a murderer."

"Well, it's certainly something to think about," Mother said.

I did not like the gleam in her eye.

CHAPTER TWELVE

THE INVESTIGATIVE COMMITTEE MEETS

*N*ED SAID YES READILY ENOUGH. Not a surprise. He was always game for an investigation. So did Marlowe and Hollingsworth. Owen Clapham didn't answer the telephone when I called, so I sent a footman to his lodgings with a note. During previous investigations, all four had been instrumental in identifying the culprit. Unfortunately, we would have to do without Sebastian and Margaret. He was busy at Wynchcombe Castle, and Margaret was at Oxford pursuing her degree.

Lady Melissande, having overheard our discussion in the library, volunteered to help. I hesitated for I didn't know how she could contribute. But after thinking it over, I accepted her assistance. Not only would another set of hands, eyes, and a clever brain make lighter work for the rest of us, but it would keep her from moping around the house. She'd played so many dirges since her arrival we could strongly recommend her for any funerals.

But the biggest surprise was Mother. "I want to help."

"Er, aren't you busy arranging for furnishings and such for Wynchcombe Castle?"

"Most of what we need has been purchased or ordered. Besides, with this madman on the loose, warehouses are leery of opening their doors."

"They think a madman would kill for a few bolts of cloth?"

"Some of it is extremely valuable." When I hesitated, she pushed on. "You need me, Kitty. You're not aware of the intricacies of the Andoverian royal line."

"And you are?"

She nodded.

"Such as?"

"Who's the heir now that the duke is dead?"

"His son."

She shook her head.

"Then who?"

"Allow me to help, and I will tell you."

I laughed. "Those cloth merchants did not stand a chance." I nodded. "All right. You may join the team. But, Mother, I'm in charge."

She fought back a smile. "Of course, dear. I wouldn't have it any other way. Now, when's our first meeting?"

"Tomorrow at two. I've already sent a missive to her royal highness agreeing to her request."

An hour later, we heard back from Mister Clapham. As I expected, he was happy to help. Good thing because we needed his expertise. With his experience as a Scotland Yard detective inspector, he knew the criminal mind and procedures better than any of us. We made quite a clever team if I said so myself, especially with the addition of Mother.

One person did concern me. Lady Melissande. After her arrival at Worthington Manor, she'd kept herself occupied playing the piano, wandering the gardens when the weather allowed, and reading books in French, English, Italian, and Greek. Obviously, she'd received an excellent education, but she'd lived most of her life among nuns, most of whom observed vows of silence. Only those who taught were allowed to speak. As a result, she did not readily enter into conversations. Eager to learn more about her, Lady Lily and I, as well as Mother, had made friendly overtures time and again. But she'd eschewed every attempt to gain her confidence. Part and parcel of an investigation was the ability to talk with people and gather whatever information one could. Would she prove effective in doing so? Or would she find it difficult? Only time would tell.

The following morning, a courier dressed in the royal livery of the House of Andover delivered an envelope for which I was required to sign. Inside was a draft made out to Catherine Worthington in the amount of 5,000 pounds.

"You should deposit it in your bank account, Kitty," Lady Lily suggested at the start of the investigative committee meeting.

"No, not mine."

"What about our agency's business account?" Lady Emma asked.

"I believe it would be best to create a separate one for this investigation. Can we do that, Ned?"

"Of course. I'll take care of that for you." English laws being what they were, a woman was not able to open a bank account on her own, and had to ask a gentleman to handle that duty. Something that would need to change in the future.

"Thank you, Ned." I trusted him implicitly to keep a careful tally over the funds.

"Why such a large amount?" Lily asked.

"It was nothing her royal highness said, but I think she anticipated our having to pay bribes."

"Informants, Miss Worthington," Owen Clapham volunteered. "We won't get anywhere without paying for information."

As a retired Scotland Yard detective inspector, he should know.

Once I called the meeting to order, I gave Mother the floor so she could explain the intricacies of the Andoverian Royal Family.

"Andover has existed for over 1,000 years," she said. "Its geography consists of mostly mountain ranges with only thirty percent arable lands. As you can imagine, its population is concentrated along the agricultural sectors. It has no direct access to a sea, so no fishing rights. With the interminable wars and skirmishes which regularly break out, it's always served as a buffer between the neighboring countries of Switzerland, Italy, and France. The Andover monarchy has kept the country neutral. So it's to the advantage of those countries to keep the Andover royal family in place. To ensure they remain so, France, Italy, and Switzerland negotiated an agreement with them which requires the heir to the crown to marry a member of the nobility from one of those countries, rotating among them. The current Queen of Andover hails from Italy, the Princess, Switzerland. So, the Duke of Andover must marry someone from France. However, the duke has refused to do so. That was more than likely the source of friction at the theatre between the prince and his son."

"Good heavens. Who would want to have a wife not of your choosing inflicted upon you?" Hollingsworth declared.

"Or any wife at all, for that matter," Marlowe exclaimed.

That remark did not surprise me, confirmed bachelor that Marlowe was.

"But that's not all," Mother said, a twinkle to her eye. "The duke is unmarried. Not a problem while the prince was alive. But now that he's died, the duke becomes the direct heir. If his grandfather the king dies and he's not married to a member of the French nobility, he forfeits the crown."

"To whom?"

"The Count of Andover."

"The dreaded cousin," Lady Emma, said biting back a smile.

"But wait," I said. "Wouldn't he need to be married to a member of the French nobility?"

"He is. His wife, Désirée, is a French viscountess in her own right."

Mister Clapham whistled. "The bloke thought ahead."

"Indeed, sir." Mayhap the Count of Andover was not as stupid as I believed he was.

"So now that we have the background in place, how do you want to go about the investigation?" Marlowe asked.

"To start off, we interview every member of the royal family," I said. "I guarantee they know something."

"Absolutely. Start with the princess," Lady Emma said.

"I'll talk to her. The son will need to be interviewed," I said.

"Either Hollingsworth or I can do it," Marlowe suggested. "He'll respond best to a man."

Normally, I would take offense at such a remark, but he was right. "He does have a rather . . . cavalier attitude toward women. Hollingsworth, why don't you talk to him? Marlowe can interview the cousin."

"Would you mind if I talked to the Queen of Andover, Kitty?" Mother asked. "A mother talking to another? She might respond to that approach."

"But she hired us."

"Doesn't mean she doesn't have something to hide,"

Mother said.

"I think your mother is right," Lady Melissande said.

"What about Désirée, the cousin's wife?" Marlowe asked.

"I'll interview her," Lady Emma said. If you don't mind, that is. She seems rather high in her instep, so she'll respond better to a lady with a title. While she's at it, she can look down her nose at me and pity my unmarried status."

"You're not married because you don't want to be," Marlowe snarked, a curl to his lip.

Everyone's head turned in his direction. But I was not about to have the meeting derailed by that cryptic remark. "Mister Clapham."

"Yes, Miss Worthington."

"We need to find out what's going on at Scotland Yard. The Queen is convinced the man they apprehended was not the murderer. So, you'll need to find out anything you can."

"Happy to do so."

"Ned, I want you to investigate the finances of the royal family and Andover itself. Is the family as flush as it seems? Is the country's economy doing well?"

"What would you like me to do?" Lady Lily asked.

I hesitated to send her on a mission as I did not wish her or Lady Melissande to get hurt. The murderer, whoever he was, would not give two figs about young, titled ladies if they stood in his way, especially if he believed them a threat.

"May I make a suggestion, Kitty?" Lady Melissande asked.

"Of course."

"Lady Lily and I can interview the staff at the hotel. They're bound to have noticed something."

"What a marvelous idea," Lady Lily said.

"You'll have a guard with you," Hollingsworth commanded. "At all times."

Seemingly offended by the directive, Lady Melissande

hitched up her chin, but she responded pleasantly enough. "Of course, brother. Whatever you say."

"I'll make the arrangements," Hollingsworth said. "Notify me of the time you intend to go on your jaunt."

"I shall," Lady Melissande said.

Heavens! She had indeed found her voice. I had no idea what had passed between brother and sister to cause such enmity between them, but clearly something had, as they were both acting decidedly strange. Hollingsworth, who'd been a happy-go-lucky sort, had now become an authoritarian, at least regarding his sister. And Lady Melissande, who'd been downright dour since her arrival had now turned amiable. Whatever it was, they would bear watching lest it derailed the investigation.

"That's everything on my list. Does anyone have anything else?"

"The equerry," Mother said. "Someone needs to talk to him."

"Who?" I asked.

"The military officer who escorted Sebastian to the Prince of Andover. That's his title."

"The one with the strong resemblance to the prince?"

"Yes. He's the prince's right-hand man. Or rather he was."

"Very well. I'll talk to him."

"He might be more forthcoming if a gentleman approached him," Marlowe said. "Either Hollingsworth or Ned or I."

"Just the opposite, I believe."

"How so?" Marlowe asked.

"He served the prince, so he might resent a titled gentleman inquiring about that relationship. He might be more forthcoming with a lady." Especially after I found out from Mother what she knew about the prince's right-hand man. With everything that had been going on, I'd forgotten to ask. "I'll talk to him. Anything else?"

"The Tower of London will need to be looked into," Owen Clapham said.

"Yes, of course. But I feel it will be better to wait until we have more information. Maybe our efforts will discover the best approach to take." I took a deep breath and let it out. "Shall we meet again in three days' time? That should give everyone enough time to conduct their interviews and perform their tasks."

Everyone nodded their agreement. "I'll see you all Friday at two o'clock then."

CHAPTER THIRTEEN

SUPPER WITH ROBERT

*T*HAT NIGHT, Robert had invited me to supper at The Ivy. The splendid restaurant, with its iconic shimmering central dining bar, signature harlequin stained-glass windows, and oak panelling, made it the place people flocked to see and be seen.

To honor the occasion, I'd chosen a sleeveless, scoop-necked, midnight blue silk cashmere evening frock with a pleated skirt and a sash tied at the hip. The pearl necklace Lord Rutledge gifted me on my twenty-first birthday completed the ensemble.

As he helped me into my fur-edged matching wool coat, he whispered into my ear, "You look very beautiful, tonight, Catherine. I won't be able to take my eyes off you."

With an impish grin, I tugged on his lapel and murmured, "That's the idea, Inspector."

He obliged by leaning down and dropping a swift kiss on

my lips. Nothing too heated as Carlton, our butler, stood nearby fondly gazing at us.

We made it down the steps of Worthington House to the waiting taxicab. Since parking was rarely to be found on the West End streets of London, Robert often chose that mode of transportation, rather than his Rolls Royce, when he escorted me to an event. I didn't mind as it allowed him to carry a conversation without having to watch out for other automobiles and pedestrians.

At the Ivy, we were welcomed warmly by the owner himself, Mario Gallati, who seemed very familiar with Robert. "Inspector Crawford. It's a pleasure to welcome you back to The Ivy. Your table is ready for you."

"Thank you, Mario."

As we were seated at a spot that provided a bit more privacy, I glanced around the space. Just about every table was occupied. As popular as the restaurant was, I imagined the empty ones would fill soon. A family party on the left was joyously celebrating an event of some kind. A birthday, perhaps. A couple ensconced in one of the semi-private areas on the other side of the room, however, did not seem to be in a celebratory mood. The lady, dressed in a glamorous black sequined frock, seemed less interested in her escort than he was in her, as her gaze kept wandering about the space.

After a server arrived at our table to fill our water glasses, a waiter greeted Robert with the same courtesy shown by the owner. "Inspector Crawford, how pleasant to see you once more."

"Thank you, Maurice."

He handed us our menus and made his recommendations. We both opted for the shepherd's pie, Ivy's signature dish, accompanied by creamed spinach and Gran Moravia cheese. For our wine selection, we agreed with Maurice's suggestion of a pinot noir.

Once the wine was poured and duly approved by Robert, our conversation turned to what we'd been doing for we'd gone several days without seeing each other. Of course, I filled him in on the Queen of Andover's visit and her request to have me investigate her son's murder.

"The Home Office will not approve of your taking on the investigation," he said pleasantly enough.

"They can address their concerns to the Queen of Andover."

His only response was a raised eyebrow.

But I knew him well enough to know what he was thinking. "Exactly. They won't as they would not wish the negotiations to be derailed."

"Did she say she would?" he asked, sipping his wine.

"She hinted at it. I can't imagine her not using that formidable ace."

Templing his hands, he gazed at me with amusement. "Miss Worthington, I do believe you're right."

"But you don't approve of my taking up this matter."

"It's not up to me to approve or disapprove of your actions. You're a grown woman capable of making your own decisions. However, I do caution you to take care. While the government may not step in, others might object to your inquiries."

"Armament manufacturers and such."

"Among others."

"What do you mean?"

"Our former enemies might want the antimony mineral for themselves. You never know what actions they'd be willing to take to stop the negotiations. You might very well get caught in the crosshairs."

"I'll be careful. I promise."

Another raised brow.

"If I need to wander into the more sordid parts of town,

I'll ask Mister Clapham to accompany me. Does that satisfy you?"

"Take Hollingsworth as well. He's handy with his fists. And knives."

It was my turn to raise a brow. I should have expected Hollingsworth to be an expert fighter, though. He was an explorer, after all. No telling how many quarrels he'd had to fight his way out of. "Speaking of Hollingsworth, do you know why he's at odds with his sister? Or she with him?"

"I haven't seen him since he returned from fetching her home."

Evasion at its finest. But then he was very good at that.

He tore a bread roll in half and busied himself buttering it. "How do you propose to go about the investigation?"

A change of subject. Obviously, he knew something about the tension between Hollingsworth and Lady Melissande, but he wouldn't tell me. Whatever Hollingsworth had shared with him, it'd been in confidence. And Robert would never betray that. Fine. I would find out another way. In the meantime, I might as well answer his question. "The usual way. I gathered the team, and everyone volunteered to interview a person or persons. The princess, the queen, the son, the cousin, and the cousin's wife for starters. Oh, and the equerry. The prince's right-hand man, as I understand."

After thoroughly chewing a morsel of bread, he said, "I expect Clapham will be sniffing around Scotland Yard."

"Yes."

"Rutherford will not be amused."

"The Queen of Andover believes he arrested the wrong man."

"Have you come up with a theory?"

"It's early days. We'll need to inspect the chamber where the prince stayed."

"That room is locked, and no one is allowed in except for

one of our own."

Before I could object, a woman slithered into my line of vision. The lady in the black sequined gown, as it turned out. With her gaze fixed on Robert, she huskily whispered, "Hello, darling."

Darling? Who on earth was she?

"Marina." Robert had barely gained his feet before she tried to kiss him on the mouth. But he turned his face, and her lips landed on his cheek instead.

A moue of disappointment rode her crimson lips. "Why haven't you called? It's been ages since Nice."

Up close she was even more stunning than she'd appeared. In her late thirties would be my guess, her dark hair pinned back into a chignon. Diamonds sparkled in her ears and flowed from her neck down a scandalous décolletage that left very little to the imagination. I wanted to claw her eyes out.

"Lady Dunstan, may I introduce you to Catherine Worthington, my—"

She cast a dismissive glance toward me. "Robbing the cradle, Robert?" She walked her blood-red fingernails up his snowy white shirt. "I can give you so much more. Practice makes perfect, as you very well know." She licked her lower lip, slowly, seductively. The witch!

Robert gently removed her hands from his chest. "Miss Worthington is my fiancée."

She choked. "Your fiancée?" she screeched. "Really, darling, she's nothing but a child."

"So glad you noticed." I tittered a laugh. "Sometimes we play tiddlywinks, other times hopscotch. Robert excels at hide-and-go-seek. He always finds me. You see, he loves my scent," I whispered in a confiding voice. "Don't you. Darling." I shot him a fulminating glance.

Taking the witch's arm, he said, "Let me walk you back to

your table. I'm sure your escort is missing you."

"He's not you, darling. No one is." Her voice faded away as they made their way across the room. Once he'd settled her back in her seat, he returned. As he arrived, the server appeared with our meals. Just as well, for it gave me a chance to calm down.

We addressed our shepherd's pie, sipped the pinot noir, chewed our food. In silence.

Finally, Robert laid down his fork. "She means nothing to me, Catherine."

"You don't have to explain. I'm not silly enough to know you don't have a past." I scrunched my lips. "But why did she have to go and ruin our dinner? We were having such a lovely time."

"Dearest," he reached across the table and captured my hand. "She can only ruin our dinner if you let her."

He was right, of course. I took a deep breath. "I'm sorry. I'm acting like an idiot."

He squeezed my hand. "I'm engaged *to you*. I'm in love *with you*."

A wobbly smile made an appearance. "I don't deserve you, Robert."

"Yes, you do. You're everything I've ever wanted and desired. I can't wait to make you my wife."

"Thank you for saying that, although I do wonder why."

He retrieved his hand and returned to his meal. "I wonder about it myself sometimes."

"You horrible man." Laughing, I launched my serviette at him which he caught before it landed on his food.

Returning it to me, he said, "Finish your shepherd's pie so you can have dessert and then I have a surprise for you."

"A surprise? What is it?"

"If I told you, it wouldn't be a surprise," he said with an impish smile.

CHAPTER FOURTEEN

THE PRINCESS OF ANDOVER

*A*FTER DINNER, Robert took me to a jazz club where we danced the night away. As a result, the next morning, I almost overslept. Thank heavens for Betsy who dragged me out of bed. It simply would not do to arrive late for my meeting with royalty.

Dressed in widow's weeds, the Princess of Andover appeared even more ordinary than before. As I'd previously noted, her eyes and hair were a dull brown. Nor did her height impress, for she was of short stature. Those attributes by themselves would not be sufficient to make her ordinary. She also made poor choices when it came to her clothes. Her black gown was appropriate. After all, she was in mourning. But it did not possess the style or flair of the countess's frock.

I'd wondered why the prince had chosen her as his consort. But Mother had cleared that up. She was a direct descendant of Swiss royalty. As such, she'd brought an unassailable pedigree to the marriage. But apparently, that's all

96

she'd brought for she lacked fortune, presence, and charm. Rumor had it that a year after their wedding, the Prince of Andover had grown bored. He remained faithful, however, until she provided him with an heir. But once that was accomplished, he'd engaged in several affairs, the latest of which was, supposedly, with his cousin's wife, the beautiful Désirée.

Feeling sorry for the princess, I vowed to treat her as kindly as I could. "Thank you for receiving me, Your Highness. My deepest condolences for your loss."

"Thank you, Miss Worthington. Please take a seat." She pointed to a burgundy chair across from her. "I've ordered coffee. But if that doesn't suit, I can request tea."

"No need. I prefer coffee as well."

"There'll be pastries." Her eyes lit up with excitement. "The hotel's pâtisserie chef trained at Le Cordon Bleu in Paris. I'm afraid I can't resist his pastries. His profiteroles are *magnifique*." The smile she flashed totally transformed her face.

Why, she was pretty! Not in an ostentatious way, but in a quiet manner. Why was she hiding her light under a bushel? A question for another time for I had a different purpose today. "They sound marvelous."

A knock on the door alerted us to the arrival of a waiter pushing a trolley with the coffee service and promised baked goods.

"Ahh, here they are," the princess said.

Once the refreshments were placed on the table between us, she poured a cup of coffee, plated one of the gorgeous pastries, and offered both to me.

After taking one bite, I couldn't help but moan.

"Lovely, is it not?" she asked.

"Absolutely."

We spent the next few minutes addressing the profiteroles. I don't know if it was due to the love we shared for excellent coffee and pastries or something else, but after a few minutes I felt a certain kinship with her as if I had known her a long while. But, of course, I couldn't allow such harmony to affect my interview. I had a task to perform.

I waited until she signaled she was ready before I asked my first question. One which hopefully would not be painful for her.

"As I understand it, the prince had a strong interest in Anne Boleyn."

A small smile bloomed across her lips as if she found the recollection endearing. "The whole of the Tudor era fascinated him, but most especially Henry VIII's second wife. Such a sad tale that was. When she failed to give the king a son, he drummed up charges of treason so he could marry Jane Seymour. My husband believed Anne Boleyn's trial was a travesty, the guilty verdict a foregone conclusion. Even as she stood at the gallows, the queen claimed her innocence."

I could see why the prince thought Henry VIII's second wife had been wrongfully accused. The facts surrounding the charges leveled against her were murky at best. While some believed she was guilty of treason, others thought the Tudor king had drummed up the charge as a way to get rid of a troublesome wife who'd proven incapable of providing him with an heir. More than likely, the truth would never be known. But even if the prince had a strong interest in Anne Boleyn, it didn't answer the question regarding his stay at the Tower of London. "Why did he want to spend a night at the Queen's House?"

"My husband was a man of science and logic and very much present in the here and now. But sometimes he had an awareness of people or things that were not there."

"Like ghosts?"

"Not ghosts precisely. Events that had yet to happen,

objects that didn't exist, whispers from absent voices. He thought if he occupied the same chamber she had during her last days, he could feel what she'd felt."

"I . . . see."

She laughed. "If you could only see your face, Miss Worthington. You think he was odd?"

I was not about to agree with her. I needed her cooperation. "Not odd, exactly. Different."

"Well, he was that." She paused. "I know of the rumors surrounding my husband. Most of which are true. That may lead you to believe I had something to do with his horrible murder." Her gaze shone bright. "But I didn't arrange for his death, Miss Worthington. I couldn't have. I simply don't have it in me."

I could see she was telling the truth.

"Did you love him?" I immediately regretted the question. "I apologize. I shouldn't have asked such a thing."

"You're not the first one to ask. To answer your question, no, I did not. He was good to me, treated me with respect and, yes, even a certain amount of affection. Crumbs, I know." She raised her chin. "But it was enough for me. His . . . affairs were just that. Affairs."

She could be telling the truth. Or lying to preserve her dignity.

"Forgive me for asking, but I heard rumors the prince was seeking a divorce."

A strange emotion flitted across her face. One I couldn't decipher. I would need to have a think on it at a later time.

"Did you?" she asked. "Divorce rumors are plentiful and varied. Not a day goes by that I don't hear a new version of it. But unlike your Henry VIII, the prince could never have divorced me. If he did, Switzerland would reclaim the land it gave to Andover."

"Really?"

"Really." She pointed to the pastry tray. "Would you like another profiterole or an eclair?"

"I shouldn't."

"One more won't hurt."

"Well, maybe just one." I held out my plate.

After the few moments I took to enjoy the pastry, I asked the question that needed to be asked. "Did you have plans for the night your husband was at The Tower of London?"

"Oh, Miss Worthington, what a clever way of asking where I was that evening. Why, I was right here. We had events scheduled for the next several days—a regatta parade on the Thames, a visit to the British Museum. I was reviewing my wardrobe with the lady-in-waiting who advises me on matters of clothes. You can talk to her if you wish. Her name is Lady VonSteuben."

"Thank you." I noted the lady's name in my journal, as I would most certainly be talking to her.

Next, I turned to the subject of the line of succession. Rather than feign coyness, I decided to be open about the subject. "I understand there's an impediment to your son ascending to the throne?"

In an instant her conviviality vanished, to be replaced by haughtiness and contempt. Directing a glacial glare at me, she sat up ramrod straight. "You are very well-informed, Miss Worthington. The queen more than likely told you."

Rather than respond yea or nay, I remained silent.

She dropped her plate on the table, the eclair barely half consumed. "As I'm sure you're well aware, my son's required to marry a member of the French nobility. He doesn't wish to do so."

"He doesn't wish to marry?"

"He's twenty-five years old, Miss Worthington. Much too young to be tied down in a loveless marriage."

Like hers remained unsaid. Clearly, she was very protective of her son. But I couldn't allow her change in attitude to impede my interrogation. I had to get to the truth. "Is he in love with someone?"

"No!"

That utterance emerged a little too quickly which made me suspect the opposite was true. But given how upset she'd become, there was no sense in pursuing that line of questioning with her. I would ask Hollingsworth to address the topic with the son.

I waited until she'd calmed down somewhat before asking my next question. "If he doesn't succeed to the throne, who will?" I knew the answer, of course, but I wanted to hear it from her so I could explore her feelings regarding it.

Her lip curled. "His cousin, the Count of Andover. He's not only next in line in succession but he's married to a member of the French nobility."

"How do you feel about such an event?"

"It will be a sad day for our country. My husband, for all his faults, always acted in the best interests of his people and Andover itself. But the count is motivated by money, and money alone. He will do what is best for him. British armament manufacturers will be more than willing to pay him handsomely for the rights to mine the antimony mineral." A strange pronouncement. The prince's vertical farming scheme would have caused the Andover people to starve. And the count's willingness to sign over the rights to mine the mineral was the same as her son's. But maybe she saw only what she wanted to see.

"Is there anything that you can do to prevent that outcome?" I asked.

"I am powerless, Miss Worthington, even less so now that my husband is no longer alive. The queen, however, can do something. It will be up to her to make it happen."

"What can the queen do?"

She seemed to shrink in upon herself. "I'm sorry. I've said too much. Whatever information you gain must come from her."

"Very well. I will ask her." I glanced at my notes to see what else I needed to ask. "The prince had an equerry, a right-hand man, did he not?"

Her gaze shifted downward. "Yes, Etienne. He's been with the prince for several years."

"Could you direct me to him? I'd like to discuss some matters?"

"I'm afraid that's not possible, Miss Worthington."

"Why?"

"Etienne, Colonel Bouchard, is no longer with us."

That sounded ominous. "What do you mean?"

"He and my husband quarreled the morning the prince was to go to The Tower of London. The prince ordered him back home. He must be there by now."

"What was the quarrel about?"

"I don't know. My husband would not tell me."

"When did he leave?"

"That afternoon. Etienne, Colonel Bouchard, came to say goodbye. That's all I know."

"You haven't heard from him?"

"No."

"Don't you think that's odd? After all, he was in the service of the prince. Wouldn't he have called?"

"There would be no reason for Etienne to contact me. He's the prince's man. We were not close. But maybe the queen has been in contact with him."

"The queen? Why her?"

"She and Etienne." She glanced off into the distance. "Well, let's just say they have a very special relationship. And no. I won't explain. You'll need to ask her."

CHAPTER FIFTEEN

SECOND MEETING OF THE INVESTIGATIVE COMMITTEE (PART 1)

*O*N FRIDAY AFTERNOON, I barely gave everyone enough time to gain their seats before calling our second meeting to order.

I suggested we make our way through our interviews with the members of the royal family before hearing from Mister Clapham and Ned. After everyone readily agreed, I reported on my conversation with the princess. The group agreed with my conclusion. She did not appear a likely suspect. I suggested, however, we withhold judgment for the moment. Subsequent information might shed a different light on her.

Next up, Hollingsworth, reported on her son, the duke. "He was otherwise occupied that night," he said, clearing his throat.

"A woman, you mean?" I asked. No sense beating about the bush.

He nodded. "I verified it with the lady in question. A widow. No need to name her."

Lady Melissande, of all people, scoffed. "Like father, like son."

An odd, emotional reaction. But maybe not so odd. Her father had been a philanderer. Was she obliquely accusing Hollingsworth of doing the same? But I couldn't afford to get bogged down by such wonderings, so I moved on. "How does he feel about being next in line to the throne?"

"He's not happy about it as he does not wish to marry a member of the French nobility. Or anyone else for that matter. He said, and I quote, *'He wants to keep his options open.'*"

"In other words, he wants to sow his wild oats," I said.

"I gathered that much."

What was it with some men's need to tup women willy-nilly? One would think they'd tire of it. But then what did I know? I was not a man. "Could his refusal to enter into an arranged marriage stem from his loving someone whose pedigree is unacceptable to the Andover crown?"

"I did not get that impression. He resents being forced to do something that goes against his grain."

"An independent young man he might be," Mother asserted, "but he owes a duty to his country."

"Yes, ma'am," Worthington said.

"Do you think him responsible for the prince's murder?" I asked.

"No. He's thoroughly upset about the prince's death, not only because he loved his father, but because it places him in an untenable position."

"Very well. Marlowe, what about the count?"

"He claims he had an early night. His wife vouched for him."

"Was she in the room when you interviewed him?" Lady Emma asked.

"She was. He requested her presence, and I couldn't find a way to deny him."

"How does he feel about the prince's death?" I asked Marlowe.

"He declared himself horrified. Apparently, he hasn't gotten over the sight of the prince's headless body, face down, blood pooled all around. He claims he hasn't slept very well since that day. His wife confirmed it."

"He would say such a thing, though, wouldn't he?" I asked. "After all, it would be expected from him. How does he feel about the possibility of inheriting the throne?"

"He dodged the question, even though I asked it point-blank. He said the King of Andover would live for many more years. All evidence to the contrary. And there would be plenty of time for the Duke of Andover to do his duty and marry."

"Do you believe him?"

Marlowe shrugged. "His words seemed well rehearsed, as if he'd expected the questions and practiced the right answers."

"We need to check his bank account. See if there are any large expenditures."

"Already handled, Kitty," Ned said, "for all members of the Andover royal family."

"Thank you, Ned. I knew I could count on you." I glanced at my notes. "Lady Emma what about the wife?"

"I was able to talk to her by herself. The count was not present. The first thing she asserted was that her husband had spent the entire night in her bed which was odd since I hadn't yet gotten around to that question. And then she pretty much parroted everything her husband said to Marlowe."

"How did she seem?" She'd appeared arrogant at the inquest, so I was curious to discover if that was her true persona. Or was she like the princess who showed one demeanor in public and quite a different one in private?

"She seemed . . . nervous about something. She kept chewing her lips, twisting her hands, looking over her shoulder. At one point, a noise went off in the other room, and she practically jumped out of her seat. If you ask me, she's afraid of her husband."

"Really? How did you reach that conclusion?"

"Her eyes were red as if she'd been crying. And, more telling, there was a suspicious red mark on her cheek."

"You think he hit her?"

"I don't know, but I don't think she ran into a door. I believe she lied to cover-up for him."

"Could she have put on a show for our benefit?"

"Maybe," Lady Emma said, "But I don't think so. At least, not in this regard."

"We'll have to look into it then. There's bound to be evidence." I made another notation in my journal. We were ending up with more questions than answers, but at least we had a path to follow. "Did you discuss the prince?"

"Yes. When I asked her about him, she froze for a second, and then she said she had nothing but the highest admiration and respect for his royal highness. When I prodded her about the rumors surrounding her and the prince, her face grew bright red. She said they were vicious lies spread by wicked people who wanted to drive her and her husband apart. And then she said quite an odd thing." She paused for dramatic effect.

"Well," Marlowe said, "don't keep us in suspense. We have enough of that already." He brushed a nonexistent speck of dust off his immaculate trousers.

Lady Emma arched a disdainful brow at him, but other

than that did not rise to his bait. "She said, and I quote, '*He can't divorce me. If he does, he won't be in line for the crown.*'"

"That is odd," I said. "Did you ask her or hint at a dissolution of her marriage?"

"No. That's why her statement was so queer. It was like she wanted me to know."

"It does make sense he would be removed from the line of succession. It's a similar situation as the prince's marriage." Except in that case, if the prince sought a divorce, Switzerland would reclaim the land it'd given to Andover.

"'Til death do us apart," Hollingsworth said.

"Indeed," Lady Emma said.

"Let's move on. Lady Lily and Lady Melissande, what did you find?"

"More than we thought we would," Lady Lily said. "Hotel staff notice *everything*. Don't they, Mellie?"

Lady Melissande returned an amused grin. "Yes, indeed, Lil."

One excursion to the hotel, and they'd become Mellie and Lil. A good thing, for Lady Melissande needed a friend. "Such as?" I prompted.

"For one, the prince and princess do not share the same bed."

"How do they know that?"

"None of her articles of clothing are in the prince's room and neither are her toiletries. It's the same for the count and countess. They keep everything separate."

"But how would the hotel staff know either couple didn't share a bed. I mean . . . how could you tell if—" I felt my face grow warmer.

"There would be clear evidence, Kitty," Ned bailed me out, "that they enjoyed conjugal relations. Any decent hotel staff would be bound to notice."

"Thank you, brother." I took a moment to gather myself before moving on. "So, what else did you find, Lady Lily?"

"The son did not sleep in his bed that night. When the count arrived with the news of the prince's death, he was nowhere to be found."

"He was probably conducting his liaison in a different hotel. One not aware of his identity."

"The Savoy," Hollingsworth blurted out. "I asked the lady."

The Savoy was one of the best London hotels. Known for its excellent service, it was rumored they knew every guest by sight. "The hotel staff would have recognized him in an instant."

"True," Hollingsworth's carefree smile which recently had gone missing suddenly reappeared. "But they're very good at pretending they don't."

"Know this from personal experience, do you?" Marlowe asked.

"I'll never tell."

There was an answer if I'd ever heard one. "Let's continue, shall we?" I turned to Lady Lily. "Do you have anything else to add?"

"Yes."

"Oh, please allow me, Lil."

"By all means, Mellie."

Lady Melissande leaned forward so eager was she to share what she'd learned. "It's about the queen. She and the prince's equerry are very close. Apparently, they spend an inordinate amount of time together."

"And," Lady Lily added, "the hotel staff suggested they enjoy a very intimate relationship."

"He's having an affair with the queen?" I asked.

"Well, they didn't come right and out and say it," Lady Lily said. "But there was plenty of giggling, nodding, and winking in the telling."

"But she must be in her mid-sixties."

"That's sheer nonsense," Mother exclaimed. "There's a perfectly reasonable explanation."

I certainly hoped so. "Go ahead, Mother."

"He's—ahem—the king's illegitimate son."

"No."

"Afraid so. The king was as promiscuous as his son supposedly was. Several months before he married the queen, he engaged in a scandalous affair. It was rumored he was so much in love, he demanded to be allowed to marry her. Of course, the crown declined, reminding him of his duty. Common sense prevailed, and he chose an Italian noblewoman as his queen. She became pregnant with the prince shortly after their wedding. A year or so after the prince's birth she discovered a child had been born from a previous liaison of the king's. She insisted on him being brought to the palace where he would be raised."

"Why would she do such a thing?"

"Apparently, the child—his birth name is Etienne Bouchard—had been abandoned in an orphanage. She thought a king's son did not merit such shoddy treatment. So she concocted an implausible tale that he was a distant relation to the king. No one believed her, of course. But they weren't about to name the queen a liar. So they kept his parentage a secret. Etienne was not only raised at the palace but received the same education as the prince. When he reached the age of eighteen, he decided to join the military. As I understand it, he conducted himself very well and rose to the rank of colonel."

"How did he become the prince's equerry?"

"Several years after the prince's marriage, the prince had already involved himself in several extramarital affairs, and the queen was afraid a scandal would erupt. So she dreamed up a scheme that would employ the colonel's strong resemblance to the prince. As part of Colonel Bouchard's responsibilities as the prince's equerry, the colonel would take his place and attend to those matters that needed attention when the prince was . . . otherwise engaged."

"And the colonel accepted such an assignment?" It was more a rhetorical question than anything else.

Still, Mother answered, "He did."

Why would he do such a thing? Something else to consider. I added it to the growing list in my journal. "Now, as far as the resemblance is concerned, there were differences between them. The prince had a prodigious mustache, sideburns, and a full head of hair. The equerry is clean shaven with hair trimmed to the skull. He also wears spectacles. How do they conduct this transformation?"

"Custom made wigs and mustaches," Mother said. "The prince wears clear spectacles at public functions."

"He wasn't wearing them at the Prince's Ball or the theatre."

"When he's challenged about it, he claims he can see well enough which, of course, is true. But he does it in such a way people believe he's simply being vain."

"Amazing. How long has this been going on?"

"Fifteen years or so. But the thing of it is, Kitty, the Queen is quite worried about the colonel."

"What do you mean?"

"He's gone missing. As you know from your conversation with the princess, the prince ordered him to return home. The colonel not only said goodbye to the princess but the queen as well. She expected the whole thing to blow over. Apparently, this is not the first time they've had a falling out. A storm in a teacup, she said. The colonel planned to fly to Paris where he would board a train to Andover. But he didn't. He hasn't been seen since the prince's murder. And nobody knows where he is."

CHAPTER SIXTEEN

SECOND MEETING OF THE INVESTIGATIVE COMMITTEE (PART 2)

"*H*EAVENS!" I'd been standing this entire time, but Mother's words rattled me enough I dropped into my seat. Where did we go from here?

"If I may, Miss Worthington," Mister Clapham said.

"Of course." I nodded my consent. If nothing else, it would give me time to arrange my rioting thoughts into some semblance of order.

"As you know, I was assigned the task of gathering information at Scotland Yard."

"Yes."

"Usually, information is not hard to come by. There's always someone willing to talk. However, for this case, information is tighter than a nun's—"

"Mr. Clapham!" —Mother interrupted— "I beg you to rethink what you're about to say."

"Yes, of course, Mrs. Worthington. I do beg your pardon. Sometimes, I forget my manners."

"Go on," I urged him, biting back a grin.

"I couldn't get anyone to open up at first, but I persisted. I worked my usual sources, spread a little blunt. And finally somebody spilled the beans."

"And that is?"

"The Yard is not sure the victim is the prince."

"What! But the count identified the body, didn't he?"

"The body was lying face down. The count bolted before the medical examiner arrived."

"A real prince that one," Hollingsworth scoffed. "No pun intended."

"With his head missing, there's no way to confirm it was the prince without bringing somebody with intimate knowledge of his, ahem, person to view the remains. That would be the princess, of course. But higher ups have refused to allow it. They don't want to offend her sensibilities."

"But how could they not know it's the prince. The head might be missing, but they should be able to check his fingermarks."

"Can't do that. The murderer chopped off the hands as well."

"Bloody hell!" Marlowe exclaimed.

"Lord Marlowe! Language!" Mother chided.

Marlowe's face grew ruddy. "Begging your pardon, ma'am."

"The medical examiner did not mention that detail in the inquest," I said.

"They don't want it made public. It would only add to the hysteria surrounding this murder. Or so they say."

"Does Scotland Yard know the colonel is missing as well?"

"Yes. That's another reason why they're keeping the identity of the body under wraps. If they discover it was the colonel who was murdered instead of the prince, it would create more panic. And they have enough of that on their hands. Right now they're operating under the theory that one was killed and the other kidnapped."

"One thing is clear, this crime was planned with meticulous precision," Hollingsworth said.

Where could we possibly go from here? Had the prince been murdered or kidnapped? If the latter, then who'd been killed? For what purpose had the prince been taken? And where could he possibly be? "Heavens!"

"Indeed," Mister Clapham said.

"Would you like my report now, Kitty?" Ned asked. "It may shed some light on the investigation."

"By all means."

After he retrieved a document from the briefcase he'd brought with him, he said, "To refresh everyone's memories, you asked me to investigate the finances of the royal family as well as the Andoverian economy."

I nodded. "Go on."

"All members of the family draw funds from the same account which is under the queen's name. She neither directs, nor manages, the amounts deposited or expended. It is simply a matter of convenience. It did make it easier for me as I only had to apply to her for permission to inspect the finances. In other words, no laws were broken."

An important point. If the issue came up, he couldn't be accused of committing a crime.

"To put it succinctly," he continued, "the royal coffers are brimming over with money. Not only have the funds been well managed, but the family owns many properties not only in Andover, but in other countries as well."

"So no chance the royal family will go bankrupt."

"No. Now as far as monthly expenditures are concerned, each member has a withdrawal limit, a quite generous one I might add. No one has withdrawn an unusual amount. The Duke of Andover is the one who comes closest to reaching his limit."

"Who is considered a member of the royal family?"

"Excellent question. The queen herself, of course, the prince and princess, the duke, and the count. The count's wife does not have access to those funds. As I understand it, she has her own account that she draws from, but it's not a large amount. If she wishes to purchase anything out of the ordinary, it would be up to the count to approve her request."

I silently thanked Father who'd settled a quite generous sum on me when I turned twenty-one. I would never have to depend on a husband for pin money, or anything else for that matter. "So she's stuck in that marriage."

"Indeed," Ned said.

"Who tracks expenditures for the royal family?"

"The missing colonel. I must hand it to him. He kept very tidy books. Not a penny out of place."

"So, nothing to be found there."

"Nothing jumped out at me." He cleared his throat as he referred to his notes. "Now, as far as the country itself is concerned, the queen ordered Andover's Chief Minister of the Treasury to be quite open with me. And, frankly, what I discovered was appalling."

"How so?" I asked.

"The country's economy has been operating on razor-thin margins for decades. Its main industries are agriculture and tourism. Sadly, the country has failed to develop an industrial sector. To the point, it's almost nonexistent. This year the combination of an especially long, harsh winter, which depressed tourism, and torrential rains, which washed away crops and killed livestock, had catastrophic effects on the economy. If the country doesn't get an influx of cash soon, it won't be able to feed its population."

"Oh, my," Mother said. "Those poor people."

"But they've discovered the antimony mineral on their lands," I said. "Wouldn't the lease of those lands to England stave off starvation and put the country on safer footing?"

"Yes, but the prince has proved stubborn about making that deal. His son, however, knows what's at stake. If Andover doesn't agree to the arrangement, it can't provide enough food for its people. As a result, there's much unrest in the country. They could be looking at a rebellion along the lines of the French Revolution."

"Will the son be allowed to step into his father's shoes during the negotiations?"

"How, Miss Worthington?" Mister Clapham interjected. "There's no proof that the prince is dead."

"So what would happen if no deal could be made?"

"Food could not be purchased to get the population through the winter," Ned answered.

"And there might be an uprising."

"Exactly."

"Couldn't the country itself take out a loan or issue a . . . What do you call it, Ned?"

"A bond," he explained. "It can't. Its financial standing is so poor no bank is willing to take on such debt."

"The question that needs to be asked," Lady Emma opined, "is who would gain from this chaos?"

"The cousin?" Lady Lily suggested. "He's married to a member of the French nobility. If I understand things correctly, he could be named the successor and empowered to make the deal."

"We don't know this, though," I said. That scenario would need to be confirmed, and I knew just the person to do it. "Mother?"

"Yes, dear."

"Can you talk to her royal highness and find out how the line of succession works in a situation such as this?"

"Of course."

"And find out her feelings on the subject. Is she willing to allow the count to step into her son's shoes so the deal can go through?"

"I'll do my best."

"Thank you, Mother. Now, Mister Clapham. We need to find out how the killer got into the Tower of London. Talk to Ned if you need funds. I imagine you'll need to make some contributions."

Mister Clapham chuckled at my euphemism. "Will do."

"Lady Emma and Lord Marlowe, talk to the count and countess individually. Tell them we know they did not spend the night in each other's company. Do what you have to do to find out where they were and with whom."

"Lady Lily and Lady Melissande, go back to the hotel. I guarantee somebody saw something that night. Hollingsworth, go with them. Make sure they don't put themselves in peril. I have a feeling things are about to get dicey. And while you're at it, find out about the colonel."

"Yes, ma'am." He gave me a snap salute.

I side-eyed him but did not say a word.

"Kitty, may I say something?" Ned asked.

"Of course."

"There's something we haven't considered, and it may very well impact the investigation."

Another avenue of inquiry? Just what we needed. "What would that be?"

"Well, our government has a vested interest to get the rights to mine that mineral. So do the armament manufacturers. Representatives of that industry are present in the negotiations. So, they would be fully aware of the status of the discussions."

"You think a member of the British government, or an armaments manufacturer could have done this?"

"Not our government, no. But an armaments manufacturer might be involved. I don't think it likely, but it's worth a look. Don't you think?"

"And you'd be ideally suited to handle that investigation."

"Well, I do have some experience in that area."

During the Great War, he'd worked for the War Department. He'd never discussed his duties since the Official Secrets Act prohibited him from talking about them. But he would know how the business side of war operated.

"Would that be possible, though?" I asked. "I wouldn't want you to break any laws."

"I know where the line is, Kitty, and I don't intend to cross it." He shared a glance with Lady Lily who was gazing starry-eyed at him.

If those two didn't end up engaged after her debut, I would eat my chapeau. "Very well. If you think we should." I sincerely hoped he wouldn't find anything. We had enough to investigate without taking on the armament manufacturers as well.

"I think that's everything, unless anyone has something else."

Everyone remained mum.

"Right. We'll meet again in three days' time if that's amenable to everyone."

As it turned out, events forced us to meet sooner than that.

CHAPTER SEVENTEEN

CEASE AND DESIST

*T*HE DAY AFTER OUR MEETING, I was tucked away in the library rearranging my notes. I normally wrote observations in a journal while matters evolved, so they were in chronological order, but this case was so complicated, I needed a new approach. To gain inspiration, I'd visited Harrods stationery department for inspiration and found something new—spiral notebooks. I bought a dozen, one for each member of the royal family, and additional ones for the Tower of London and the antimony issue. The extras I would save for additional matters of interest which were bound to come along. I couldn't help but think that my sister Margaret, a meticulous organizer and planner, would have approved.

I was happily consolidating the information in the notebooks when Carlton knocked on the library door.

"Pardon me, Miss Worthington, but two gentlemen from

the Home Office have called. They would like an audience with you. I've shown them to the drawing room."

I recalled Robert's warning that the Home Office would not be pleased with my investigation of the prince's murder. Is that why its representatives were here? Well, there was only one way to find out. "Thank you, Carlton. Please inform them I will join them in a few minutes. Could you arrange for tea and refreshments?" Even if they were unexpected, and more than likely unwelcome, Mother would want to be hospitable.

"Very well, Miss." He bowed and stepped out.

After I closed the notebook I'd been writing on, I stacked it with the others and tucked them all away in a desk drawer to which I had the only key. During an earlier investigation, I'd commandeered one of the library desks for my private use. That way, I would not have to cart journals and papers back and forth from my bedchamber. In a way, this desk had become my own home office. I smiled at my own joke.

Two dour-faced gentlemen, one fair-haired, the other dark, waited for me in the drawing room. Neither had availed himself of the numerous chairs, settees, and sofas that dotted the room.

"Gentlemen, won't you take a seat?"

The dark-haired one answered. "We prefer to stand. Thank you. I'm Joseph Wharton, and my colleague is James Stirling. We're here on behalf of the Home Office." Each flashed a document which I inspected. They were who they said they were.

Whatever they had to say, I was not willing to listen while standing up. So, I settled on the couch. "What can I do for you?"

Before they could say a word, Mother rushed in, seemingly out of breath. "Kitty. I've just heard. Carlton told me."

"May I introduce my mother, Mrs. Worthington?"

They bowed their heads.

"Mister Wharton and Mister Stirling are here from the Home Office," I explained.

With a questioning glance, Mother settled next to me. "Kitty, dear. What is going on?"

"I have yet to find out. Gentlemen, if you could state your purpose."

"It has come to the Home Office's attention that you're investigating the unfortunate matter that occurred at the Tower of London."

Unfortunate matter. Euphemism at its best. Well, I wasn't about to let them get away with it. "The Prince of Andover's murder, you mean." Call it what it was. Or what it supposedly was.

"As that matter is under investigation, I can neither confirm nor deny your statement."

Government obfuscation at its finest.

A knock on the door preceded the arrival of two footmen, each carrying a tray with the tea service and assorted biscuits. I offered both to the gentlemen, but they both declined. Mother and I, however, helped ourselves. Whatever they had to say, it was better if we were fortified.

I took my time pouring Darjeeling into a cup, stirring cream and sugar into the tea, plating two biscuits. Only after I'd taken a sip, did I comment on the last statement. "Someone was murdered at the Tower, Mister Wharton. You can't deny that much."

"Yes, well. Regardless of what may have happened, your investigation is causing some distress in government circles."

"What kind of distress?"

"As you may, or may not, know, the Andoverian and British governments are negotiating for the rights to mine a mineral located in Andover territory. This mineral would provide us with a great advantage in the manufacturing of armaments."

He thought me an idiot. I clasped my hands together to keep them still. Last thing I wished them to see was my state of agitation. "The mineral is antimony. And yes, I know."

"The negotiations are at a sensitive stage. Any interference may result in the discussions being called off. We're afraid that your investigation may very well upset the applecart, if you will."

"And you wish me to cease my efforts?"

"Yes, Miss Worthington. It may very well impact national security."

He was pulling out all the big guns. Not that it would get him anywhere. "I'm afraid that is not possible, Mister Wharton. You see, I've been entrusted with this responsibility by the Queen of Andover. If I am to stop looking into this matter, I'll need to hear it from the queen herself."

Almost in unison, their jaws dropped. I'm sure they weren't often denied a request.

"You do understand it's the Home Office making this entreaty?" Mister Wharton said, his eyes practically bugging out.

"I do."

"And you refuse its mandate."

"I believe I've made my feelings perfectly clear." I calmly sipped the tea.

"Very well, Miss Worthington. We will inform our superiors of your decision."

"Please do so. With my regards, of course." I walked to the bell pull and yanked it. Carlton appeared so quickly he must have been standing right outside the door.

"Carlton, I believe these gentlemen are ready to leave."

Our butler bowed his head. "Very well, Miss. Gentlemen, if you will follow me."

Once they were gone, Mother wasted no time making her feelings known "Kitty, don't you think we should accede to their wishes? It is the Home Office."

"We're not breaking any laws, Mother. We're conducting a proper investigation upon the request of the Queen of Andover. If they want us to stop, they'll need to approach her." I doubted they would. Her royal highness would not take such a demand lightly. She might become so upset, she would direct the negotiations cease in their entirety. That's the last thing they and the Home Office wanted. So I was safe enough denying their request.

"Well, when you put it that way."

"I do."

"Your father will need to be informed."

"Please do tell him. I'd like to know his thoughts. I'll also need to move up our next meeting. The committee members will need to be informed. Although the Home Office might not approach the queen, they might impede the investigation in other ways. Forewarned is forearmed." Ironic, given the goal of the negotiations.

That night after supper, Father pulled me aside. "Your mother told me about the Home Office visitors and their request you cease your investigation."

"I asked her to. What are your thoughts?" As much as I wished to continue, he could forbid me from carrying on.

"I'm concerned, of course. One does not take a directive from the Home Office lightly."

"I promised the Queen of Andover we would undertake this mission, Father. We have a duty to perform."

"You don't think Scotland Yard can get to the truth?"

"The queen believes Scotland Yard apprehended the wrong man. I agree with her. The man they caught is a common thief, not a murderer."

"What does Robert think?"

"He won't criticize another inspector's actions, but I know him well enough to believe he agrees with me."

"I talked to Ned. He shares your belief about the suspect. He also thinks this matter might impact national security. You might have a certain level of expertise with murder investigations, but the safety of our nation is nothing to meddle with, Kitty. I am concerned."

"Do you want the investigative committee to stop?" I would hate to do so. We were making progress. Not great by any means, but it was early days.

"No."

I breathed a sigh of relief.

"I do have a condition, though."

"Very well."

"If you discover anything—and I mean anything—that affects the welfare of England, you will cease your investigations."

"How are we to determine such a thing?"

"Ned will make that determination. Are we agreed?"

I had no choice but to say, "Yes."

CHAPTER EIGHTEEN

THIRD MEETING OF THE INVESTIGATIVE
COMMITTEE

"*T*HE HOME OFFICE ORDERED US TO STOP INVESTIGATING? The cheek of them." This from Marlowe.

"I share your sentiment, Lord Marlowe. Regardless, we need to vote on whether we should continue. I can't make that decision for the group." I may have asserted to the Home Office representatives that we would cease only if the queen told us to do so. But we couldn't proceed if the committee decided against it.

"Of course, we'll continue," Hollingsworth said.

There were head bobs all around.

"If I could see a show of hands, please."

Hands shot up around the room. Mother kept hers tucked against her.

"You don't approve, Mother?"

"I'm just concerned. It is the government, Kitty."

"We're not breaking any laws, and we were asked by the Queen of Andover to look into this."

"Very well, dear, whatever the group thinks is best." She raised her hand, hesitatingly, but she did it nonetheless.

"Wonderful. We all agree to continue then."

Mother made a noise.

"Mother's reservations are noted." I wrote them into my journal.

"Thank you, dear," Mother said.

"The government phrased their request in terms of the impact on national security, but I wonder if there is more to it than that?" I asked.

"Such as?" Marlowe asked.

"They don't know whose body was found at the Tower. That's what Mister Clapham learned from Scotland Yard. If it was the colonel's, then where is the prince? Kidnapped? Or did he disappear of his own volition?"

"Why would he opt to vanish?" Lady Emma asked.

"To delay the vote on the negotiations," Marlowe responded.

"For what reason?" I asked.

"His advisors and his own son wished him to accept the deal which he didn't want to do. By disappearing, he effectively caused the negotiations to cease without taking the blame for it."

"Again, why?" I asked.

"More than likely, he hoped his advisors would see his point of view and agree to his vertical farming plan."

"Not likely when winter is coming."

"May I make a point, Kitty?" Mother asked.

"Of course."

"If he chose that course, it would mean he planned the

colonel's murder. That does not seem likely. The prince did not strike me as coldblooded."

"I can't see it either, Mother. Which means somebody else planned it. So the question now becomes who killed the colonel and kidnapped the prince?"

"Same reason," Marlowe said. "To delay the negotiations."

"For what purpose?" I asked.

Mother raised her hand. "I have something to contribute in that regard, Kitty."

"By all means, Mother, take the floor."

"Well, the Queen, who was once more very gracious, explained the process regarding the line of succession in a situation where the heir is missing. Someone thought far enough ahead, it's written into their constitution. As things stand, the duke cannot succeed to the throne because he's not married to a member of the French nobility. But, even though the count meets that requirement, neither can he."

"Why not?"

"Because it is up to the Andoverian Parliament to make the decision regarding who will be named the heir apparent, and thus able to rule in the king's stead. A member of Parliament makes the motion, presents all the facts and circumstances, and the entire body votes. But a motion can't be made until thirty days have elapsed after the disappearance of the prince."

"Thirty days?" Marlowe exclaimed. "Their country could erupt into chaos during that time, seeing how they're running low on food and winter is drawing near."

"Is there no exception?" I asked.

"None."

"If I may, Kitty?" My brother asked.

"Yes, Ned."

"I spoke to Sir George Gordon. He represents the armaments manufacturers at the negotiations. He said all the right things during our discussion. He's shocked about the prince's murder. What a horrible thing to have happened. He feels for the Andoverian royal family. But underneath it all, his main worry is the status of the discussions. They're at an impasse. Without the prince's participation, it cannot move forward unless someone is assigned to take his place."

"Couldn't somebody be authorized to do that?" I asked. "That is a separate issue from who inherits the throne."

"The Andoverian Minister of the Treasury would be the logical candidate, but he would need some sort of approval. The question now becomes who would be authorized to do that? There's a difference of opinion regarding that matter. Andover scholars are parsing through their constitution to find a solution. But until they do . . ."

"The negotiations can't proceed," I said.

"No."

"One thing is clear. The identity of the body takes precedence over anything else," Hollingsworth said. "Without that, they can't move forward."

"But Scotland Yard has done that. Hasn't it?" Melissande asked.

"They have yet to make an official ruling that the victim is in fact the prince," Mister Clapham responded.

"But at the inquest the medical examiner declared him dead," I said.

"He never actually said it was the prince. It was the count who identified the body."

I glanced at my inquest notes. I'd written that the medical examiner referred to the body as the prince's. But maybe I'd injected my belief rather than what the medical examiner said.

"I checked with the court reporter to make sure my recollection was correct," Mister Clapham said to bolster his argument.

"Splendid, Mister Clapham. So glad we have you on our team." The Gordian knot we were trying to unravel was proving too difficult. For the moment, it would be best to let it rest. "Let's table these issues for the moment and move on. Lady Lily and Lady Melissande, did you discover any additional information at the hotel?"

"Quite a lot, actually."

"Oh?"

"The royal suite, where the prince and princess are staying is located in an eighteenth-century mansion connected to the hotel. It features a sitting room, a dining room for private dinner parties, and two bedrooms. It also contains a study, two dressing rooms, and lavish marble bathrooms. But here's the interesting part. The suite has an additional set of rooms which are approached through the study. It contains not only a bedroom, but a sitting room and a private bathroom. That's where the colonel's been staying."

"That would make sense, wouldn't it?" I asked. "He would need to be available to the prince."

"We discovered that the door was always kept unlocked."

A wild thought occurred to me. "Is it unlocked on the prince's side as well?"

"Yes."

We all stared at each other as our imaginations took flight.

"There's a perfectly innocent explanation," Mother offered. "The prince wouldn't desire to walk down the corridor to reach him."

"What about the princess? She has attendants as well, doesn't she?" I asked.

"Two," Lily answered. "Their bedrooms are two floors down."

So, the equerry was kept close by, but the princess's attendants were not. Was something to be made of this?

"One additional thing we discovered about the colonel," Lady Melissande said. "He entertained guests. In his bedroom."

"A lady, you mean?"

"That's what the hotel staff suggested."

A thought occurred to me. "Did the room also have an exit into the corridor?"

"Yes."

"Somebody could have come in that way."

"True. However, a security guard is posted day and night by the elevator. Nobody gets past him unless the guest has been approved by the colonel or the prince."

"Who was on duty that night?"

"We were not able to discover that information from the hotel staff. But it stands to reason somebody was."

"We'll need to find out who. The duke should know. Hollingsworth, can you ask him?"

"Will do."

"Were you able to discover information about the colonel?" I asked him.

"A great deal, although I'm still waiting on a few more reports from Andover. He's indeed acknowledged, although unofficially, as the king's illegitimate son. Everything I learned tallied with what Mrs. Worthington said. He was the result of an affair the king had before he married his queen. When the queen discovered his existence, she had him brought to Andover Palace where he was raised alongside the prince. They received the same education, participated in the same sports."

"So he was treated like another son."

"Seems that way. When he turned eighteen, he and the prince went their separate ways. The prince remained in the palace to perform his royal duties; he joined the Andoverian army. From what I've learned, he rose through the ranks on his own merit. He was thirty-five when the prince offered him the position of equerry which he readily accepted. By that time, he'd reached the rank of colonel."

"Rather young to achieve such an honor."

"From what I was able to gather he distinguished himself during his service. Andover might be a neutral country, but that doesn't mean it does not engage in confrontations. Some years ago, the capital city was attacked by insurgents dissatisfied with the way the country was being run. He took charge of the troops and soundly defeated them. For his bravery and leadership, he was awarded the rank of colonel by the prince himself."

"So he knows his way around a battlefield," Marlowe said.

"Yes. He's a legend among the soldiers," Hollingsworth answered. "And he's thoroughly trusted in the palace. Apparently, nobody has a bad thing to say about him. His allegiance is to Andover and the prince, in that order."

"Is the colonel married?" I asked.

"No."

"So, he would be allowed liaisons, as long as he was discrete, which he seems to have been. He supposedly entertained in his quarters. Did you learn anything about the identity of his lover?"

"I did ask. But if there was one particular lady who caught his interest, no one knew of it."

"How old is he?"

"Fifty."

"A man doesn't live that long without forming some sort of attachment," Lady Emma said.

"And you know this how?" Marlowe asked.

"I have eyes, ears, and a sound mind."

By way of response, Marlowe arched his brow.

"I agree with you, Lady Emma. Keep looking, Hollingsworth."

"Yes, ma'am." His mischievous grin made an appearance as he offered me a salute.

"Sorry, did that come out too harshly?"

"Not at all." But he didn't lose the smile.

A glimmer of something was beginning to appear, but it was nowhere clear enough for me to see. But the pattern was there. All I needed to determine was what were lies and what was truth. Something that, in this case, was proving very difficult.

"What about the Tower of London, Mister Clapham?"

"I've greased the palms of those likely to be in the know. Should find out something in the next day or two."

"Very well. Keep us apprised. In the meantime, let's look at the information we have about how the murder was carried out. The window was broken from the inside which means the colonel let somebody into the room. Do we all agree?"

Some head bobs. Some yeses.

"It had to have been somebody he trusted," Lady Emma said.

"Not necessarily," Marlowe offered. "His supper tray was brought in."

"And removed. That was mentioned in the inquest," I said.

"Nothing to stop whoever took away the tray from doing the murder, though," Lady Emma opined.

"Mister Clapham," I said, "find out who performed that duty. It had to be somebody who works at the Tower."

"Noted."

"Let's assume for the moment, it wasn't the manservant. That means somebody else came calling that night. Who could it have been?"

"A member of the royal family," Marlowe suggested.

"His lover," Lady Emma opined.

"Which could be a member of the royal family," Marlowe said.

"Like whom?" Lady Emma asked.

"The countess. Maybe she was the one having an affair with him."

The room became quiet while we considered that theory.

"There's no evidence about that."

"There wouldn't be. They would want to keep anyone from finding out."

"We'll have to look into that. Lady Emma?"

"I'll add it to my list of questions when I finally manage to talk to her."

The countess was guilty of something. Whether it had anything to do with the investigation was anybody's guess. "Let's get back to the basics. Where were all the members of his family that night?"

"The queen was in her suite," Mother said.

"You'll need to verify it. Consult with her ladies-in-waiting. At least one of them should know."

"Very well, dear."

"The princess said she was in her chamber reviewing her wardrobe options with Lady VonSteuben. I'll confirm it with her."

"The son was at The Savoy enjoying a tryst," Hollingsworth said. "Verified by the lady in question."

"The count and countess?"

"They refused to talk to Marlowe and me," Lady Emma said.

"Do they realize that makes them suspects?" I asked.

"More than likely. I believe I can get the countess to talk to me. I just have to get her away from her husband. He's watching her like a hawk, though."

"Well, if that's not suspicious, I don't know what is. Mother, coordinate with Lady Emma. See if you can get the queen to request the count's company. Since there's no love lost between the queen and the countess, she can tell him she wishes the discussion to be private."

Turning to Lady Emma, she said, "I'll call as soon as I know."

"Thank you, Mrs. Worthington."

"Whoever removed the head had to do it for one simple reason," Mister Clapham said. "To obfuscate the identity of the corpse."

"Exactly," I said. "The prince was not clean-shaven. He was proud of his mustache. Even if they'd taken a razor to him after death, there would have been signs that he'd been recently shaved. Wouldn't there?"

"Yes," Mister Clapham answered.

"And if the corpse is the colonel's, he couldn't grow a mustache overnight," I said.

"Absolutely."

"At last, we're getting somewhere." I had no idea where it would lead, but at least we were moving forward. "It seems likely somebody within the royal family or entourage arranged this. But we can't ignore the armament manu-facturers."

"Who's the leader among them at the negotiations, Ned?"

"Sir George Gordon."

"I doubt he would've committed murder, but he could've arranged it with somebody else. Is he nefarious enough to plan something of this nature? We'll need to look into his business dealings. Can you do that?"

"Of course," Ned replied.

I glanced once more at my notes. "I believe that is all for today. We'll meet again in three days' time. But leave the day after tomorrow open in case we need to meet earlier than that."

The meeting broke up and as usual they formed groups to discuss the evidence. Leaving them to it, I made my exit. More than anything, I needed to clear my head.

CHAPTER NINETEEN

A THREATENING NOTE

*A*FTER FETCHING MY OUTER GARMENTS and Sir Winston, I headed for our garden. For once, the weather was fair, with neither rain nor wind to spoil my walk. So, I spent the time wandering through the neatly laid out paths while allowing my mind to roam. With so many theories to explore, there was a strong possibility we would never get to the truth. But I had to try. I refused to give up.

After a half hour, lengthening shadows and rapidly dropping temperatures forced me inside. I stepped into the house through the back door to leave Sir Winston at his favorite spot. A basset hound he might be, but he loved nothing so much as his warm bed in the kitchen.

"Miss Worthington," one of the footmen said when I handed over my coat and scarf by our front door. "A letter came for you. I handed it to Betsy. Would you like me to fetch it for you?"

"No, thank you. I'll go up to my room." By now, Betsy was probably laying out my clothes for supper.

Sure enough, I found her studying the gowns in my wardrobe. I had so many, I only kept the fall and winter ones in my room. The others had been carefully packed in trunks and stored in the attic where they would remain until spring.

She turned as soon as she heard me walk into the room. "Oh, Miss, I was wondering what you'd like to wear tonight?"

"I think the turquoise silk cashmere with the pleated skirt. The one that arrived last week from Angelique's. I'll need a warm shawl as well. It can get drafty downstairs."

"Yes, Miss. I'll set it out. You received a letter. I placed it on your desk. Would you like me to run you a bath?"

"Please. Thank you, Betsy. Oh, and pour some rose oil in it."

While she rushed off to the bathroom, I opened the envelope. No return address. Curious. Wondered who'd sent it. Well, there was only one way to find out.

I almost dropped it when I read the contents. "Stop looking into the prince's murder. If you don't, the prince will not be the only one to lose his head."

"Miss. Miss. Anything wrong?" Betsy's voice seemed to come from a place far away.

Snapping back to the here and now, I said, "No. I just have a bit of a head, that's all." I choked out a laugh at the non-intentional pun.

"Well, a warm bath will put you right as rain, Miss."

"Yes. You're right. Thank you, Betsy."

An hour later, bathed and dressed, I entered the drawing room to find a lovely surprise. Robert. Since he was considered a part of the family, Mother had issued him an open invitation to come for supper anytime he was free. "How lovely," I said walking up to him.

He greeted me with a smile which, as always, made my heart melt. "Hello, Catherine."

Although I was eager to share the news of the threat I'd received, I couldn't very well do it in front of the entire party. It would have to wait until after supper.

As everyone was drinking cocktails, I asked Carlton for a sidecar. A combination of cognac and orange liqueur, it hailed straight out of the Paris Ritz.

Guests and family alike engaged in desultory conversation. By tacit agreement, we did not discuss the investigation. No surprise. Everyone was probably as exhausted about the subject as I was.

To my surprise, however, Mother addressed one particular question toward me. "Did you receive a letter this afternoon, Kitty?"

I stiffened. I couldn't tell Mother the truth. She'd worry. So, I made up a story. "Yes, a friend from finishing school. She's visiting London over the holidays and wanted some suggestions. Where to stay, what restaurants to visit, what sites to see. Those sorts of things."

"Lovely. You'll have to invite her for supper."

"Afraid that won't be possible. Her visit will coincide with Margaret's wedding. We'll be at Wynchcombe Castle during the length of her stay."

"How very unfortunate. It would have been nice to renew your acquaintance with her."

I may have fooled Mother but not Robert as he scrunched his brow at me. When Mother turned to say something to Father, I whispered, "Later," to him.

Supper was a merry affair. Along with Mother and Father, and Ladies Lily, Melissande, and Emma, a trio of gentlemen—Ned, Hollingsworth, and Marlowe—had joined us. So were seated ten to supper. A nice enough number which wouldn't strain the conversation. After supper, using the excuse there was something I wanted Robert to see, we headed to the library. No one believed me. But then he was my fiancé. If we didn't stay away too long, we were allowed a certain amount of privacy. But in this case, I was speaking the truth. I fetched the letter I'd locked away in my desk and showed it to him.

It didn't take him long to read it or react. "Catherine, this is serious."

"You don't see me laughing, Robert. I know it is."

"What are you going to do?"

"Tell everyone, of course."

"That's all fine and good. But this threat is directed at you, not them."

"It encompasses everyone. After all, I'm not the only one looking into things."

He took a deep breath. Head down, he strolled about the space, no doubt pondering the best way to present his argument. Finally, he ended his wandering in front of me. "I had a visit from the Home Office."

"Oh." I should have known the government would reach out to him.

"When were you going to tell me about their request? Or weren't you going to inform me at all?"

"Of course, I was going to tell you. They were here only two days ago," I argued in my defense.

"Long enough for you to call. There's this marvelous contraption called the telephone."

"I wanted to do it in person."

"And yet, you did not set up a meeting with me."

"I apologize. I should have told you right away. I was just afraid . . ."

He tilted his head. "Afraid?"

"You'd demand I stop the investigation."

A shake of his head. "When we got engaged, I said I would not interfere with a path you wished to take."

"And yet, here you are, suggesting I quit the investigation."

"I'm presenting my point of view, as I promised I would."

Much as I hated to admit it, he was right. He'd promised not to interfere with my chosen course of action, but he'd reserved the right to make his feelings known. I couldn't fault him for doing what we'd agreed upon. "You're right. I apologize once more."

"Apology accepted." His lips quirked into a crooked smile before they turned serious again. "Did you inform the investigative committee about the Home Office's request?"

"Yes. I told them, and we voted to continue the investigation."

"When will you tell them about this letter?"

"I'll inform Ladies Lily, Melissande, and Emma tonight when we retire for the night. Everyone else, I'll contact early tomorrow morning."

"I would *advise* the ladies be kept at Worthington Manor."

"Would that include me?"

"Well, you are a lady."

"You are avoiding the question, Inspector."

"No, my advice would not encompass you, mainly for the reason you would not heed it. I would caution you, however, to be careful when you wander outside."

"I'll ask Lily and Melissande to organize my notes. That should keep them engaged in the investigation without venturing forth. But Lady Emma is planning to meet with the countess. I'll ask Marlowe to escort her."

"Let's hope he'll keep her safe."

"He will. She's actually very dear to him."

"Marlowe and Lady Emma? Every time I've seen them, they've been at daggers drawn."

"The course of true love never does run smooth, Inspector. They'll work it out. If they don't kill each other first, that is."

"Hope not. I would hate to arrest one of them."

I shook my head and smiled.

"You'll have to tell your mother about the note, you know. She'll see right through your scheme to keep the young ladies home."

"I fear you're right. She's also due to talk to the queen tomorrow. I can't let her go by herself. Somebody must accompany her. Mister Clapham, Hollingsworth, and Marlowe are all occupied. And so is Ned."

"Let me do it."

I gazed at him with surprise.

"I am peripherally attached to this matter."

"But not in charge of it."

"No."

"A shame. You would have done a much better job than Rutherford. Very well. I'll let Mother know. Her appointment with the queen is at eleven."

"That's unusually early. Most ladies don't rise before noon."

"The queen is made of stronger mettle. Apparently, she likes to take a walk in the park before breakfast. Claims it keeps her mind sharp and her body strong."

"She's more than likely right. Very well. I'll be here by ten. That should give us plenty of time to drive to the hotel."

We rejoined the party to find several of the guests had departed, and only those who resided with us remained. Robert soon said his goodbyes as he had an early meeting in the morning. Shortly after, Father and Mother retired for the night.

That's when I took the opportunity to tell the ladies about the letter. "We will need to be extra vigilant. For the moment,

I'm afraid some of us will need to keep to Worthington House. At least until this matter is cleared up."

"Some of us meaning?" Lady Lily asked.

"You and Lady Melissande." I squeezed her hand. "I'm sorry. I know how much the investigation has meant to you."

"That's so unfair," Lady Melissande said, her expression crestfallen. "I was just beginning to enjoy myself."

"And you will again." I hoped she wouldn't become melancholy and start playing funeral dirges again. "In the meantime, I'm sure Hollingsworth will escort you to wherever you wish to go. The theatre, for example."

"That would be nice."

She didn't appear thrilled by the idea, but then she seemed to be nursing a grudge toward her brother.

"I have to talk to the countess, Kitty," Lady Emma said.

"Marlowe will escort you."

She rolled her eyes.

"I think I will say goodnight," Lady Lily said. Her sentiment was echoed by Lady Melissande. Together they exited, clearly despondent.

"It's not your fault, Kitty," Lady Emma said.

"Then why do I feel so guilty?"

"Because you're a good and kind person, that's why. Come. Tomorrow will be a better day, you'll see."

Unfortunately, she was wrong. Dead wrong.

CHAPTER TWENTY

A GRUESOME DISCOVERY

*W*E'D CONGREGATED in the drawing room before luncheon was served when Mother and Robert returned from their meeting with the queen.

"How did it go?" I asked.

"As well as could be expected. The queen will arrange a private audience with the count. She'll telephone with the details, so Lady Emma can schedule her meeting with the countess."

"You've been such a great help, Mother. I don't know what we would have done without you."

As usual, she took the compliment in stride. "You would have figured it out, Kitty. You're rather good at that." Glancing at my fiancé, she said with a smile, "Robert will be joining us for luncheon. His reward for escorting me today."

"No need, ma'am. It was my pleasure," he said with an elegant bow of his head.

Carlton stepped into the room, I thought to announce the

luncheon was served. But I was wrong. "A letter, Miss Worthington, from Mister Clapham. The messenger said it was urgent."

What on earth could it be? Mister Clapham was scheduled to visit the Tower of London this morning. Had he discovered some alarming news? Only one way to find out. I tore the envelope and read the contents of the note inside. *"Suspicious body parts found by a Thames waterman. Turned over to Scotland Yard."*

I handed the missive to Robert. "You need to read this."

"What is it, dearest?" Mother asked.

"It looks like they found the missing head and hands."

"Oh, dear." Mother's face grew pale.

"My apologies," Robert said. "I must go."

"Yes, of course," I said. "Let us know what you find out. If you can."

"I will."

He rushed out the door. At least, he'd driven his Rolls Royce Phantom this morning, so he wouldn't need to hail a taxicab.

"Do you think it really could be—" Mother didn't finish her thought.

"More than likely. We'll just have to wait and see."

"I think I'll go have a lie down. This is becoming much too real."

"Shall we send up a tray? You have to eat."

"Something light."

"I'll let Cook know."

"Shall I go up with you, Mrs. Worthington?" Lady Lily said, wrapping her arm around Mother's elbow.

"You don't have to, dear. I'm fine."

"Please indulge me," Lady Lily offered with that sweet smile of hers. "I won't feel comfortable until I see you settled."

"Very well."

"I'll ring for Cummings," I said. Mother's maid knew exactly what do for Mother. She might be a martinet to everyone else, but she treated Mother with kindness and love.

"Thank you, Kitty."

We waited for Lady Lily to return before proceeding to luncheon.

"How is she?" I asked.

"A little pale. Cummings took over the caring of her."

"Cummings will give her something to lift her spirits and tea. By suppertime, Mother will be right as rain, you'll see."

"Maybe Mrs. Worthington should take a lesser role," Lady Emma suggested. "One of us can step in if need be."

"I'll offer that option to her. But we'll have to see how she feels about it. It's up to her to decide."

"Yes, of course."

"After luncheon I could play some piano pieces," Lady Melissande said. "Maybe that would help."

"No," I said a bit too harshly. The last thing Mother wanted was to hear funereal music. "Thank you, Lady Melissande. But quiet is what she needs right now."

It wasn't until later that afternoon that we heard from Mister Clapham. He came in person to deliver the news. "It hasn't been confirmed, but there are strong indications it's the missing head and hands."

"How do they know?"

"They were chopped off with a heavy axe. The edges match the cuts on the body."

"Well, at least they'll be able to identify the remains now."

"I don't think that will be possible."

"What do you mean?"

"The remains were tossed into a sack which has been in

the Thames several days. The fingerprints would have deteriorated by now."

"But the face" —I gulped— "wouldn't they be able to identify it?"

"The face is clean shaven. The hair was close cut to the
skull. The facial features are not recognizable as waterlogged
as they are."

I swallowed hard while thanking heaven Mother was not
around to hear this. "Wouldn't that indicate it's the colonel,
not the prince?"

"One would think so. However, whoever performed this
deed could have very well shaved the prince to make it look
like it's the colonel. The chief medical examiner is not willing
to make that conclusion. Not without further evidence."

As he had an appointment with a person who had information about the Tower of London, he barely had time to
gulp down a cup of tea and eat a sandwich before he made
his way out once more.

Mother joined us for supper but remained quiet during
the meal. After we retired to the drawing room, she didn't
remain long. Claiming she was tired, she excused herself.

Father accompanied her upstairs but soon returned. "This
is growing serious, Kitty."

"Yes, Father."

"Can't she be kept out of this?"

"It's up to her to decide. I'll make that option available to
her."

He let out a heavy sigh. Claiming he had some business
matters to attend to, he said goodnight and headed for his
study.

Ladies Lily and Melissande set up in a corner to peruse
fashion magazines and discuss the upcoming season while
Lady Emma took up her embroidery. To my surprise, she not
only excelled at plying the needle but rather enjoyed it. Since

I had no interest in either, I made my excuses and took the stairs to my room.

The following morning, the discovery of the remains was splashed all over the news with each journal seemingly trying to outdo each other with the goriest of details. Since under no circumstances was Mother to see them, much less read the accounts, I ordered Carlton to burn all the papers.

By eleven, I hadn't heard from Robert, so I telephoned him to see if he had information to share. Unfortunately, he was not in his office. I thought to leave a message but decided against it. He knew I was anxious to hear from him. He would contact me when he could.

As it stood, the investigative committee was at a standstill. Since we had been commissioned by the Queen of Andover to discover her son's murderer, we could not move forward until the body was identified. If it was the prince's, we could continue our investigation. But if it was the colonel's, we couldn't forge ahead without the queen's permission. And if in fact it was the colonel's, it begged the question. Where was the prince? Would the purpose of our investigation change from investigating a murder to discovering what had happened to her son?

I'd almost decided to drive to Scotland Yard when Robert showed up. Although as always, he was immaculately dressed and shaved, his eyes were bloodshot. He'd probably gotten little sleep.

"Did you get some rest?"

"Some, not much," he said, with a tired smile.

"Would you like some coffee? Or something to eat?"

"Coffee. Thank you."

I ordered the service. Once it arrived, I allowed him to enjoy a sip or two before I asked, "Any news?"

"The medical examiner can't positively identify it as the prince's. The fingermarks have been too degraded by water."

"Mister Clapham said the hair was closely shorn, and the mustache was missing. Wouldn't that prove it's the colonel?"

"It would indicate so, but it can't be positively proven. After all the mustache could have been shaved off and the hair trimmed."

"So what's Rutherford going to do?"

He straightened. "Nothing. He's been replaced."

"Let me guess. You?"

"Yes."

"They should have chosen you in the first place. What precipitated this decision?"

"The Queen of Andover was furious with the direction of the investigation. Apparently, she made her feelings known to the higher-ups. After this latest discovery, she demanded I be assigned to the case."

I suppressed a grin. "Your manly charms must have impressed her."

An arched brow. "I released the suspect."

"The thief?" Well, that surprised me.

"Yes. Turns out the night of the murder he spent the night in the clink. He instigated a pub fight."

"And Rutherford didn't verify his whereabouts?"

"He should have."

I sensed that was all he would say on the subject, so I asked another question, an open-ended one which was bound to draw a response. "What happens now?"

"Once Rutherford apprehended the thief, he didn't continue to investigate. And with all the time that's passed, the trail has gone cold. It's a good thing you took on this matter for you'll give Scotland Yard a path to follow." He took a sip of the coffee. "I'll need to talk to your team."

I could have crowed in triumph, but I didn't. It wasn't his fault Rutherford was an idiot. "Of course. We have a meeting tomorrow at two."

"Can you move it to the morning? Time is of the essence."

"I'll telephone everyone right away."

"Thank you for not gloating."

"I'll need a favor, though." Might as well press him on it.

He stiffened in response. "Is this boon required to have access to your team?"

"No. You'll have their cooperation whether you grant the favor or not."

He crossed his arms across his chest. "Very well. What do you want?"

"Access to the Queen's House, specifically where the prince, or the colonel, stayed. Mister Clapham needs to examine it for clues. He'll also need access to any witnesses."

"Very well." He lowered his arms. "An officer will need to accompany him while he's performing this inquiry."

"I'm sure he won't mind."

After he left, I told the ladies and then telephoned every member of the team who did not reside with us. Everyone agreed readily enough to meet at eleven. Except for Marlowe, that is, who had a thing or two say about the ungodly hour.

Mother joined us for supper that night, seemingly recuperated from her ordeal. "I must apologize, Kitty. I have no idea what came over me."

I hugged her. "No need to apologize, Mother. You've been stalwart throughout. Not only did you provide vital information, but you established rapport with the queen. We wouldn't be this far along if it weren't for you." When I explained about Robert taking command of the investigation and his request to talk to the team, she was fully on board. "Absolutely. So glad they put him in charge."

"Mother, if you want to withdraw from the investigation, Lady Emma is willing to step in."

"Withdraw?" she asked, seemingly affronted by the

suggestion. "No. Absolutely not. That was just a temporary weakness. I mean to see this through to the end."

"Mildred. Are you sure?" Father asked.

"Absolutely. I've never shirked my duty, and I don't mean to start now."

"Very well," I said, with a glance toward Father.

"Now, what are we going to serve at the meeting?" Mother asked. "That early in the morning, gentlemen need something heartier than tea and cakes."

Mother's way of ending the discussion to show she was fully in command of herself. I'd never been prouder of her than right this moment. She may have been temporarily down, but you could never count her out.

CHAPTER TWENTY-ONE

THE INVESTIGATIVE COMMITTEE'S FOURTH
MEETING

*T*HE FOLLOWING MORNING, to compensate for
the early hour, we added ham and cheese crois-
sants to our usual fare of coffee, tea, and pastries. While the
ladies satisfied themselves with the sweet goods, the
gentlemen seemed particularly appreciative of the
sandwiches.

Everyone filled their plates before arranging themselves
around the room. Lords Marlowe and Hollingsworth, as well
as Ned, in leather wing chairs. While Ladies Lily and Melissande settled on a settee upholstered in a light blue brocade,
Lady Emma opted for one close to Marlowe in a darker blue
shade. Mother had chosen her favorite camelback sofa
finished in distinctive blue satin silk. Interestingly enough,
Mister Clapham had commandeered the most expensive
piece in the library, a hooded porter's chair which hailed

from the 17th century. Robert and I had no preference other than comfort, so we settled on a blue grey Chesterfield sofa. While everyone ate their fill, we enjoyed desultory conversation. But once everyone's hunger was satisfied, I stood and brought the meeting to order.

"As I informed you yesterday when I telephoned or talked to you, Chief Detective Inspector Crawford has been put in charge of the investigation. He asked for permission to address the committee which, of course, I granted."

Marlowe raised his hand. "I'm happy to share what I learned. Will Chief Detective Inspector Crawford be happy to share as well?"

"Interesting question," I said.

Robert came to his feet as well. "May I answer that, Catherine?"

"Of course."

"I will share what I can. But some information will need to be kept confidential."

"Absolutely," Ned said.

"Such as?" Marlowe was not giving up.

"Matters of national security, for one," Ned answered, rather tersely.

"Children!" I clapped my hands, and the room grew quiet. "We benefit as well. Chief Detective Inspector Crawford has very kindly given permission for Mister Clapham to inspect the Queen's House at the Tower of London and for him to interview the witnesses surrounding the murder. Now why don't we let Chief Detective—"

"Robert will do, Catherine," Robert gently said. "They are fully cognizant of my title."

"Very well." I addressed the group once more. "Let's hear what Robert has to say."

Calmly and methodically, he brought them up to speed

on the investigation. The remains had not been positively identified. Water had deteriorated the surface of the skin making it nigh impossible to get fingermarks. They'd contacted the Bureau of Investigation in the states and the International Criminal Police Commission to see if they could provide assistance in this matter.

"I've heard of the Bureau of Investigation but not the International Criminal Police Commission," Lady Emma said.

"It's a newly created organization meant to address the rising criminal rate in Europe. As you can imagine it's to everyone's advantage for our agencies to cooperate with each other."

"Makes sense," Lady Emma said.

"This morning before the meeting," Robert continued, "Catherine provided me with a summary of what you've discovered. As you can expect, I have questions."

"Stands to reason," Hollingsworth said.

The rest of the committee nodded their assent.

"If we could start with your impressions of the royal family, beginning with the queen," Robert said before turning to Mother. "Mrs. Worthington, if you would?"

"Of course." She provided information not only about the queen but the entire royal succession and the problems they were experiencing. While she spoke, Robert made notations in his journal. He'd used a similar one during a previous investigation when I'd been the subject he interviewed.

From Mother, he moved on to me, Hollingsworth, Marlowe, and Lady Emma. Finally, he asked, "That's the lot then?"

"Yes," I answered for the group.

"It appears the members of the royal family are not who they seem to be. The princess turned amiable. The son does not appear to be a wastrel but deeply concerned for the people of his country. The count is not as mealymouthed as he seemed, and his wife fears him. Is that about right?"

"Yes." Everyone agreed.

"What about the prince?" Robert asked. "Did you get a sense of him?"

"Well," I said, "We heard different points of view. According to the queen, he's honorable and wants to do his best for his country. His son begs to differ as he thinks him a fool. His wife knows about his affairs but refuses to speak a word against him. The count is saying everything that's proper, just as we would expect him to do. So does his wife."

"What about Colonel Bouchard?"

Hollingsworth shared what he knew.

"So, he's a right and proper soldier whose allegiance is to the country first and then the prince," Robert said.

"That's what I understand," Hollingsworth confirmed.

"Ned suggested another avenue of investigation," I said.

Robert nodded. "The armament manufacturers."

"Specifically, Sir George Gordon," Ned explained. "He's representing them in the negotiations. He said everything that was proper. But same as the count, it seemed well rehearsed."

"He may have something to hide as well."

"Yes. But I fear there's only so much I can do. I don't have the authority to look into his armament's enterprise. Because it would involve matters of national security, that investigation would be best handled by a branch of the government."

"MI5 handles matters of national security, so my investigation into Lord Gordon and his activities might be curtailed as well. Be assured, though, I will push that limit to the utmost." Robert stated with a glint to his eye. "Anything else?"

"Ladies Lily and Melissande interviewed the staff," I said.

He listened politely while they revealed what they'd

learned. But it wasn't until they got to the part about the colonel sleeping in a bedroom attached to the study that his interest was well and truly caught. "He entertained in his bedroom?"

"Yes. But nobody knows who," Lady Lily answered.

"In order to reach the prince's suite, someone would need to take the private elevator," Lady Melissande offered.

I followed up with, "And they could not have access to that suite, including the colonel's chamber, without going past a guard stationed there at all times."

"I'll need to discover who was on duty that night," Robert said, noting it on his journal.

"The colonel has not been located?" I asked.

"No," he answered. "We telephoned the Superintendent of Police in Andover. He never made it there. We couldn't find any record of him taking an airplane to Paris or a train to Dover, either."

"The Golden Arrow?" I asked.

"Yes." We shared a private smile.

That's where we first became acquainted, although we'd actually met at the Gare de Lyon train station in Paris when I literally ran into him. "May I ask a question?" I asked.

"Of course."

"The thief you released. Where did he find the pocket watch?"

"He says he found it on one of the streets, close to the Tower of London. He was too inebriated to remember which one."

"Do you believe him?"

"No. I'm having him followed. Sooner or later, he'll meet up with someone who knows something."

An idea blossomed in my idea, one which Robert would most surely not approve, so I fought to keep it from showing on my face. His raised brow told me I hadn't succeeded. Still, he didn't voice an objection. Not in public anyway. But honestly, he had nothing to worry about. I would ask Mister Clapham to accompany me and Hollingsworth as well.

"I've arranged to interview the princess tomorrow," Robert said. "Since you've already established rapport with her, I'd like you to accompany me," Robert said.

"Be happy to."

He turned back to the group. "Now that we've discussed your findings, I'd like to hear your opinions regarding the murder. Who do you think is responsible?"

"The count," Marlowe said. "He stands to gain the most from this scenario."

"Why?" Robert asked.

"With the prince out of the way, he would be next in line to the crown."

"The son could marry and take that option off the table."

"Somehow I don't think he would have waited for the king to die a natural death."

"You think he would have killed the king as well?"

"He's already at death's door. Surely it would take only a push to have him cross over."

"Very well. Any other theories?"

"The princess," Lady Melissande said. "She was tired of her husband cheating on her."

"A reasonable assumption."

"I vote for a foreign source," Ned said.

"Such as?"

"Enemies of the state. They would not have wanted England to be given the rights to obtain the antimony. It would provide England with a great advantage should another war come along."

"You think that's possible, Ned?" I asked in dismay. It was one thing for Mother to suggest such a thing. But Ned's opinion was based on not only his experience but a deep knowledge about issues surrounding wars.

"Not only possible, but likely. That region of Europe is very unsettled. Too many actors hunger for power, and they won't stop until they get it."

"That's horrible," Lady Lily said, gazing at him with a stricken gaze.

"Not to worry, dear," Mother said. "England will always prevail."

Yes, but how many would die if another war came along.

Robert cleared his throat, recalling us back to the issue at hand. "Anyone else?"

"The prince himself," Mister Clapham said.

"He arranged for his own death?" Robert asked.

"Not bloody likely."

"Mister Clapham," Mother protested. "Language."

"Begging your pardon, ma'am."

"Go on," Robert said, biting back a grin.

"The victim is the colonel which means the prince sent him to his death."

"The murderer could have confused him with the prince."

"He didn't. This was a well-planned operation. Feel it in my guts." Mister Clapham patted his belly.

"Let's say, I agree with you," Robert said. "Why would the prince kill his right-hand man?"

"I don't know. Yet. But we will find out. We're a bl-fine group of investigators, if I say so myself."

"Thank you, Mister Clapham," I said. "Does anyone else have a theory to share?"

When all remained mum, I brought the meeting to a close.

As Robert had to return to Scotland Yard, I accompanied him back to the foyer. "What time is your appointment with the princess tomorrow?"

"Three. I'll pick you up at two, if that's amenable."

"It will be." I just hoped we wouldn't discover information that pointed to the princess as the perpetrator of the crime. She didn't seem the type to plan such a complex operation. But then it wouldn't be the first time I'd been fooled.

CHAPTER TWENTY-TWO

INSPECTOR CRAWFORD INTERVIEWS THE
PRINCESS

*R*IGHT AT TWO THE NEXT DAY, Robert appeared at our door. I'd purposefully waited for him in the drawing room, so we didn't waste time with pleasantries.

"Who was playing the piano?" he asked after we'd climbed into his motorcar.

"Lady Melissande. When she first arrived, it was nothing but funeral dirges. Mozart's *Lacrimosa* from his *Requiem in D Minor* was in constant play. She's lightened her repertoire since then. *Für Elise* and *Moonlight Sonata* are her current favorites."

"Did you ever discover the source of her sadness?"

I shook my head. "Not even Lily has gotten to its root. She may very well be naturally predisposed to melancholy. She had such an unusual upbringing. I can't imagine what it must have been like to grow up in a convent."

"Was she the only student?"

"There were others, all of whom were meant for the veil. She was the only one who was not. Although all the students received the same classical education, the others were further instructed on their faith. She, on the other hand, was taught how to paint, draw, and, of course, play the piano. She reads not only in English and French, but Latin, Italian, and Greek."

"She seems to have received a first-rate education. Does she intend to make her debut in the spring?"

"She seemed reluctant at first, but Lady Lily has convinced her to do so. If Hollingsworth hasn't found her a chaperone by then, I'm sure Margaret will be happy to sponsor her. After all, she'll be squiring Lady Lily about town. One more debutante shouldn't make a difference."

"She should do well."

"In the marriage mart, you mean?"

"That is the goal of most debutantes."

"I'm not so sure she wishes to marry. At least not at the moment."

"Reminds me of another young lady I know." We shared a grin.

Although at the start of my season I'd been against marriage, by the end of it I'd become engaged to him. But then, I'd never expected to fall in love.

"What about Lady Lily?"

"She'll go through the motions, but I believe her heart's set on Ned. And his on her. I imagine at some point, they'll announce their engagement."

"Your mother will be pleased."

"Yes. She adores Lily, and Lily adores her."

As we pulled into the hotel, the doorman opened the door and held an umbrella for me as the day had turned drizzly. After a valet rushed to the other side to take over behind the wheel from Robert, he and I made our way into the hotel. Although the prince's suite was located in a private residence next to the hotel, one could enter through the hotel lobby. The only way to reach the suite, though, was through a private elevator which took us to the top floor where the prince's suite was located.

A hotel employee ensured our name was on the list of approved guests before we climbed into the car. Upon our arrival at the top floor, a military guard dressed in the Andoverian colors checked Robert's Scotland Yard credentials, while another guard accompanied us to the actual suite.

"Was this the procedure you went through before?" Robert enquired on the way.

"They added this additional guard. I was only met by the one next to the elevator."

"They're being more cautious now."

"Shouldn't a member of our police force be assigned as well?"

"We're not allowed to do so. Only Andoverian security can safeguard the royal family."

As before, we were shown to the sitting room, a gorgeous chamber lined with gilded mirrors and cream and gold wallpaper. Chandeliers sparkled above richly upholstered furnishings and Aubusson rugs. The princess, dressed in widow's weeds, a white handkerchief caught in one hand, was waiting for us seated in the same sofa she'd occupied during my previous visit. This time she seemed more somber, as if she'd finally realized the impact of the murder.

"Please take a seat, Miss Worthington, Detective Inspector Crawford. As you can see"—she pointed to the silver service on the table in front of her—"I've arranged for coffee and tea."

"Thank you."

After we'd duly sipped the offerings, Robert rested his

cup on the tray and retrieved his journal. "Do you mind if I take notes?"

"No. I'd prefer it actually. That way my words can't be misconstrued."

He discussed the events leading up to the prince leaving for the Tower of London. By taking it hour by hour, he was able to obtain a clearer image of what happened that day. "When did the prince leave?"

"Around four in the afternoon. He'd scheduled a tour of the Tower before he settled into the Queen's House."

"What time was he due back the next day?"

"By nine. He'd scheduled a meeting with representatives of our government to discuss the negotiations."

"What were his feelings on the negotiations?"

"He preferred it didn't go through. He very much thought we could grow sufficient food ourselves. That's why he discussed vertical farming methods with Miss Worthington's future brother-in-law, the Duke of Wynchcombe."

"And what was the position of the Andoverian ministers?"

"They were very much in favor of arranging for the lease, especially the Minister of the Treasury. He was concerned about the state of the country's finances. The Minister of Agriculture thought the prince's plans were not feasible as Andover only has thirty percent arable land. Now, of course, nothing can be determined."

"The prince's absence has caused a disruption to the negotiations?" Robert asked.

"Yes. Nothing can be agreed upon without his presence."

"Could we address Colonel Bouchard for a moment?" Robert asked.

The princess's demeanor drastically changed from reluctant politeness to slight belligerence. "Why? He's not here, nor does he have anything to do with the negotiations."

"I'm sorry to tell you this, but Scotland Yard has in its

possession certain . . . remains which match the body found at the Tower of London."

The princess raised the white handkerchief to her mouth. "Do we have to discuss this?"

"My most sincere apologies, but I'm afraid we must."

She lowered her trembling hand. "Very well. Proceed, Inspector."

"There's a strong belief that the remains at the Tower of London are those of Colonel Bouchard, not the prince."

To my great surprise, she let out a sob. "It can't be. It just can't be. He left."

"You prefer it be your husband's?"

"No!"

"Do you know of any marks or scars we could use to identify the body?"

"My husband did not have scars or birthmarks or moles."

"What about Colonel Bouchard?"

"How could I possibly know such a thing?" Her lips trembled. Why was Robert pushing her so hard? She was about to break.

"He was a soldier, wasn't he? Stands to reason he might have been hurt in a skirmish. Maybe you heard about it."

"He suffered a wound on his right leg. A saber slash which left a puckered scar on him." She held the handkerchief to her mouth once more. Clearly, she was at her limit. "I'm afraid I'm not feeling well. I need to lie down."

"My apologies if I caused you any distress," Robert said.

"Shall I ring for your maid?" I asked.

"Yes, please."

We waited in silence for her maid to appear before we led ourselves out.

Although I was eager to discuss what we'd just heard, it was better to hold off until we were somewhere where we would not be overheard.

Finally, when we were in Robert's Rolls once more, I said, "She totally fell apart when you brought up Colonel Bouchard."

"Yes, she did, didn't she?"

"Could they have been lovers?" All this time, the rumor has been about the prince having extramarital affairs, but no one connected Colonel Bouchard to the princess.

"There isn't the slightest hint of such a thing."

"He was sleeping in a room only a few feet away from hers. She could have easily made her way there."

"Without her husband finding out?"

"They sleep in different beds, and by all accounts, he never visits hers. Or maybe he knew and didn't care."

"An affair of such magnitude wouldn't have started after they arrived in England. It would have been an ongoing thing. I would need confirmation."

"Can you obtain it?"

"Maybe."

I sensed that's all he would say on that subject, so I moved on to the question burning in my mind. "Does the body in Scotland Yard's morgue have a scar on its right leg?"

"Yes. Yes, it does."

Which meant the person who'd been murdered was Colonel Bouchard.

"So, where's the prince?"

"That we have still to find out."

* * *

As soon as I arrived home, I was pounced upon by Lady Emma. Of course, she wanted to know what I'd learned.

"Has afternoon tea been served? I'm perishing for some sustenance. The princess offered tea and coffee but no pastries."

"How very odd when she'd been so accommodating before."

"She probably deemed my earlier visit as unofficial. Today, however, was a different matter as she was being interrogated by a detective inspector from Scotland Yard." I glanced around the drawing room. "Where's everybody?"

"Hollingsworth took Melissande to a picture show. Can you believe she's never been to one?"

"She was stuck in a convent for her entire life. So, yes, I do. What about Mother and Lady Lily?"

"They got word from one of the cloth merchants. Apparently, a shipment of Japanese goods arrived. As soon as they heard, they pelted out the door."

I laughed. "I hope Margaret loves oriental motifs as much as Mother does."

"Your sister doesn't give two figs about decorating matters. She'll accept whatever they decide upon because it brings them joy."

I squeezed her hand. "You know Margaret so well. Shall we ring for some food? I can tell you what we discovered while we eat."

A smile was her response. Once the spread was before us, we fell upon it like starving wolves.

"I don't know if it's detective work or the colder temperatures," I said, "but I've grown ravenous in recent weeks."

"A little of both, I would think." She bit into a scone with relish. "So, what did you find out?"

As Robert had not sworn me to secrecy, I did not hold back. "The body is definitely Colonel Bouchard's."

"No!" she said, sipping her tea.

"It appears that way. Now the question becomes, who was the intended victim. The colonel or the prince?"

She glanced off into the distance while she pondered the

issue. "The prince must have arranged for the colonel to take his place. There really is no other explanation."

"I agree."

"Why would he do such a thing?"

"Maybe he had an assignation with a lady and wanted to spend the night with her," I conjectured.

"But it's been over a week. Shouldn't he have returned by now?"

"If he indeed planned an affair, he would have been horrified about what happened to the colonel. More than likely, he's trying to come up with a plausible explanation about his disappearance. Heaven knows a tryst won't do. It will not only make him a laughingstock but might put the negotiations in peril."

She dismissed my suggestion with a wave of her hand. "Oh, he need not worry about that. Our government would craft a reason as to his disappearance."

"You think so?"

"I know so." She glanced at me over the rim of her cup. "He's not the first member of a royal family to be caught on some escapade. Higher-ups are very good at covering up such matters."

"What excuse could they use?" I asked.

"They could say he was kidnapped."

"For what reason?"

"To prevent him from signing away the rights to the mineral," Lady Emma said. "That would place the prince in a sympathetic light. He'd be so grateful to our government for saving him from such a colossal embarrassment, he would approve the lease."

The obvious had to be said. "But he was leaning away from that position."

"Only the ones involved in the negotiations knew that, though."

A thought suddenly occurred to me. "They probably thought it was a stratagem to obtain more money from them."

"How did you think of that?" Lady Emma asked.

"I am my father's daughter, so I know how business-people think. It's always about money."

Having had her fill, Lady Emma leaned back against her seat. "I shouldn't have enjoyed so many scones. I'm fitting into my clothes again."

"Betsy can always let them out if they grow tight."

"You horrible creature!" She tossed a cushion at me which I dodged.

Taking advantage of her convivial mood, I asked, "Lord Marlowe made a rather cryptic remark the other day. He said you could have married if you wanted to."

"I wondered how long it would take you to ask." She plated another scone and took a bite.

"Well?"

"He asked me to marry him."

"What! When?"

"It's the how that's the important part. But I'll take pity on you and satisfy your burning curiosity. As you know, he asked me to dinner. At your prompting, I know."

I didn't even think of denying it. "Where did he take you?"

"The restaurant at the Ritz."

"Wonderful."

"It was rather." A dreamy expression surfaced in her eyes. "The food was beyond marvelous. He paid attendance upon me at every turn. He's quite an amusing conversation-alist when he wishes to be. In short, it was a perfect evening." A frown crinkled her brow. "Until the dessert was served."

"Oh, no. What happened?"

"Instead of the *charlotte russe* I'd ordered, I was presented with an empty plate on which the words 'Marry Me,' had been spelled out in dark chocolate."

I sighed. "That's so romantic. What did you say?"

"*What's this?*" That's when the waiter fled.

He would. Waiters know when a man's about to be refused.

"*It's clear, isn't it?*" Marlowe said. "*I think we should get married.*"

"*Why?*" I asked.

"*We suit each other.*"

"Of course, I countered with the obvious. '*We're always arguing.*'"

"*That's what I mean. A peaceful woman would bore me to flinders.*"

"*What about what I want?*"

"*You're attracted to me. I can tell.*"

"*One of my many failings. It's not enough, Marlowe.*"

"*Why not? We'll have a grand old time. In and out of bed.*"

"*For a few months. And then we'd be miserable.*"

"He rather took umbrage to that. '*I can assure you I would not be.*'"

"*What about my role at the Ladies of Distinction Detective Agency?*"

"*You wouldn't need to do that anymore, of course. You'd have wealth, position, a title. You could do anything you wanted.*"

"*What if I wanted to work as a lady detective?*"

"*Why?*"

"*Because I'd rather use my intellect to help people in distress than waste my life gossiping about them. Can we leave? I seem to have lost my appetite.*"

"*Yes, of course.*"

"And that was that." She glanced at her hands to hide the glimmer of tears in her eyes. "The thing of it is, Kitty, I so wish we could."

"Marry?"

"Yes."

"Maybe things will work out."

"Only when pigs might fly."

CHAPTER TWENTY-THREE

THE TOWER OF LONDON

*T*HE FOLLOWING MORNING, Mister Clapham paid a call. He'd been to the Tower of London and had substantial news to report.

As he always appreciated a nice spread, I arranged with Carlton to serve refreshments as soon as he arrived.

"Ah, ginger biscuits," Mister Clapham said helping himself to one. "My favorite."

"That's why I specially requested them." After allowing him sufficient time to enjoy the food, I asked, "So, what did you discover at the Tower?"

"Well, for starters, the guard outside the Queen's House was drugged."

"No!"

"All signs point to it, although it can't be verified. Too much time has passed."

"What happened?"

"He was scheduled to be on duty from midnight to four.

When his relief showed up, he found him slumped against the wall."

"But why didn't the relief say anything?"

"He thought the guard had taken a nip or two to ward off the cold and ended up drunk. He didn't report it because he didn't want to impact the guard's record."

"And Rutherford missed that?"

"No. He didn't. He knew. After my visit to the Tower, I dropped in on him. Rutherford had much to share. Much as the relief, he thought the guard took a nip or two to keep warm. It was a cold, raw night. But when questioned the guard flat out told him he hadn't taken a drop. Apparently, he's known throughout the barracks as a teetotaler, so Rutherford believed him. That led him to realize the guard had been drugged."

"But why didn't Rutherford say anything?"

"Scotland Yard didn't want word to get out. They already had a murdered prince on their hands. They didn't want to add a drugged guard as well."

"How was he drugged?"

"The guard has no recollection of what happened to him. But he was adamant he'd taken neither food nor drink. Best guess, he was injected with something."

"Did anyone hear what happened in the Queen's House?"

"Nothing out of the ordinary. The Queen's House guard would have been the only one close enough, and he was out of commission."

"The colonel must have been as well, don't you think. He would have put up a fight if he'd been in possession of his faculties."

He stopped scarfing down biscuits and stared at me. "The body is definitely the colonel's then?" he asked.

"Yes. During Robert's interview with the princess, we discovered that the colonel had a scar on his right leg.

Earned during a hard-won fight, apparently. Only a few people knew, including the prince. That's how the princess learned about it. I will share that information at tomorrow's meeting."

"I take it that the corpse has a scar on his leg."

"That's what Robert said."

"But if she knew, then why the bloody hell—pardon me, Miss Worthington."

"No need for apologies, Mister Clapham. I feel the same way."

"Why didn't the Yard ask her? It would have taken only one simple question," he said.

"Because they have no idea as to the whereabouts of the prince would be my guess. They were probably hoping to find him alive before identifying the remains."

"Did Inspector Crawford say that?"

"No. He never discusses an investigation while it's in progress. So who killed the colonel?" I asked.

"You know my theory. The prince himself."

"But why? Did you learn anything from Rutherford?"

"The man's an idiot. He still thinks the prince was the target, and the murderer killed the wrong man."

"But if the prince staged the argument so he could send the colonel to his death, where is he? Why hasn't he returned? Could he have arranged a tryst far from London where he'd need a few days? It would provide an excuse for his absence."

Mister Clapham laughed. "A slap and a tickle, by Jove."

"He's notorious for it. That's why the queen convinced him to hire the colonel as his equerry in the first place. Such maneuvering would not seem out of place."

"But if that's the case, why hasn't the prince reappeared?" I asked. "The jig's definitely up."

"He's alive somewhere. He'll show up when the time's

right. Probably when he comes up with a valid reason for his absence. That time's quickly approaching, though. I can't imagine Robert waiting to identify the victim as Colonel Bouchard."

"That should draw him out. He'd have no reason to remain least in sight after that announcement is made."

"I agree." I paused for a second before I mentioned my next concern. "There is one thing that bothered me about the prince's stay at the Tower of London."

He arched a brow. "Only one? I have several."

"I'll be happy to hear about them but let me first bring this up. At my visit to the royal family's quarters, and Mother's visit as well, a guard has been present. Always one by the door; other times an additional one by the elevator. And yet, no guard accompanied the prince when he supposedly visited the Tower."

"That concerned me as well. So much so, I made a point of asking if anyone had visited the prince that night. They hemmed and hawed for a bit, but I pushed them on it. Turns out there was a visitor. He arrived just before the Ceremony of the Keys."

"The Ceremony of the Keys? What's that?"

"It's an ancient ritual that happens every night at 10 o'clock when the Tower of London is officially locked up. No one knows when it got started. Middle Ages is the best guess."

"And no one comes in or goes out after that time?"

"Supposedly."

"Who arrived?"

"A gentleman, tall, clean-shaven. He carried a satchel with him with some papers that the prince needed to see."

"At ten o'clock at night?"

"They thought it odd. But he had the right credentials, so they let him through."

"And when did he leave?"

"That's just it. He didn't."

"What?"

"At least not through the front gate as it had been locked for the night."

"So, he just disappeared into thin air?"

"No one knows how he made his getaway. He had to have been known to the colonel, though. Otherwise, he would not have admitted him. My guess is he brought a bottle of wine that had been laced with some drug. At some point after midnight, after the new guard reported for duty, the murderer must have stepped out, probably claiming he needed a bit of fresh air. That's when more than likely he injected the guard with some substance. Once there was no one to hear, he returned to the bedroom where the colonel had been rendered unconscious and performed the deed. He then stuffed the head and hands into the satchel, walked out, and disappeared into the night."

"And nobody thought anything of it."

"They thought he spent the night. Wasn't the first time a visitor had overnight guests, apparently."

"When did they realize he'd disappeared?"

"The morning they discovered the body."

"And they said nothing?"

"They told Rutherford who requested a search of the Tower. But the man was never found."

"Unbelievable."

"My thoughts exactly."

"Anything else?"

"No. That about covers it."

"Very well. Could you report your findings at tomorrow's meeting?"

"Be glad to. Unless you have anything else, I thought I'd

head back to Scotland Yard. I'd like to confirm Rutherford's tale. He's been known to slant the truth."

In other words, lie. More than likely, to please his superiors. "Yes. Do that." I paused for a second. "There was one thing I wanted to ask you about."

He raised an expectant brow.

"The thief who pawned the prince's pocket watch."

"Yes." He gave me a side-eye.

"He knows something." I put on my brightest smile. "Do you know where he might be found?"

"I have a strong suspicion."

"Wonderful. How about we go in search of him?"

He shook his head. "Now, Miss Worthington. It was one thing to do this when you were an unattached lady. But you're now engaged to Inspector Crawford. Do you know what he'll do to me if he finds out? Have my guts for garters, he will."

"Oh, it won't come to that, Mister Clapham because he'll never know. We'll take Hollingsworth as well."

His gaze took on a look of horror. "Hollingsworth is his best mate!"

"I'll swear him to secrecy. He won't go back on his word."

"Blimey, Miss. You'll turn my hair white, you will."

"Too late, Mister Clapham." I pointed to his full head of hair. "It's already white."

Of course, that was not the end of it. He argued for another fifteen minutes. But in the end, I prevailed.

Since I suspected we'd be visiting the dodgy neighborhood of St. Giles, I would need something suitable to wear. Betsy knew all the best rag shops, so, of course, I consulted her.

"I can go, Miss, same as before and fetch you something suitable."

"You're not going alone this time. I want to go too." This

was information I needed to know as Betsy might not always be available to visit the shop.

"If you say so, Miss. But you can't arrive looking all flash. They'd charge you an arm and a leg, they would."

"Grace's about my size. Why don't you ask her if I can borrow a dress and a coat."

"And a pair of shoes, too. You can't go in those." She pointed to my Italian leather t-strap heels.

"That's why I need you, Betsy. I never would have considered a change of footwear."

Since Mother would ask when she noticed I was missing, I left word I'd gone shopping for a new hat.

The store Betsy favored was in a step down from the street in Covent Garden. The place was not large by any means, but it did have some quality merchandise in their front window.

"What you lookin 'fer?" The proprietor asked as soon as we walked in.

"Me friend 'ere's lookin' fer a dress," Betsy said. "She ain't got much blunt." She and I had agreed that she would do all the talking. They would know I was quality as soon as I opened my mouth.

He sniffed. "The cheap stuff is back there in that bin." He pointed to a wood box in the back of the store that had all manner of clothes spilling over.

"'Ta," Betsy said.

After a good rummage, we chose a dress one size too big that had a rip down the side.

"I can fix that, Miss," Betsy whispered.

"I don't know if I want you to."

"You can't go out there like that!" She sounded shocked. "You'd be half naked."

"Yes, well, there is that. All right. But only enough to make me decent."

175

"Blimey, Miss."

When we took our purchases to the proprietor, he said, "Three and seven."

"Go on with ye," Betsy said. "It wasn't worth that when they was new. I'll give you a pound for the lot."

"Give it over then," he prompted her.

After Betsy paid, he wrapped the dress, a pair of scuffed shoes, and a moth-eaten hat in brown paper, corded it, and handed it back to us.

"Thank you." I'd forgotten to keep mum.

"Wot's this?" the proprietor asked, staring googly eyed at me.

"She's learning to talk flash," Betsy rushed to say. "'ow's she doing?"

He scratched the back of his head. "Could 'ave fooled me."

'Ta," I said, wiggling my fingers and winking at him.

Grabbing my arm, Betsy yanked me out of the store. "You're going to be the death of me, Miss, you are," she said once we were out on the street.

"Funny. You're the second person today to fear retribution from my actions."

"It's a wonder it's not more."

Giggling, I linked arms with her and, together, we headed back home.

CHAPTER TWENTY-FOUR

THE LAMB AND FLAG

ORKING HIS CONTACTS, Mister Clapham discovered that Billy 'the Pincher' Murrow liked to frequent the Lamb and Flag, a Covent Garden pub which once upon a time hosted bare-knuckle prize fights in its upstairs room. So, after I contacted Hollingsworth and swore him to secrecy, we set about our jaunt the following night.

Hollingsworth had gotten right into the act and donned clothes of questionable quality. Pants held up by suspenders. A vest topped by a bottle green corduroy jacket that had seen better days. A grimy collarless dark grey flannel shirt I doubted had ever been washed. I could tell by its smell. From somewhere he'd managed to obtain a pair of scuffed brown boots and a soft, small-brimmed wool cap with fold-down flaps, presumably to keep his ears warm. He'd done something to his hair to make it look greasy.

"What have you done to yourself?" I asked.

"Have to look the part, don't I?"

"As long as you don't talk, you'll be all right," Mister Clapham said.

"I'll confine myself to grunts then." He flashed one of his devil-may-care grins.

A reasonable distance from Grosvenor Square, we hailed a taxicab and asked to be dropped off two streets from the meeting place. Since Mister Clapham had set up the assignation with Billy the Pincher, he would go into the pub by himself. It was explained to me that attractive females tended to cause a commotion at this particular establishment, so I was to remain outside with Hollingsworth. Once Mister Clapham caught Billy's eye, he would return to the street. Billy would follow, and all three of us would retreat to an alley so we could have a private word with him.

The plan should have worked perfectly. A quick in and out with none the wiser. We'd failed to account for a group of three men, passing a bottle around. They appeared to be three sheets to the wind.

"I don't like the look of those men," Hollingsworth said.

No wonder. I sensed not only curiosity but an avid interest in me. Where were my nunchucks when I needed them?

"I'm going to get amorous," Hollingsworth whispered. "Play along." He threw his arm over my shoulder and tried to steal a kiss from me. I swapped him a good one. "Stop it."

"That's right, sweetheart. Give 'im what fer," one of the men slurred.

"Blast it. I don't want to start a fight. It'll draw too much attention. I better go hurry Clapham along," he said. "You going to be all right? It'll only be for a second."

I glanced at the men, all swaying on their feet. I could take one, but not all three. "I'll be fine. But hurry."

Just for show, he tried to steal another kiss.

I cuffed his ear. "Go on with you."

When he slinked off inside the bar, the men had a good laugh on him.

Unfortunately, one of them wasn't satisfied with a laugh. "Why don't you come over here and let me give it to you good and hard."

"Stuff it."

That did not deter him. Just the opposite. He strutted over to me. "You want a real man between your legs, don't you, Gooseberry Pudding? Yeah, I can tell. You're gagging for it." He pushed me against the hard stone of the pub wall while making for the flap in his trousers.

Before he could do much more, Hollingsworth was there, thrusting a knife against his side. "I'd reconsider that if I were you."

So much for him not talking.

The man froze. "Bloody 'ell. Who the devil are you?"

"Your executioner if you don't let go of the lady."

The man freed me and took a step back. "I ain't done nothing."

Hollingsworth's knife flashed in the light of the lamppost. "Good. Let's keep it that way. Now, scram."

Not waiting to be told twice, the man quickly disappeared into the fog. His friends had already done so.

"Are you all right?" Hollingsworth asked, a worried look in his eyes.

"Yes. Sorry. He caught me by surprise."

"Clapham got Billy around the corner." He curled his arm around my elbow, lending me his support.

"Thank you for your help, Lord Hollingsworth."

"I didn't do it for you, Miss Worthington, but myself."

He was lying, of course. He was as honorable as they came.

"Robert would skewer my liver if anything happened to you."

I couldn't let that remark go by. "Really?"

"The man's smitten with you. Head over heels. And if you ever repeat that, I'll call you a liar."

"My lips are sealed, milord."

We found Clapham and Billy "The Pincher" Murrow behind the pub in an alley barely wide enough for two to stand abreast. The cold and drizzle worked in our favor, as nobody was loitering about.

"Now Billy, 'tis too cold to stand out here jawing," Mister Clapham said, "so the sooner you start talking the sooner you can get back inside and have a nice ale with your friends."

"It's brass monkeys out here," Billy said, blowing on his bare hands. "Where's my blunt?"

Flashing a couple of notes, Clapham handed them to Billy.

"Two quid? Stop faffing around." Billy seemingly objected to the amount.

"There's more, if what you have to say is worth it." Mister Clapham grabbed Billy by his lapels. "Now talk."

"All right." Billy shook off Mister Clapham's hold on him. "Someone came to St. Giles looking for a cove who knew how to burgle a place."

"How long ago?"

"I don't know. A couple of weeks maybe. I don't keep a calendar, Inspector."

"I'm not an inspector anymore, Billy."

"Could have fooled me."

"Never mind that. Go on."

"A couple of me mates put the word out that I was the best." He puffed out his chest like that was something to be proud of. "Next thing I know I'm being kidnapped."

"Kidnapped?"

"Dark hood over my head, arms yanked back, dragged into a motorcar. Gotta tell you. I almost pissed meself."

"Watch your language. There's a lady present."

He turned to me. "Sorry, miss."

"It's fine, Billy," I said. "Go on."

"Well, they took me somewhere dark, lashed me to a chair. Kept the hood on me the whole time. Could hardly breathe."

"What did they want?"

"They wanted to know the best way to burgle the Queen's House. Told them that was a laffer. Couldn't steal into the Tower of London. Not with that many guards around. They said that part was handled. All they wanted to know was how to break into the house itself."

"And you told them?"

"They offered me twenty pounds. What do you think?"

"How many men?"

"Three. But only one asked questions. A toff with an accent. Not a frog. I know what they sound like." He spit on the ground.

Obviously, Billy was not a fan of the French.

"What happened after you told them?"

"They tossed me back in the motorcar. Drove for a long time until it got quiet like. When the car stopped, well, I knew I was done for."

"Obviously, you weren't as you're here."

"No thanks to those toffs. They dumped me on the side of the road. In bleeding Greenwich, the wankers. Took me hours to get back to St. Giles."

Like that was a pleasant address, but then home is home.

"How did you end up with the watch?" Mister Clapham asked.

A grin rolled over Billy's face. "Found it, I did."

"Where?"

"In the motorcar. Can you believe it?"

"Your hands were tied. How did you manage that?"

"It was just me and the driver in the motorcar. The toff and his wankers weren't there. I was not going down without a fight. So, I loosened the ropes quiet like, felt around the seat for something to use as a weapon. That's when I found it. The toff must have left it behind. Couldn't believe me luck. A watch that fine would fetch a pretty penny, which it did. And then I went and got arrested for it. Should have known it was a stitch up."

"Is that it?"

"You want more? Blimey, I almost got meself killed. Now, where's the rest of my money?"

Mister Clapham gave him the rest, and Billy fled back to the pub.

By tacit agreement, we waited until we climbed into a taxicab several streets away before discussing what we'd just heard.

Squeezed between Mister Clapham and Hollingsworth, I was, if not toasty warm, less cold than they must have been. "He was framed," I whispered. By necessity I kept my voice low as I didn't want the driver to hear our conversation.

"It appears so," Mister Clapham responded in kind. "They knew he would pawn that watch. And the pawnbroker, hearing about the murder at the Tower of London, did his duty and called Scotland Yard."

"Quite clumsy, though," Hollingsworth said. "Anyone with a working intellect would have seen right through it."

"We're meant to interpret it as clumsy, when in reality it was quite clever," I said.

"Rutherford didn't figure it out, though," Hollingsworth said.

"He must have," Mister Clapham said. "But higher-ups needed somebody to blame for the murder. And Billy came in awfully handy. He had the watch, after all."

"But who could have crafted this plan?" I asked. "And who was the intended victim?"

"You already know what I think," Mister Clapham said.

"If the colonel was the target, where is the prince? Why hasn't he come forward?" I'd asked myself that question many times and had yet to come up with an answer.

None of us could hazard a guess, so we remained silent for the rest of the drive. After we bid Mister Clapham goodnight at his address, we proceeded to the mews behind Worthington House where Hollingsworth had parked his sleek Vauxhall Tourer.

Figuring there was no time like the present to satisfy my curiosity, I casually asked, "You first met Robert at Oxford?"

He scrunched his brow as if he found my question odd, but he answered readily enough. "That's right."

"What was he like then?"

"Serious about his studies. He read jurisprudence; you know. I thought he'd become a barrister or a solicitor, but he had his heart set on Scotland Yard. I daresay one day he might very well be named commissioner."

"Heaven knows he has the intellect and the drive for it. What did he do when he wasn't studying?"

"He joined the lads at the pub. Drank only enough to be social, a pint or two of dark ale. Unlike me. Don't know how many times he had to carry me back to my room."

"What did you read?"

"Anthropology. I'd always been fascinated by other cultures. Father did not approve, of course. He thought people of other nations were savages." He gritted his teeth. "Once I inherited the title, I did bloody well as I pleased."

Hollingsworth would have resented such control over his

183

life. "And now you travel the seven seas in search of adventure."

"Yes. But not anytime soon again. I'll need to get Melissande settled before I venture forth once more. I won't abandon her."

"Your heart does you good, Hollingsworth." Now came the question that had me sleeping poorly some nights. "What about ladies? Three years is a long time to go without female company, especially since you're both handsome fellows."

Assuming that devil-may-care air of his, he said, "Ah, lass, a man never discusses affairs of the heart. Most especially those of a mate."

"There was a lady in Robert's past?"

"You'll need to ask him about that." All his gaiety vanished as his gaze turned toward the window, effectively shutting me out.

A sense of shame filled me. Why did I have such a sharp need to know? All that mattered was that Robert loved me. And he did. Hollingsworth had just confirmed it. "I'm sorry. You're right. I shouldn't have asked."

He veered back toward me. "No need to apologize. No harm done."

The gentlemanly thing to say, but I had to wonder if my wretched curiosity hadn't ruined our friendship. I sighed. Only time would tell.

CHAPTER TWENTY-FIVE

ALARMING NEWS

*T*HE NEXT DAY, we'd scheduled a meeting of the investigative committee to review what we'd learned. Mister Clapham and Hollingsworth caught everyone up on the information we learned from Billy the Pincher. Since Mother was present, we kept my participation out of it. I'd sent notes around to everyone about the identification of the remains, so the conversation regarding that topic was minimal. A more extensive discussion ensued about what Mister Clapham discovered at the Tower of London.

Once everyone spoke, I glanced at my notes to make sure we'd covered everything. Satisfied, I said, "Unless someone has something else to report, I believe that's all for now."

When nobody spoke up, I adjourned the meeting.

As usual, the committee broke up into smaller groups to discuss what we'd just learned. I was gathering my things when there was a knock on the door and Carlton entered.

"My apologies for the interruption, Miss Worthington. A gentleman has arrived. He claims he has urgent news from the Queen of Andover."

What could have happened? Had the prince been found? "Show him in, Mister Carlton, by all means."

It took but a minute for the gentleman to appear in the library—the Duke of Andover himself. He'd barely entered the room before Lady Melissande came to her feet, clutching her chest. "Paolo."

He turned toward her just as surprised as she. "Lissande. What are you doing here?"

"I could ask the same of you."

"You know each other?" I asked. Here was a turn up.

"Yes," Lady Melissande said. "We met in France. I was roaming the convent grounds one day, gathering herbs for the kitchen, when suddenly Paolo was there." The way she whispered his name told me this was no mere acquaintance. Maybe this was the source of her melancholy. "Are you the queen's emissary?"

I would have thought it an odd question, except for the fact she knew not what the Duke of Andover looked like.

His complexion grew ruddy. "In a manner of speaking. I must beg your indulgence for a moment, Lissande. I'm on a mission."

"Of course." She resumed her seat, but her gaze never wavered from him.

"My grandmother received a note this morning." He handed it to me. "It was dropped off at the front desk of the hotel."

"You're the Duke of Andover?" Lady Melissande asked.

The ruddiness on his face grew more pronounced. "Yes. I will explain as soon as I can."

Her gaze turned downward to her clenched hands.

"What does the note say?" Ned asked, recalling us from the melodrama that was playing out.

I read it quickly as there was not much to it. "It claims they kidnapped the prince. They want ten thousand pounds to free him."

"As proof, they are holding him hostage they sent this." Paolo handed over a signet ring. "It's my father's."

"Did you alert the police?" Mister Clapham asked.

"The note says not to," I said. "'*Tell the coppers and the prince dies,*'" I read.

"Grandmother thought it best to let you know, so you can get word to Scotland Yard," the duke said.

"Yes, of course."

"How did you travel here?" Mister Clapham asked.

"By taxicab."

"Blast it. You were more than likely followed."

The duke stiffened, apparently taking affront at the remark. "I'm not as much of a numbskull as that, sir. I took the service elevator, walked out the back of the hotel. Hailed a taxicab several streets away. I asked the driver to stop at Adams Row and walked from there to here. I'm certain no one followed me."

Clapham's expression turned from accusatory to approval. "Good lad."

"Mister Clapham," I said, "you'll have to be the one to alert Scotland Yard. If anyone sees you, they won't think anything of it since you visit often enough. Talk only to Robert and no one else. We don't want word to get out. Once you've accomplished that task, please come back here." I didn't mention he should return with a report. He knew what was expected of him.

"Of course." He held out his hand. "If I could have the note and the ring. He might notice something we don't." After I handed both to him, he quickly made his way out.

Turning to the duke, I said, "Your Highness, you must go back to the hotel. Inspector Crawford will more than likely contact you by day's end."

"If you don't mind, I prefer to remain until we hear back. I don't wish to return to grandmother empty-handed." As he said this, he looked at Lady Melissande who was clasping her hands while darting glances at him.

Obviously, waiting for Mister Clapham to return was not the only reason he wanted to stay, but I couldn't order him to leave. "Very well."

His gaze took stock of the committee members. "Were you discussing the investigation?"

"Yes, but we were just done when you walked in."

He folded his hands behind him. "What have you discovered?" The question came out as a command.

Which I wasn't about to obey. "I'm afraid I can't share that information with you. I report our findings to your grandmother, as she's the one who hired us. It will be up to her to tell you what we've learned."

He lowered his gaze. "She hasn't exactly been forthcoming."

"I'm sorry."

Raising his head, he looked straight at me. "I imagine some of the information you discovered had to do with my mother and Colonel Bouchard."

Everyone's attention snapped to the duke.

"The princess admires him," I said.

"She more than admires him, Miss Worthington. They're close. Very close."

Was he intimating that the princess and the colonel were lovers? "I . . . see."

"I don't blame her for seeking . . . comfort with him. Father has been rather horrid to her."

"Why are you telling me, us" —I waved my hand around the room— "about this?"

"If Father was kidnapped, it stands to reason that the person who was killed was the colonel. I think she's known for some time. Inspector Crawford's questions confirmed it. She's . . . taken to her bed."

"I'm so sorry."

"Would you like some tea, Your Highness?" Mother asked. Her solution for everything that ailed a person.

"Yes, thank you."

She pointed to the table where the food had been served. "We have sandwiches and pastries and cakes. If there's something else you wish, I can ring for it." With those simple words, she'd taken over the handling of the duke.

"This will be fine. Thank you." After helping himself to a cup of the fragrant Darjeeling, he went in search of Lady Melissande.

Needless to say, Hollingsworth frowned the entire way.

Whatever they were going to discuss, we couldn't stay and listen in on their private conversation. It would be beyond rude. "Luncheon will be served soon. Won't it, Mother?" It was close to one.

"Yes." She'd already extended a luncheon invitation to the entire committee, and everyone had accepted.

"Let's await the announcement in the drawing room, then," I said.

"I'm staying," Hollingsworth said, taking a seat across from the duke and his sister.

"Of course." It wouldn't do any good to argue. Wild horses couldn't drag him away.

The rest of us, however, headed toward the drawing room.

As soon as that door closed, Lady Lily said, "Did you see?"

"How could I not?" Lady Emma answered. "They have eyes only for each other."

"Do you think that's why she's so sad?" Lady Lily put a hand to her heart. "She had to leave her love behind."

"You don't know that Lady Lily," Ned opined.

"I do so, Ned," Lady Lily snapped back. "She perked right up when she saw him."

I was glad to hear her challenging Ned. On occasion, he tended to be a bit of a know-it-all. It augured well for their future that she was willing to take him down a peg or two.

"Well, I'm sure you ladies will get the story out of her soon enough," Marlowe said with a smirk.

"Are you calling us gossips?" Lady Emma challenged; one hand propped on her hip.

"Oh, look at the time," Mother said, not glancing at any timepiece. "Best I consult Cook regarding our luncheon."

"I'll go with you," I said threading my hand around her arm.

After we made our way into the hall, she whispered, "Wouldn't it be better for you to remain? Someone must keep the peace between Lord Marlowe and Lady Emma."

"Ned can handle that duty."

"Are you sure? I wouldn't want any blood shed on the furnishings."

"It won't get to that point, Mother. But if it does, you'll have an excellent excuse to buy new furniture."

"Umm, there is that," she returned with a grin.

"Why do you think the duke mentioned his mother's affair with the colonel?"

"He didn't quite say that, dear."

"He might as well have. He used all the right words. How much his mother cared for the colonel, how she sought comfort with him. And then there's her behavior. When I first met her, she was all smiles, focused more on pastries than the alleged death of her husband. Now that it's become clear the colonel was the one killed, she's utterly devastated. So much so, she's taken to her bed."

"Do you think the prince knew?" Mother asked.

"He must have. After all, the son did." Now the question became whether the prince had cared enough to do something about it.

CHAPTER TWENTY-SIX

LADY MELISSANDE'S REVELATION

*M*ISTER CLAPHAM RETURNED
MIDAFTERNOON with the news Scotland
Yard had activated a new team to investigate the prince's
alleged kidnapping.

"Alleged?" The Duke of Andover, who'd joined us for
luncheon, seemed less than satisfied with that explanation.
"There's nothing alleged about it."

"We don't know that Your Highness," I said, eager to take
the focus away from Mister Clapham. He was only the
messenger, after all. "It could be a ruse."

"I'm sorry." The duke brushed a hand across his brow.
"You're right. It could be a ploy to obtain ill-gotten gains."

"The inspector in charge will be visiting the queen, sir, to
make further arrangements." Mister Clapham said. "It'd be
best if you returned to the hotel so you could support those
efforts."

"Yes, of course." The duke extended a hand to Mister

Clapham. "Thank you for your assistance. I apologize for my curtness."

"No need, sir. You're under a lot of pressure," Mister Clapham responded.

The duke thanked Mother for our hospitality, and then, following Mister Clapham's suggestion, exited through our kitchen. The mews, located behind Worthington House, would lead him to Grosvenor Square where he could hail a taxicab.

Mister Clapham would have further news that he wouldn't wish to report in the presence of the duke. But Mother would not allow him to do so until he'd had his luncheon. So she had it brought to the drawing room.

Eager to hear what he had to say, we arranged ourselves in the room. Except for Lady Melissande who made a beeline for the door.

"Mellie? Anything wrong?" Hollingsworth asked, coming to his feet.

"I'm fine, brother," she said with a soft smile. "I just need some rest. It's been a rather eventful day." And then she excused herself and wandered out of the room.

Even as he regained his seat, Hollingsworth kept his eye on the door, a slight frown to his brow. Undoubtedly, he was worried about her. With good reason. The realization she'd met the duke, a known womanizer, while she was at the convent had to be weighing on his mind.

But that was neither here nor there as far as the kidnapping investigation was concerned. "Please enjoy your meal, Mister Clapham. When you're ready, let us know what else Scotland Yard had to say."

As it didn't take him long to satisfy his hunger, he was soon addressing us. "When the prince did no reappear, Scotland Yard assumed he'd been kidnapped. So, they're taking the matter quite seriously."

"It's the only theory that makes sense," I said.

"The note was tested for fingerprints. They found some, but there's not knowing to whom they belong. That's one of the reasons they will be visiting the queen."

"To take her fingerprints?"

"Hers and every member of the royal family. The staff's as well."

"That's why you sent him back to the hotel," Hollingsworth said.

"Every member of the royal family and their attendants will be interrogated and fingerprinted."

"So Scotland Yard suspects it's somebody within their world?"

"Stands to reason, doesn't it? Who else would be so familiar with the prince's schedule and be near enough to kidnap him?"

"What about the hotel staff?"

"Oh, they will be interrogated and fingerprinted as well."

"Will Robert be involved in this matter?"

"No. He will continue with the inquiry into the murder at the Tower. The team in charge of the kidnapping matter will keep him apprised, of course. But he will not be directly involved."

"That's good," I said. "He has enough on his plate."

Once he finished his report, the group dispersed. Since I hadn't finished gathering my materials, I returned to the library. That's where I found Melissande. It was obvious she'd been crying.

I took a seat next to her in the settee and clasped her hand in mine. "What's wrong?"

"Nothing." She turned her face away in an attempt to hide her tears. But I wasn't having it. It was past time she shared what was troubling her.

"Poppycock. You're crying."

"I shouldn't be." Her blue eyes were filled with emotion. "You have been so kind, and here I am turning into a waterpot."

Shades of Lady Lily who'd acted in a similar fashion when she'd sought refuge at our door. "One thing doesn't have anything to do with the other. Is it the Duke of Andover? Is that what's causing you heartache?"

She nodded. "I was such an idiot."

Oh, dear. That did not augur well. "What happened in France?"

"Well, as I said, I was gathering herbs for the kitchen. The convent had quite an extensive garden where they grew all sorts of produce."

"That's where you met the duke?"

"He told me his name was Paolo and was part of a group of travelers who'd camped nearby."

Travelers, or gypsies as they were sometimes called, wandered from place to place, never staying long in one spot.

"They usually arrived in late spring and stayed until midsummer when they pulled up stakes and wandered somewhere else. They were always welcome at the convent."

"Had you seen him before?"

"No. That's why I was so surprised. He explained he'd joined the group but a few months earlier."

"You spent time together?"

"Yes." She blushed. "I knew I shouldn't have done so. Convent rules prohibit interaction with the outside world. But I was fascinated by him."

She would be after leading such a sheltered life.

"Did you do anything . . . untoward, Lady Melissande?" The question needed to be asked.

"No!" An emphatic reply. "We held hands, that's all."

That was good to know. I wouldn't put Hollingsworth

beyond skewering the duke if he'd violated his sister. And then we'd have an international incident on our hands.

"So, why the tears?"

"I'd dreamt of meeting him again, getting to know him better. That's an impossibility now."

"Why?"

"He's a royal duke from a country far away. Once the prince is found, he'll leave, and I'll never see him again." She clenched her hands. "I've been such a fool."

"Did he say that when you talked earlier?"

"He didn't have to. But it stands to reason, does it not?" A gleam of hope shone in her eyes, more than likely a wish I'd contradict her.

I couldn't reassure her as to the duke's intentions as I had no knowledge of them. But there was something I could offer. "If there is something I've learned from Mother it is not to anticipate trouble." I pressed her hands for support. "Did he mention visiting you again?"

"He did. Hollingsworth said he would allow it, but only if he was present."

I bit back a smile. "I fear your brother intends to be a strict chaperone."

"I don't blame him. The duke does have a reputation."

"But his actions were honorable toward you." I took a moment to formulate my next question." He was surprised to see you here. Do you know why that is?"

"He thought I intended to become a nun. When we met, I was dressed in the habit of a novice."

"A reasonable conclusion then."

"Yes." Something seemed to ease within her, as if a weight had been lifted from her shoulders. "I think I'll play the piano. That always makes me feel better."

"Not the *Lacrimosa*, please," I begged.

"Something cheerier." She kissed me on the cheek. "Thank you, dear Kitty. I feel better after talking with you."

I squeezed her hand. "You can come to me anytime, Lady Melissande. I'm aces at listening."

"Yes, I do believe you are." And with that she drifted out of the room, a spring to her step. I waited a few minutes, curious to hear what she would play. She didn't disappoint. Although I did not recognize the particular composition, it definitely had a lighter feel to it.

CHAPTER TWENTY-SEVEN

THE PRINCE RETURNS

*T*HE NEXT TWO DAYS were extremely frustrating. We felt matters were proceeding at a rapid pace. Unfortunately, we were not able to discover anything about them. Not for lack of trying, though.

Mister Clapham visited Scotland Yard several times to obtain information. Unfortunately, he failed. "Loose lips, sink ships," he grumpily reported every time he returned without an iota of news. I didn't dare request an audience with the Queen of Andover or the princess. They had enough to deal with. And Robert wouldn't reveal a single thing about the case. So we were forced to wait until the matter played itself out.

Eager for news, every committee member made an excuse—not that they needed one—to visit Worthington House. Hollingsworth claimed he wanted to further his sister's acquaintance. A noble enough cause to be sure. Wanting to check on Mother's welfare, Ned was there morning, noon, and evening. Strangely enough, he spent more time with Lady Lily than Mother. Marlowe came up with the flimsiest reason of all—he'd lost his tiepin once more, probably in the library.

"Again?" Lady Emma asked, a doubting tone to her voice.

"Er, yes. The clasp is loose, don't you know?"

"Maybe you should have it fixed then."

"I will, as soon as I find it."

I refused to dedicate any of our staff to look for the thing since it was clearly a ruse. But to my surprise, Lady Emma volunteered her efforts. Why would she help him when it was clearly a ploy? The reason was soon made clear. She would charge him for her time. After all—she argued—she'd be employing her detective skills. After Marlowe reluctantly agreed to her fee, they headed for the library to hunt for the thing which, of course, they never found.

In my opinion, Mister Clapham was the only one with a valid purpose, as he was the intermediary between us and Scotland Yard. Not that he was able to discover anything. So, we sat and waited and talked and waited and ate and waited.

Finally, after three days of agony, news about the prince's kidnapping made its way to the papers. Of course, some of them sensationalized every detail, but somehow, they managed to report the truth.

The queen had received a ransom demand of 10,000 pounds for the return of the prince unharmed. Anxious about her son's safety, she had the funds withdrawn from the bank. The money was then deposited in a black satchel which was to be delivered at midnight the next day to a shack located on the Hyde Park grounds.

The location surprised me. "Why would they choose such a public place?"

"With so many trees, bushes, and what not, they could

easily make their getaway under the cover of darkness," Mister Clapham pointed out.

At first, everything had gone along as scheduled. On the night in question, the person assigned to deliver the satchel, an Andoverian military officer, entered the structure. Soon, however, gunfire erupted, and London policemen swarmed the shack. Simultaneously, the prince, who'd been set adrift on a boat on the Serpentine, hit the deck, as it were, as soon as he heard the shots. Several policemen, however, had spotted the prince and jumped into the water to rescue him. Thankfully, he hadn't suffered an injury, either during his kidnapping ordeal or during the volley of fire. The same could not be said for the kidnapper who was mortally wounded, or the Andoverian military officer, who'd suffered a superficial wound.

The dead kidnapper was identified as a known rabble-rouser who hated the monarchy and everything that went along with it. His partner in crime, seen fleeing the shack, had somehow made his getaway and hadn't been found.

"Well, there you go," Mother said, reading the latest newspaper account. "All is well."

The gentlemen members of the investigative committee had already come and gone. Grateful for the happy resolution to the prince's disappearance, they'd all breathed a sigh of relief. The ladies, after sharing that same sentiment, had withdrawn as well. Ladies Melissande and Lily to pour over fashion magazines, Lady Emma to make further plans for our agency. Only Mother and I remained in her personal parlor.

"But we have no idea how he was kidnapped in the first place," I protested.

"And we likely never will," Mother said. The last thing the police would do is reveal those details. It might give ideas to other nefarious sort." Her shoulders eased as if a weight had been lifted from her shoulders. "This means your investigation can draw to a close. And for that, I am truly grateful."

"A person was murdered, Mother. A colonel in the Andoverian army. Surely that deserves an investigation."

"But you were hired to find out who murdered the prince. Since he's alive, and well by all accounts, I doubt the queen will wish you to continue."

I would have further argued the point, but for Carlton, who arrived to inform us the Duke of Andover was eager for an audience.

"Show him in, Mister Carlton," Mother said.

I was thrilled to say the least for he would most certainly be better acquainted with the facts than the papers. Whether he was willing to share was another thing altogether.

"Mrs. Worthington, Miss Worthington." He offered an elegant bow, something he had no need to do since we were not members of the nobility. "I came to tell you the news."

"We've been reading the papers, Your Highness. We trust your father is well?" Mother asked.

"He suffered a few bumps and bruises. Nothing major."

"That is great news," I said.

"Would you care for some tea?" Mother asked.

"No, thank you." He gazed around the room. Not finding what he sought, he asked, "Is Lady Melissande at home?"

Ah, his real reason for coming to see us. "She's in her room, I believe. Would you like us to send for her?"

"If it would not be an inconvenience."

I rang for Carlton and asked him to alert Lady Melissande as to the duke's presence. It would take but a few minutes for her to arrive, time I would use to learn as much as I could about the prince's disappearance.

"Forgive my curiosity, Your Highness, but we were wondering how it happened? How was your father taken?"

He must have expected the question because he didn't

hesitate to respond. "As you know, Father had arranged to change places with Colonel Bouchard. He had an, er, assignation that evening."

With a lady, no doubt. Somehow, I managed to keep a straight face. "Yes."

"The motorcar was waylaid along the way."

"Where?"

"Father's not familiar with English roads, so he has no idea. He was no longer in the streets of London, though, heading south."

"What happened to the driver?"

"Father doesn't know. They were separated, you see."

"Oh, no," Mother said.

"We're fearing the worst, to tell you the truth."

"Where was the prince kept?" I asked.

"A cottage somewhere. At first, he feared for his life, for there was a definite interest in ending it. But as the days progressed, there was a change of leadership. The one who talked of killing him was replaced by another who was more interested in ransoming Father than anything else. When they brought up the subject in front of him, he suggested the 10,000 pounds. They got right jolly after that."

"Yes, I imagine." Ten thousand pounds is a huge amount of money. A person could live comfortably off that bounty the rest of his life.

Lady Melissande breezed in, out of breath and flushed, effectively ending the conversation. Curtsying, she said, "Your Highness. I understand you wanted to see me."

The duke immediately rose to his feet and bowed deeply to her. "I do." He turned to us. "Would it be possible to have a private audience with Lady Melissande?"

"I'm afraid that can't happen, sir," Mother said. "One of us must be present."

"I'll be glad to play chaperone, Mother. Maybe we could retire to the library?"

"Of course, dear. That will be fine."

I'd forgotten Lady Emma was there, so everyone was surprised all around after we arrived. When she understood the status of things, she started to leave, but I signaled for her to stay. "We can discuss the agency's future plans, Lady Emma." Taking her arm, I guided her to a corner on the opposite side from where the duke and Lady Melissande took a seat. We'd be close enough to see but not hear them as long as they spoke in low tones.

Sparing only an occasional glance at the couple, we settled ourselves around a table. Needless to say, we didn't discuss anything, as we were too busy watching the play of emotions on the duke's and Lady Melissande's faces. From his earnest expressions and her blushing responses, I surmised he was asking for something which seemed to flatter her. I caught the occasional word. "Hollingsworth . . . approve" and "no objection" from Lady Melissande and "I will" from the duke.

The whole thing was over in less than fifteen minutes after which the duke bowed and left.

"Well," I asked once he made his exit.

Lady Melissande's face grew pink once more. "He wants to court me."

Both Lady Emma and I rushed to her side. "Is that what you wish?" I asked taking a seat next to her.

"I think so."

"But you're not sure."

"I need to know him better, don't you think? He does have a reputation."

"Absolutely," Lady Emma said, settling on Lady Melissande's other side.

"So what did you say?"

"That he would need to get Hollingsworth's approval. And that I wanted to have a season, and I couldn't commit to anything until after then."

I squeezed her hand. "How very wise of you."

She let out a giggle. "Yes, I thought so."

Who knew she had such fortitude within her? She definitely was not a fool.

"But how is the duke going to manage a courtship?" Lady Emma asked. "Assuming Hollingsworth approves it, that is. He'll be returning to Andover soon, after all."

"I asked him that as well. He said he would find a way."

"Interesting," I said.

"Could you excuse me?" Lady Melissande asked coming to her feet. "I'd like to inform Lady Lily."

"Of course."

Lady Melissande practically ran out of the room.

"I didn't know she had that much common sense in her," Lady Emma said.

"She'll need it if she's to lead the life of a royal."

"But how's the duke going to manage that courtship?" Lady Emma asked.

"I guess we'll find out."

"You think Hollingsworth will approve?"

"Of course. He would not dare go against his sister's wishes, not when they've just managed to establish rapport. He'll be watching the duke like a hawk, however. If he commits an indiscretion, he'll put paid to the whole thing."

"Then, let us hope, for Lady Melissande's sake, he doesn't."

"Only time will tell."

CHAPTER TWENTY-EIGHT

THE QUEEN REQUESTS AN AUDIENCE

*T*HE DAY AFTER THE DUKE'S VISIT, I received a note from the Queen of Andover requesting my presence at her hotel suite. She suggested a time of two in the afternoon if it was convenient. Although she'd phrased it in polite terms, it was clearly a command, and one I could not deny. So, of course, I accepted.

The next afternoon, I dressed in one of my best dresses, a blue tunic frock with a satin flounced collar and cuffs. I could have taken my Tourer since it was a bright, sunny day. But I didn't want to appear windblown, so I asked Neville to drive me. Since I expected her to request an update on the investigation, I'd written a report which I asked Betsy to type. She'd done a bang-up job of it, but then I'd expected no less from her.

As before, I took the elevator to the floor where the queen's suite of rooms was located. A guard stood sentry outside her door. She was waiting for me, seated in one of the gold and cream sofas that dotted the room. After I curt-sied, she asked me to take a seat across from her.

She wasted no time in telling me why she'd requested to see me. "I would like you to stop the investigation."

"What?" The single word, impolite as it was, burst out of me, followed by another one just as improper, "Why?"

She dismissed my questions with a flick of her hand. "My son has returned to us, Miss Worthington. A little worse for the wear, true, but he'll be back up to snuff in no time."

"Don't you want to discover who murdered Colonel Bouchard?"

"Of course, I do. His death was tragic. The way he was killed—" She shuddered. "He will be honored back home. Given a state funeral." Her voice shook as she raised a trem-bling hand to her lips. "I don't wish to pursue the investiga-tion. The idea is abhorrent to me."

"But we've made such great progress, and we are so close," I pleaded. "Won't you please reconsider?"

She pinned me with a hard stare. "Miss Worthington. I have spoken my piece. You will honor my request."

"Very well." I tucked the report Betsy had so carefully typed back in my handbag. "I will provide you with a full accounting of our expenses and return the amount we did not spend."

"There's no need. You may keep the money. I don't want it back."

I was astounded, to say the least. "It amounts to thou-sands of pounds. We barely touched it."

"Donate it to a charity or allocate it to your detective agency. It doesn't matter to me."

If that's what she wished, so be it. But I would require proof. "I'll need that authorization in writing. For our records." If anyone called into question our retaining the funds, I would show it to them.

"I'll have my personal assistant convey it to you. Goodbye, Miss Worthington."

Given my curt dismissal, I retreated as gracefully as I could.

Neville was waiting in front of the hotel. He must have noticed my mood because he didn't engage in chatter on the way home as he usually did. Betsy, however, was another matter altogether. As soon as I entered my room, she was there. Apparently, she'd been on the lookout for me.

"How did it go, Miss? Did the queen like the report?" Her joyous face expected no less.

Unfortunately, I couldn't provide it to her. "I'm afraid not, Betsy. She ended the investigation."

Her face fell. "Oh, no. It wasn't"—she gulped—"it wasn't my typing, was it? I was ever so careful."

"No, Betsy, it wasn't." I'd been so immersed in my own misery, I hadn't measured my words, and inadvertently hurt her feelings. Something I would never do intentionally. Well, that needed to be corrected. I patted the bed. "Come sit, next to me."

Once she had, I put my arm around her. "I read the report three times and did not find a single mistake. Not one. You did a marvelous job."

"Then why did she fire us?" Her gaze showed nothing but despair.

"Well, she hired us to find her son's murderer. As he's now returned to her safe and sound, she thought it best to end it." For professional reasons, I had to phrase our dismissal in positive terms, rather than the way I really felt.

"But, Miss, the colonel was killed. Doesn't she want to find his murderer?"

"She has no more taste for the investigation and wants to put the entire matter behind her."

Her gaze tilted downward. "That's a shame, Miss. You all worked so hard."

I couldn't bear to see her like this. "I tell you what. Let's have a celebration. I'll invite all the members of the committee, including you. We'll have a grand time." I infused as much excitement into my words, even though I was just as upset as her.

"But Miss, there's nothing to celebrate. We haven't found the murderer."

My shoulders slumped. "Yes, you're right. We haven't."

"Just because the queen doesn't want to continue doesn't mean we have to stop."

"No, it doesn't." I squeezed her tight. "Oh, Betsy, you're a treasure."

A knock sounded on the door. Betsy opened it to find all three ladies on the other side.

"Well," Lady Emma said, a hopeful look on her face.

After I provided a summary of my discussion with the queen, Lady Lily asked, "We're not really quitting, are we?" She had a despondent air about her.

"No, we're not," I said. "But we can't tell Mother what the queen said. She's a stickler for propriety."

"She will ask, Kitty." Lady Emma had only stated the obvious.

"I'll come up with something to tell her."

"Fib, you mean?" Lady Lily's voice held a scandalized tone.

"More like skirt the truth. Who's with me?" I stuck my arm out, the way I had done with Margaret and Lady Lily during a previous investigation.

"Are we doing the Three Musketeers?" Lady Lily asked. "One for all and all for one?"

"Yes."

Getting into the spirit of the thing, Lady Emma placed her hand on mine. "Count me in."

Lady Melissande giggled before she did likewise. "Me too. Paolo would want us to continue."

I wasn't so sure of that, but I wasn't about to decry her.

"Lady Lily?"

She bit her lower lip. "Do we have to hide it from your mother?"

"Afraid so."

"Be brave, Lil," Lady Melissande said. "A faint heart never wins."

Lady Lily took affront at that remark. "I'll have you know I was brave enough to escape the clutches of my grandfather *and* my odious cousin."

"That's right, she did," I said.

"Join us in our quest, Lady Lily," Lady Emma said.

"Oh, very well." She slapped her hand on top of ours. "Ned better never hear of this."

"I won't tell him," I said. The other ladies echoed my sentiment.

Seemingly eager to swear the oath, Lady Emma said, "One for all, and—"

"Wait, we have one more Musketeer," I said. "Betsy, join us."

"Me, Miss, but I—"

"You're as much a member of the team as the rest of us."

With a proud smile, she very gingerly placed her hand on top of all.

"Ready?"

Head nods all around.

"One for all and all for one." We yelled and threw our hands in the air.

We were giggling so hard, no one noticed the soft snick of the door as it quietly closed.

CHAPTER TWENTY-NINE

THE GOVERNMENT TAKES ACTION

SINCE MOTHER WAS SURE TO ASK about my meeting with the queen, I had to devise a reasonable explanation that, while not an outright lie, embellished the truth. My moment of reckoning arrived the next day when she called me into her parlor.

"How did the meeting with the Queen of Andover go, dear?"

"She's very pleased with the investigation."

"Is she?"

"Yes. Unfortunately, she won't be here to see its conclusion since she's returning to Andover, along with the rest of the royal family. When I offered to refund the money we did not spend, she said we could keep them."

She templed her hands. "That is very generous of her. What will you do with the funds?"

"I'll put it up to a vote with the committee, of course.

There should be quite a surplus after we pay Mister Clapham for his services." Although the rest of us were reasonably wealthy and had no need for the money, such was not the case with Mister Clapham. I would make sure he received not only the pay we'd agreed upon, but a generous bonus.

"Do you have any thoughts on how to allocate that amount?"

"I'd like to donate half to the Ladies Benevolent Society so you can use it for your good works—The Magdalen House for Fallen Women, the Children's Home Orphanage, and such. The other half I'd like to allocate to our detective agency since our participation in the investigation precluded us from taking other business." I felt that was a fair assessment. After all, business had picked up shortly before our involvement in the matter.

"I'm sure the committee will agree with your suggestion. What about Betsy?"

"B-Betsy?" Whatever did she mean?

"Yes. Between her duties as your maid and the secretarial classes, she's been rather busy, don't you think? I think she deserves a bonus."

"You knew?"

"Yes, dear."

"Who told you?" Who snitched more likely. I would have something to say when I found out who it'd been.

"No one."

That surely couldn't be true. Mother never lied, though. "Then how did you find out?"

"About two weeks ago, Mrs. Simpson grew quite concerned about water leaks in the staff quarters. Of course, when she told me, I insisted on inspecting the premises. To my surprise, I heard clickety-clacks coming from Betsy's room. Having heard that sound before when Margaret was typing her university papers, I knew exactly what it was—a typewriter."

"So, Mrs. Simpson spilled the beans." Should have known. She could never keep anything from Mother.

"No. She did not. I simply used the faculties the Lord gave me to make a logical deduction."

"Did you find water leaks?"

She nodded. "In the ladies' bathroom. I asked Mrs. Simpson to notify the plumber we've used. He visited the next day; and in no time at all, it was fixed."

"Ummmm." Mrs. Simpson probably manipulated the whole thing. I wouldn't put it past her to create the water leak in the first place knowing Mother would want to see for herself. "That's wonderful. We wouldn't want the staff to go without water."

"Of course." She pinned me with a hard stare. "Now about the queen, what else did she say?"

I heaved out a sigh. Why did I think I could keep this from her? She always found out. "She wants to end the investigation."

Her brow scrunched. "Why?"

"She claims the idea is abhorrent to her. Her son is safe. That's all she cares about."

"You would think she would want to pursue justice for the colonel. He's a hero to Andoverians."

My feelings exactly. "I thought the same thing, but she's adamant about terminating the investigation."

"Something you'd find difficult to do. You've never given up on something you're passionate about."

She knew me so well.

"Do you plan to obey her wishes or proceed with your inquiries?"

An honest question which deserved an honest answer. "I will bring it up for discussion with the committee, but, yes,

I'd like to continue."

"They'll go along with your suggestion. The gentlemen, especially, won't want to give up."

I hitched up my chin. "The ladies as well, Mother! We've sworn an oath."

"Yes, I know." A hint of merriment crossed her lips.

Had she learned about our Three Musketeers vow? Yes, more than likely. Probably from Cummings, her maid. The woman had the ears of a bat and the nose of a busybody. What she couldn't scent out was not worth knowing.

Still smiling, she said, "It's a good thing you enjoy the support of your friends, Kitty." But then she suddenly grew serious. "But have you thought about the ramifications?"

"Such as?"

"The Home Secretary was not pleased with your investigation. Now that the queen has withdrawn her support, they may take action."

"As you've often told me, dear Mother, 'Don't borrow trouble before it arrives.'"

Unfortunately, Mother was right. Trouble arrived the next day.

* * *

FOR THE FIRST TIME in a long while, both Lady Emma and I were present at the detective agency. We'd decided we would once more function five days a week. But there was much to do before we could do so. For one, the place needed to be cleaned from top to bottom. Happily, we could depend on our charwoman for that. For another, we would need new business. The plan was to post new adverts in the papers announcing our full return. I'd already drafted them. All I needed to do was send them to the papers.

Third, we wanted to apply modern marketing techniques

to our business. Adverts were fine, but by themselves not enough. Along that vein, Lady Emma had written an article based on her investigation into the alleged theft of a brooch. That matter turned out to be a miscommunication between the lady and her companion. She'd sent the brooch to a jeweler to be cleaned shortly before leaving town to attend to a sick relative. Until her return, however, every servant had suffered under a cloud of suspicion. They'd been so fearful of losing their positions, several had succumbed to tears during their interviews.

Lady Emma had been so moved by them, she'd written "*The Servant's Plight.*" Without naming names, she'd detailed the vicarious position of servants when a wrong supposedly committed by one person impugned the entire staff. She wanted to submit it to one of the newspapers for publication, as she thought it would bring great publicity to the agency.

I talked her out of it, of course, since just the opposite was true. Once a newspaper published that article, we would be seen as tittle-tattles. However, I did encourage her to offer it to a woman's journal using a pseudonym. She'd need to change some of the details, however, so it wouldn't be associated with us. But it was very much a story that needed to be told.

The matter I'd taken on regarding the man of business stealing from a widow, Ned had handled. When he'd proven it as true, I'd presented the proof to the widow who'd insisted on talking to the man of business himself. With me alongside her for moral support, she had done just that, getting a great deal of satisfaction upon seeing the dastard's guilty expression when she fired him. She'd been so grateful to Ned that she'd accepted his recommendation for a new man of business and placed her accounts under the management of Worthington & Son.

Having settled all open matters, we had no open current

investigations. So, Lady Emma and I were looking forward to our grand reopening plans. We'd just gotten around to discussing them when a knock sounded on the door. Looking at her, I exclaimed, "A client, by Jove!" and raced to open the door. Unfortunately, I couldn't have been more wrong.

Rather than the new business we would happily welcome, the two gentlemen who stood outside were not likely to bring good tidings.

"Miss Worthington," the taller of the two said, doffing his hat. "I don't know if you remember us. I'm Joseph Wharton and this is James Stirling. We're from the Home Office. May we come in?" They were the same representatives who visited Worthington House.

"Of course." I threw the door open wide.

We'd been discussing our plans in my office, but there was no room there for four people. So, we settled into our reception area where there was more than sufficient space.

"I apologize we're unable to offer refreshments, gentlemen. We're not fully open for business just yet." I pointed to the chairs across from where Lady Emma was sitting. "Won't you take a seat?"

"We prefer to stand," Mister Wharton said.

Same thing he'd said before. I couldn't help but think it was a precursor to bad news. "What can we do for you then?"

Mister Wharton retrieved an envelope from inside his jacket and handed it to me. "We've been charged with delivering this to you."

"What is it?"

"Best you read it first," Mister Wharton said.

I tore open the envelope and retrieved the single sheet of paper within. Leaning closer to Lady Emma so she could see it, I read the document silently to myself. It didn't take long to get the gist of it. "You're shutting us down? Why?"

The gaze I shot at Mister Wharton would have withered a lesser man, but apparently, he was made of sterner stuff as he didn't react in any way. "It's a matter of national security, Miss Worthington, as the letter states."

It had. I just wanted him to explain it. "What is that supposed to mean?"

"Must have something to do with the negotiations, Kitty," Lady Emma said.

She was more than likely right, but I was not closing our doors without a fight. Too much depended on our staying open. "This order is an abomination. I will appeal it."

Mister Wharton remained cool and collected. "That is your privilege, of course. But in the meantime, you will cease your business. Failure to obey an order from the Home Secretary will open yourself to prosecution and possibly incarceration."

Lady Emma gasped.

I jutted out my chin. "Are you threatening us?"

"No, Miss Worthington, simply providing the facts. Do you have any questions about what the order requires you to do?"

"No. You've made it quite clear."

"Then we will let ourselves out."

They left silence behind. For a little while anyway. "They can't do this, can they?" I asked more to myself than Lady Emma.

"I think they can, Kitty. Mister Wharton was quite adamant about it."

"But that's not fair."

"Life rarely is." She came to her feet. "If you'll excuse me, I need a moment." After reaching her office, she softly closed the door behind her.

For a long while, I sat despondent. An appeal wouldn't go anywhere as national security trumped everything else. But surely our doors wouldn't need to remain closed forever. Once the negotiations were finished, we could ask the Home Office to allow us to reopen our business. In the meantime, we'd just have to muddle through as best we could.

CHAPTER THIRTY

GUY FAWKES DAY

*T*HE NEXT DAY, I suggested to Lady Emma that she remain home. I would take care of the paperwork the government had requested in which we'd assure them we had closed our doors. However, I was not going to allow her to sit home and mope. So, as soon as I arrived at the agency, I telephoned Marlowe and strongly suggested he invite her to lunch.

Having done that, I attacked the paperwork which was lengthy to say the least. It not only required my oath but a detailed account of our income and expenditures, as well as a summary of our most recent investigations. A tad intrusive, I'd thought. Last night, I'd telephoned Ned to get his take on it. He advised me to fully comply with it as it would show good faith on our part.

It took most of the day to gather the documentation. Once it was done, I arranged a messenger from a service we often used to deliver it to the Home Office. I barely had the opportunity to breathe a sigh of relief after he picked it up. Robert and I were planning on watching the Guy Fawkes celebration at Victoria Park tonight.

Guy Fawkes Day, observed in the United Kingdom on November 5, commemorates a failed assassination attempt from roughly three hundred years before. The titular gentleman, along with a group of radical English Catholics, plotted to assassinate King James I by blowing up the House of Lords. Of course, such a thing could not be kept secret. Somebody had indeed informed on them. Before the deed could be accomplished, they were promptly rounded up, tried for treason, and executed. Britons, who never allowed a good excuse for a party to pass them by, soon started celebrating the survival of their king by burning effigies, lighting bonfires, and setting off fireworks. All in the name of good fun, of course.

Robert and I had decided on seven as the time he would pick me up. That would give us time to wander through the food stalls at the park before the great bonfire was set ablaze. It was already past five which meant I would barely have enough time for a bath once I arrived home. I would need to get my skates on.

After grabbing my wool coat and settling my cloche at a rakish angle—a lady must always look her best— I wrapped my scarf snugly around my throat and locked the agency door behind me. As I rushed up the pavement toward my motorcar parked half a street away, I ran into two boys, no older than ten, pushing a cart with an effigy of Guy Fawkes. "Taking him to a bonfire?" I asked.

"Yes, Miss. A penny for the guy?" The smaller one asked, flashing a gap-toothed smile.

"Of course." I rummaged around for the coin purse inside my handbag. But it was beginning to grow dark, so I had a hard time finding it. That's when I heard it. The explosion, followed by a blast of air so strong it knocked all three of us down flat. Things were flying at us, careening down the street. From somewhere seemingly far away, people were screaming. I couldn't breathe, much less think. When an object flew by too close for comfort, I covered my head. That's when I caught the panic on the boys' faces. When one started to rise, I yelled, "Stay down," as I rolled over their bodies to keep them safe. But then something hit me, and I knew no more.

* * *

I BLINKED. Slowly. It hurt to do more than that.

"She's awake!" Somebody said. Mother.

I blinked again. Forced my eyes to stay open. I felt muzzle headed, as if there was cotton inside my head. I raised an arm, my right one, I thought.

"Don't move." Mother again. Signs of tears streaked her face.

"Am I dying?" I whispered. I would hate for that to happen.

"No, dear. But you do have a nasty bump on your head."

"Oh."

She made room for Father. "How are you, my darling girl?" There was moisture in his eyes, as well.

"Muzzle . . . headed."

"Stands to reason."

"Robert?"

"Right here," his deep voice answered as he took Father's place.

"What—what happened?"

"Somebody bombed your motorcar."

"No."

"Afraid so."

"The boys. With the Guy. Are they hurt?"

"Just scrapes and bruises. You took the brunt of the hit. You saved them from something worse."

"Good." I was fading. I could tell. "How long?"

Somehow, he understood. "You've been unconscious for a day."

"Robert."

"Yes, my dearest love."

"I know who killed the prince."

CHAPTER THIRTY-ONE

KITTY COMES HOME

*A*FTER TWO MORE DAYS IN HOSPITAL, I was finally released. Honestly, I didn't know what the fuss was about. Yes, something had hit me on the back of the head. But it'd barely registered as an injury. They only had to shave fifty millimeters or so to clean the wound. It was small enough I could easily arrange my coiffure to hide the bare spot. Once they removed the bandage, that is.

I'd been discharged with a list a mile long of what I could do or couldn't do. Basically, it amounted to only one thing—lying in bed and resting. After an entire day of doing that at home, I was going barmy. So, I decided to take matters into my own hands. With the help of Betsy, I'd bathed and dressed and then, by myself, carefully negotiated my path down the stairs. I was so focused on putting one step in front of the other, I failed to notice Mother standing at the bottom, frowning at me.

"What are you doing up? You're supposed to be resting."

"I've been resting for four days."

"One of which you were unconscious."

"I'm fine, Mother."

A hitched brow "Are you? Then why are you clutching that post for dear life?"

"I was exercising caution, that's all. But I'm perfectly able to stand without help. See." To prove my point, I released my grip on the post and stood straight with barely a wobble.

"Ummm." Mother did not seem to agree. "Why don't you keep me company in my private parlor? I have some correspondence to attend to."

"Fine. But only for a little while. I need to go out."

She did not respond until she'd tucked me into a sofa with my feet up and my back propped with a cushion. "You are in no shape to go gallivanting around London, especially with this bomber on the loose. He failed to kill you. He'll try again."

"He only wanted to scare me. If he wanted to kill me, he would have done so."

She pinned me with a hard stare. "Is that statement supposed to make me feel better?"

I should have remained mum. Maybe I was a bit more addled than I thought.

Turning her back on me, she set about rummaging through her pile of correspondence. "How do you intend to move about London? Your motorcar was destroyed."

I spared a condolent thought for my Tourer. I'd loved that motorcar. But certainly, there were other ways to move about. "Neville?" I suggested hopefully.

"Your father forbade him from driving you anywhere."

Figured. "I'll take a taxicab then."

She turned to gaze at me. "You barely made it down the stairs. How do you figure you'll walk to the end of the driveway to hail one?"

"One of the footmen could fetch one?" After all, they did that all the time.

"Think again."

"Fine, I'll rest. But only for one more day."

"Three more. Doctor Crawley's orders."

"What does he know?" A stupid question for Doctor Crawley was the finest of physicians.

Something which, of course, Mother pointed out. "He was a military doctor, Kitty, during the Great War. He's seen these types of injuries before. You may suffer from dizziness, blurred vision, ringing of the ears, a whole myriad of things."

It would be difficult to rest for three more days, for there was so much to do with the investigation. At least I could take solace that the gentlemen on the team hadn't given up on finding the colonel's murderer and were still following leads. Maybe they would discover something that would lead us to a solution. In the meantime, I could discuss the case with the ladies, who'd been kept home, and Robert, of course.

"Is Robert planning to call on me?" The day I was injured he spent every minute by my side. Not that I was aware as I was unconscious. The next two days he'd stopped by the hospital in the morning to check on my progress and returned in the evening to spend it with me. So I didn't expect him to wait too long before he visited me again.

"He is, but not until this evening. He apologized he can't come sooner, but he's investigating the bombing. Along with the murder, of course." She finished addressing an envelope and turned to me. "Would you like something to eat? You missed breakfast."

My stomach grumbled at the mention of food. A good sign, I thought. "Yes, please. Some scrambled eggs, bacon, toast with butter and orange marmalade. Some coffee will go down a treat."

She retrieved a piece of paper from her desk and read from it. "The eggs and toast are fine. But not the bacon or coffee. You may have tea."

"All right." At least it wouldn't be the bland, tasteless meals I'd been offered at the hospital.

After thoroughly enjoying my breakfast, I spent the rest of the morning in her parlor. When she left to attend to some household matter, Ladies Lily and Emma took over as the 'keep Kitty entertained' brigade. Lady Melissande was missing so I enquired after her.

They exchanged amused glances.

"What?" I asked.

"Mellie is in the library enjoying an audience with the Duke of Andover."

"By themselves?"

Lady Lily giggled. "Hollingsworth is playing chaperone."

"Poor Lady Melissande," I said.

"She doesn't mind. It will prove the duke's mettle if he can put up with Hollingsworth's frowns."

"She's right about that. So, is it really serious?"

"Seems to be," Lady Emma said. "Although I don't know how such a romance can proceed. The royal family is due to return to Andover within the week."

For the rest of the time, Lily and Emma talked about only inconsequential things, as they'd been given strict instructions not to discuss the case. Apparently, my mind was not to be strained. If they kept up the mindless conversation, however, it was bound to wither away. After lunch, I was allowed to take a walk in our gardens with Lady Emma by my side. But the weather was too brisk to stay out long, so I returned to my room to review the case notes.

The next day passed much the same way. Bored to flinders, I requested an audience with Father which thankfully he granted that afternoon. After arguing I was both mentally and physically fit, and proving it by doing sums in my head, and standing on one foot, he allowed me to continue the investigation as long as I took precautions.

When it was time for supper, I dressed in one of my favorite frocks, a midnight blue gown adorned with a sash below the waist from which a pleated skirt flowed. Since my face was a bit pale, I rouged my cheeks and lips to lend them some color. I'd just draped a silver shawl around my shoulders when a knock sounded on the door.

I opened it to find all three ladies—Lily, Emma, and Melissande—on the other side. All of whom were wearing identical sheepish expressions.

"Do I really need all three of you to escort me down?"

Lady Lily laughed that tinkling laugh of hers. "We couldn't decide which one should have the honors, so we opted to do it en masse."

"Very well." Melissande led the parade down the stairs, while Lily and Emma curled their arms around mine to make sure I didn't fall. I was beyond frustrated about being cosseted about, but I didn't complain. Their intentions came from a good place. We'd almost reached the bottom when I discovered Robert waiting for me. Breaking rank, I ran down the rest of the steps and threw myself at him. He caught me, as I knew he would.

"You shouldn't have done that," he said his arms tight around me.

I grinned. "I've never been very good with shouldn'ts."

"Yes. I know." Seeing as we had an audience, he limited himself to a quick peck on my lips. "Should we proceed to the drawing room?" With a glance, he included the three ladies, all of whom were grinning like loons. Honestly, they'd all gone mad.

"Lead on, Macduff," I said, curling my hand around his elbow.

Although cocktails were served prior to supper, I was not allowed any. Doctor's orders, Mother explained. Supper was a bland affair. A plain potato and chicken breast, with no accompanying sauces, water to drink, and custard for dessert. Everyone else got to enjoy coq au vin, potatoes Dauphinoise, chardonnay, and trifle. I sighed. Life was very hard.

After supper, I was allowed to go for a drive with Robert, so we fetched our coats, scarves, gloves, and a motoring robe for me, before heading out in his Rolls. To my surprise, he took me to his Eaton Square townhouse which I'd never been to before.

"I obtained permission from your father to bring you here."

"You don't see me complaining." I'd been perishing to see his home.

"I've arranged for champagne. Your doctor said a small flute of the bubbly wouldn't hurt."

I laid a theatrical hand on my chest. "Be still my heart."

As soon as we stepped inside, we were greeted by an older gentleman, dressed in immaculate butler's livery.

"Catherine, this is Mister Grant, a grand fellow, who keeps this house running tip-top."

"A pleasure to make your acquaintance, Miss Worthington." Mr. Grant's bow was exquisite. Seemingly, he'd been trained in the best of butlering schools.

"The pleasure is all mine, Mister Grant," I returned with a smile.

After we handed off our outer garments, Robert led me to the library where a fire had been lit. It was warm and cozy; its walls lined with books. I'd barely had a glance around when Mr. Grant entered carrying a platter of strawberries dipped in chocolate. Another manservant followed with an ice bucket into which a bottle of champagne had been tucked.

Once the door closed behind them, I curled my arms around Robert's neck. "Champagne and strawberries, Inspector? Are you trying to seduce me?"

He shook his head at my antics. "I thought you would enjoy a respite from all the bland food and drink. Your doctor approved the menu."

"Good old Doctor Crawley." I helped myself to a strawberry, bit into it. Predictably, juice ran down my chin. "Oops."

"Here." He handed me a serviette.

"I have a better idea."

He quirked a brow.

"Why don't you lick it off me?"

He tilted his head. "Miss Worthington, are you trying to seduce me?"

"Yes." I flashed him a saucy grin. "Am I succeeding?"

Rather than take me up on my invitation, he used the serviette to clean my chin.

Pouting, I dropped into the leather settee. "You're as dull as dishwater."

Not bothering to respond, he simply handed me a champagne flute. After joining me on the seat, he offered a toast. "To your quick return to health."

I scrunched my mouth. "I am fine, Robert."

"It will take weeks for you to feel like your former self." When I started to object, he said, "I've seen these injuries on the battlefield, Catherine."

He rarely mentioned his days as a soldier, so I went whole weeks without remembering he fought in the Great War. "I'm sorry. I should take your words more seriously. But honestly, I feel fine."

"You might think you are, but, trust me, you're not. Dizziness, blurred vision, headaches. Those symptoms and more are likely to come and go. They will affect your daily life. You'll need to curtail your activities until you're well and truly healed."

"Is that why you brought me here? To caution me against overexerting myself?" If it was, I'd be rather disappointed, for I expected more from him.

"That's part of it, yes."

"What's the other part?" I asked with a lilt to my voice.

"To discuss the investigation."

That perked up my spirits. "Well, I'm totally on board with that." Tucking my feet under me on the settee, I turned toward him.

"Catherine, in the hospital, you mentioned you knew who the murderer was."

That was a surprise. "Really?"

He nodded.

"How very odd. I have no idea who killed the colonel. I'm sorry I said such a thing."

"No need to apologize. You were not in your right mind at the time. It could have simply been a wish you had."

"More than likely that was foremost in my thoughts." I sipped some champagne. "What about the bombing? Have you made some headway?"

"Yes. The explosives were grenades, German made."

"German? How could you tell?"

"They have long wooden handles, pull cord arming and cylindrical warheads. Enough detritus remained they could be identified."

"Where would someone obtain such a thing?"

"An illegal shipment would be my guess. MI5, a branch of the Home Office, investigates such things. I consulted with them. They took notes, thanked me, and sent me on my way."

"They didn't tell you anything?"

"No. I didn't expect them to. That's not how they operate."

"So, you're on your own?"

"Not quite." He pinched my chin, a loving gesture of his. "I do have Scotland Yard behind me. We've deemed your car bombing and the colonel's murder are connected, so I've been assigned additional staff to investigate both."

"Well, there's no better inspector to head the effort. I trust you completely. You'll get your man." Smiling, I curled my arms around his neck. "I certainly have mine."

He didn't join in on my mirth. "I worry about you, Catherine. You will take care?"

"I convinced Father to allow me to continue the investigation. Mister Clapham will accompany me wherever I go. Neville will drive us."

He let out a heavy sigh. "I suppose that's the best I can hope for."

"It will be fine, Robert, you'll see."

CHAPTER THIRTY-TWO

A REVIEW OF THE CASE

$\mathscr{B}$ETWEEN MY HOSPITAL STAY AND RECUPERATION, I'd been out of the know for days. Now that Father had allowed me to continue the investigation, I asked the ladies—Emma, Lily, Melissande—to gather in the library. They could fill me in not only on what they had heard but what Marlowe, Hollingsworth, and Ned had discovered. As far as Mister Clapham was concerned, I'd scheduled another meeting with him this afternoon.

"So, what happened while I was out of commission?"

"Well, the negotiations are done," Lady Emma explained. "The prince is scheduled to sign the agreement tomorrow. The royal family is making plans to leave two days after that. Our king and queen offered to hold a farewell ceremony for them, but the Queen and Prince of Andover turned down the proposal. Given the colonel's horrific death, they didn't feel it would be appropriate. They're planning to have a state funeral for the colonel once they're back home."

"Did the kidnapping story hold?" I asked.

"Yes, the prince has been very forthcoming about his ordeal and the reason behind the murderous and kidnapping schemes," Lady Lily explained. "The newspapers, of course, are in alt. They don't often have access to individuals who suffered grievous wrongs. They printed every word the prince spoke verbatim. The telling was so convincing, the public believes he was the victim of a murderous plot."

"How did the papers explain the death of the colonel and the kidnapping of the prince?"

"Apparently, word spread about the argument between the prince and the colonel," Lady Melissande responded. "Since the colonel would no longer be guarding the prince, the assailants thought it would be the best time to kill him. Apparently, they'd been planning the prince's murder for some time and were only waiting for the right place and time."

"Why did they wish to murder him?"

"To stop the negotiations from taking place," Lady Emma answered. "Supposedly, some enemies of the state do not want England to have the antimony. So by killing the prince, the negotiations would stop."

"But they killed the colonel, not the prince," I pointed out.

"Apparently, the kidnappers only realized they had changed places when they spotted the prince climbing into a separate car," Lady Emma continued. "By then, the plan was in motion and couldn't be stopped."

"And so the poor colonel ended up dead while the prince was kidnapped," Lady Lily said. "Not that the colonel would have survived. They were planning to kill him as well."

"But then they decided to exchange the prince for money?" I asked. "That doesn't make sense."

"According to the prince, there was a change of leadership among those who kidnapped him," Lady Emma said. "Some were purists who wanted to stop the negotiations from taking place. They were the ones planning on murder. Others, however, were interested in money. Guess who won that argument?"

"The ones who wanted money," I said.

"Exactly. So they wrote the ransom note, arranged to pick up the funds, and return the prince," Lady Emma said. "As we know, it didn't quite happen that way. The kidnapper responsible for retrieving the satchel was killed."

"What happened to the others? I imagine there was more than one."

"Scotland Yard is searching for them, but so far, no joy," Lady Lily said.

"Maybe Mister Clapham learned more from his visits to Scotland Yard," I said.

"One can only hope," Lady Lily said.

That afternoon, I met with Mister Clapham who indeed shed more light on the case.

"The murder victim has been officially identified as Colonel Bouchard."

"In a strange way, that's good to know." The poor colonel would be buried in pieces. I sincerely hoped he hadn't suffered.

"The Andoverian royal family has requested his remains, all of them. His coffin will accompany them to Andover where plans are already under way to provide him with a hero's funeral."

"Have they made progress on the murder or kidnapping investigation?"

"They've been cautioned against speaking about the matters, so, I couldn't discover much."

"That's disappointing." I'd been hoping for more.

"Except for one thing."

"Well, don't keep me in tenterhooks, Mister Clapham. I'm dying to know."

"MI-5 has taken over both the murder and the kidnapping investigations. Apparently, they're deemed a matter of national security."

"All they have to do is wave those magic words and everyone kowtows to them." I couldn't help the tone of resentment in my voice.

He grew serious. "We suffered a war, Miss Worthington. A great many soldiers died. If these investigations are threatening our hard-won peace, I welcome them handling the matters."

I breathed a heavy sigh. "You're right, of course. I'm just afraid we'll never learn the outcome of the cases."

"More than likely. They're a closed-mouth bunch."

After I bid goodbye to Mister Clapham, I fetched my spiral notebooks and retired to my room for I had much to think about. Once I filled in the details about the kidnapping, I spent an hour studying the information we'd gathered about the murder, the royal family, the Tower of London, the royal family, the colonel, the kidnapping, the royal family. I kept returning to them for good reason. One member of that illustrious group had planned the colonel's murder, of that I was certain, but who?

Supper came and went. Everyone acted normal, but underneath the polite discourse, there was a decided unrest. And I knew why. We'd worked too hard not to know. Somehow, I would figure it out. And once I did, I would do something about it.

CHAPTER THIRTY-THREE

DISCUSSION WITH ROBERT

*T*HE FOLLOWING MORNING, I arranged to meet Robert at Scotland Yard. "Thank you for seeing me. I know how busy you must be."

"Actually, I'm not." For once, he seemed disgruntled. A rare occurrence for him.

"Oh?" I didn't want to reveal what I already knew. That he'd been taken off the murder investigation. Mainly because I wanted to hear it from him.

"I've been stopped from further investigating the murder. Nor can my counterpart look into the kidnapping."

I adopted a shocked expression. "Why?"

"They've been deemed matters of national security. As such, MI5 is best equipped to handle them." He may have been saying the right words, but he didn't appear happy about the decision that had been made.

"I'm so sorry. You've worked so hard on it."

"Yes, well." He fiddled with a pen on his desk. "There's not much I can do."

"What about the bombing of my car?"

"Transferred to them as well. I did manage to discover some details before it was taken off my hands, though." His expression brightened somewhat.

I flashed a smile in return. "Pray tell."

"We know how the bombs got into the country. An illicit shipment of weapons was found in a warehouse near the London docks. They included, among other things, German-made grenades, similar to the ones used to torch your car. We've apprehended those involved."

"Were they involved in the bombing?"

"They claimed they were only importers and had no knowledge of what was in the containers."

"Do you believe them?"

"No. We were in the process of tracking down the group who'd purchased the weapons, probably the anarchists who kidnapped the prince."

"And then you were stopped."

"Yes."

"Awfully convenient, don't you think?"

He nodded. "It was a well-planned operation from beginning to end."

Might as well spell it out clearly. "You are talking about the murder, the kidnapping, and the bombing. Are you not?"

A light of admiration shown in his eyes. "You figured it out then."

"Yes. Finally. And it only took a knock on the head to make everything clear."

"So, you did know."

"I did, but I was muzzle-headed at the time. I thought it was my imagination that dreamt up the scenario. Yesterday, I talked to the ladies and Mister Clapham, and then I sat in my room and wrote it all out. There were so many pieces, it took me until late into the night before the solution surfaced. Or rather resurfaced. It was only a matter of setting everything aside and looking at the one bare fact."

"That Colonel Bouchard was murdered."

"Yes. That was the key to everything. What will you do?"

"Nothing much I can do."

"Because England wants the antimony mineral."

"Yes, and nothing can interfere with that."

"Nothing to stop us from sharing our conclusions, though. We wouldn't be investigating, after all."

He glanced up. "Share with who?"

"The member of the royal family who had nothing to do with the murder, of course," I opined brightly.

"Do you think that person will listen?"

"I do."

He pondered my suggestion for a minute or so before he focused an appreciative gaze on me. "Yes. I believe that's the right course."

"Shall I arrange it then. Say tomorrow afternoon at two?"

"That should work." He came to his feet and approached me, tilted my face up to him. "You will be careful in how you arrange things."

I shot him a devilish grin. "Aren't I always?"

An arched brow was all I received in response.

CHAPTER THIRTY-FOUR

KITTY ISSUES HER FINAL REPORT

"*T*HANK YOU FOR SEEING US, Your Highness."
I'd arranged an audience with the Queen of
Andover so I could provide her with the final report on the
investigation. She hadn't been keen on the idea, said there
was really no need. But after I explained it was something we
provided to all our clients, she eventually agreed.

Still, she didn't exactly welcome Robert and me with
open arms. "My time is not my own, Miss Worthington,
Inspector Crawford. As you can imagine, we're quite busy
with our departure preparations. I'm hoping you'll be brief."

"We won't keep you long."

But before I could act, a knock sounded on the door that led
to the corridor, shortly followed by the entrance of the Duke of
Andover dressed in stunning regimentals of red and gold.

"Paolo, what are you doing here?" The queen asked. "And
why are you wearing your uniform?"

"I have a duty to perform, and Miss Worthington felt it would be to my benefit to attend."

The queen scrunched her face. "Very well. Take a seat then."

"If you don't mind, Grandmother, I prefer to stand."

She hesitated before nodding her consent. "Suit yourself." She turned back to me. "Now, Miss Worthington, if you could get on with your business."

I retrieved the revised report from my satchel. Different from the one I'd written before, it contained the conclusions I'd drawn. Taking a deep breath, I started, "From the moment you asked me to conduct this investigation, I knew it would be a difficult one. In my earlier inquiries, I knew the suspects. But that was not the case this time."

"An investigator is rarely familiar with those suspected of a crime," the queen said.

"Yes. That was one of the reasons this matter appealed to me. Would our team be able to discover the murderer when we had no acquaintance with the parties involved? I now have that answer, Your Highness."

Her lip curled. "And what is that?"

"We were successful."

"You think so?"

"I know so."

"And who, pray tell, murdered Colonel Bouchard?"

"You did. You and the prince."

Her eyes practically bulged from her head. "That's outrageous. How dare you?"

"I dare because it's the truth."

"My son would never—I would never—do such a thing."

"I'm sure he didn't commit the murder himself. You hired someone for that. A loyal operative easily found among those you command. While the foul deed was committed, your son planned to travel to some secluded spot where he would await the appropriate time to return."

"He was kidnapped!"

"No, he wasn't, Your Highness," Robert said. "We dug into the past of the individuals who allegedly took your son. You had dealings with them in the past. When they stirred up trouble in Andover several years ago, you made a deal with their mercenary leader. You paid him to lose the fight. Interestingly enough, Colonel Bouchard was hurt at that time. Maybe that was your first attempt to end his life."

"How do you know this?" She didn't deny Robert's allegations.

"We have excellent sources throughout Europe."

"Sources?" She cackled. "Spies, you mean."

Robert remained mum. Even if the Official Secrets Act did not preclude him from sharing that information, it would be personally abhorrent to him.

"Why would I want Colonel Bouchard dead? I advised my son to hire him as his equerry."

"Your son's frequent absences required the colonel to spend a fair amount of time with the princess in the execution of official duties," I said. "They ended up falling in love."

"Even if that were true, it would not require the colonel's death. My son could have simply assigned him to other duties far away from the princess."

"Something changed. Something that forced you to act. But you couldn't commit such a heinous deed in Andover. The prince was too closely guarded, and the colonel was too well loved. So you crafted your evil scheme to be executed in England. Here, you believed, you could carry out your plan."

Her mouth twisted with arrogance. "If all you're saying were true, your system of justice can do nothing about it. Not only are we protected by diplomatic immunity, but if your country acted against us, we would nullify the agreement for the mining of our mineral."

"You're right, of course," Robert said. "The proof isn't there. It would be extremely difficult to obtain a conviction in court, even if such a thing could be carried out."

"So why come to me with these nonsensical conjectures?"

She hadn't called them lies. If she were innocent, she would have. Her reasoning was not hard to fathom. She wanted us to know she'd gotten away with murder.

"That's where I come in, Grandmother," the Duke of Andover said. "You see, they might not be able to prove it, nor would England charge you and Father with such a heinous crime. I, however, believe what they say."

Her lip curled. "And what will you do about it?"

"I will not be returning with you to Andover, and neither will Mother. We will set up our household here in London. I will only return when I inherit the crown."

She scoffed. "And how will you live?"

"As you know, I'm provided an allowance, which will increase when I marry. Mother has her own funds as well. Between our fortunes, we'll muddle through."

Ned had told me about the monthly allowances paid to the duke and his mother. They amounted to quite astronomical sums. To avoid any future shenanigans, the duke had already arranged for those funds to be placed under the management of Worthington & Son.

A nasty grimace rolled over the queen's face. "I can arrange otherwise."

"No, you can't. The allowances are set by law. The royal coffers are brimming over with gold, which is only bound to increase with the funds collected from the lease agreement Father just signed. As it stands right now, Mother gets ten percent while I get fifteen. When Grandfather passes away, which I hope won't be for a long time, I will become the prince and my allowance will increase to twenty-five, the same amount Father receives now."

"I can go on a spending spree and reduce the size of the royal coffers."

"The Minister of the Treasury is in charge of those expenditures. If you exceed a 'reasonable limit,' he will cut you off."

"You have him in your pocket, do you?"

"No, Grandmother. He's an honest sort, totally loyal to Andover. He will not allow you to dissipate those funds."

"How do you plan to become the Prince of Andover? You can only do so if you're engaged to marry a female descended from French nobility."

"I believe" —he cleared his throat— "I hope that will happen."

He was talking about Lady Melissande, of course. Her mother was descended from French nobility. Therefore, so was she.

"Found a fool to marry you, did you?" The queen asked.

"She's not a fool. She's a lady. It's my desire one day she'll accept me as her husband."

The queen's eyes narrowed. "Who is she?"

The duke's lip curled. "If you think I will share that information with you, then you are the fool."

The queen cackled. "Sooner or later, I'll find out."

The duke stepped forward to tower over her. "If you hurt so much as a hair on her head, Grandmother, I will reveal your deepest, darkest secret. Where will you be then? Out on the street, penniless, no longer a queen, that's where."

The queen's face paled. "You wouldn't, you couldn't. How could you even know?"

Resuming his stance by our sofa, the duke calmly said, "You've made many enemies through the years. After I turned twenty-one, they came to me with proof. Churches keep wonderful records of marriages, don't you know? The truth of the matter is that Etienne was the true heir to the throne. That's why you brought him to the palace when he was but a few years old. So you could keep your eye on him and ensure he never found out."

"You will lose everything if you speak!"

"I will already have lost it all if the lady I love is gone."

The queen bared yellowed teeth. "You bastard!"

The duke allowed himself a smile. "That's one thing I'm not. Your son, on the other hand, very much is. You see at the time you married Grandfather, he was still married to Etienne's mother. So your marriage was not legal. Ergo, Father is a bastard, and he has no right to the throne."

"You wouldn't dare bring all that to light. Think, Paolo! The count would inherit the throne."

"*Au contraire*, Grandmother, I very much can, and I will if you hurt anyone I love. And don't think you can hurt me, either. If I perish or suffer a grievous injury, the proof of Etienne's mother's marriage to the King of Andover will make front page news."

"How will I explain your absence to the country?"

"Tell them Mother is ill, and I remained in England to support her. If you breathe one word against her or me, I will take my revenge. Do you understand?"

Defeated, she collapsed in her seat. "Yes. I do."

"Good." He turned to us. "Colonel Bouchard's execution was carried out because Mother wished to divorce Father so she could marry him. Such an event would require Andover to return the lands Switzerland had given to our country. Grandmother and Father couldn't allow that." A look of disgust rolled over his face as he veered back to the queen. "Isn't that true, Grandmother?"

The queen withered from the intense hatred in her grandson's eyes.

"Miss Worthington, Inspector Crawford, I'm sincerely sorry that justice can't be carried out. On behalf of my country, I beg your forgiveness." And then he snapped a salute, I'm not sure to whom, and exited the room.

The queen did not wait long to end our audience. Practically frothing at the mouth, she spit out. "Get out."

But I couldn't leave without learning one specific answer, "Why did you hire me to investigate the murder?"

She bared her teeth. "Your connection to Scotland Yard. If my son and I became suspects, I needed to know so I could act. Now, I've answered your question. Leave. I no longer wish to suffer your presence."

Without another word, Robert and I stood and, in unison, walked out.

"Well, that was . . ." I couldn't even think of the right word.

"Revealing."

"Yes, it very much was that." I threaded my hand through his as we entered the private elevator. With an operator present, I couldn't say much more than, "What shall we tell the team?"

Pulling me into him, he whispered into my ear, "Enough and no more."

CHAPTER THIRTY-FIVE

THE LADIES OF DISTINCTION DETECTIVE
AGENCY REOPENS ITS DOORS

*I*T TOOK A WEEK TO WORK OUT THE DETAILS, but we finally obtained permission for the agency to reopen its doors. The credit was equally shared between Robert, who worked assiduously through government channels, and the Count of Andover who worked his charm through the British press.

Almost overnight, the duke became their darling as he provided interview after interview. In every one of them, he praised our laurels. Miss Catherine Worthington and her fellow detective, Lady Emma Carlyle, had been instrumental in the investigation. It was their behind-the-scenes diligence that helped crack the case. Faced with the mounting pressure, both publicly and within, the Home Office relented and approved our request.

The resolution of the Tower of London murder, the prince's kidnapping, and his rescue drew the nobility back to

London like a moth to a flame. Everyone, and I mean everyone, wanted to gossip about the juicy details.

Lady Emma's and my names may have been the only ones mentioned in the papers, but society was fully cognizant of the names of the rest. As a result, Marlowe soon found himself lauded as a 'hail-fellow-well-met' at his club with plenty of pats on the back and hand pumps. Hollingsworth's sea crew threw him a party which culminated in, well, he wouldn't say, but I could well imagine. They were sea adventurers, after all.

"Unseemly," Mother said when she heard about it. But she secretly smiled. Hollingsworth had been a favorite of hers since they met.

Ladies Lily and Melissande, guests of honor at Lady Clinton's afternoon tea, were assailed with plenty of questions from those present. The busybodies ended up disappointed, however. As part of the deal with the government so we could reopen our doors, every member of the investigative team had been sworn to secrecy. Needless to say, that only added to the mystique surrounding the case.

As far as Lady Emma and myself were concerned, on the first day the agency officially reopened, we arrived to find several individuals waiting outside our office. We'd thought far enough ahead to bring Betsy along, but I soon realized we were not enough for the steady stream of traffic coming through the door. After I put out a call, Mother arrived with not only Ladies Lily and Melissande but enough biscuits, cake, and tea to feed an army.

It took us the better part of the day to talk to the prospective clients. Half of them turned out to be gossips, eager to get the details about our investigation. So, as politely as we could, we sent them on their way. Another fourth had matters that were better handled by the police and were referred to them. The last fourth, however, had real needs and concerns that we could investigate.

By the end of the day, we had eleven new clients, including a lady who suspected her husband was cheating on her. If that was the case, she would need grounds for a divorce.

"I don't know if we should take that one on, Kitty," Lady Emma said when we sat down for afternoon tea sans Mother, Lady Lily, and Melissande. They'd returned home when the crowd had died down.

"The lady has deep pockets, Lady Emma."

"You don't intend for us to follow him, do you?" Her voice held a note of horror.

"No. Mister Clapham can do it. He'll need to catch him in the act, though, so the lady may have proof."

"And how will he manage to obtain the evidence? A court of law won't simply take his word for it."

"Photographs, of course. I think I'll buy Mister Clapham one of those new pocket cameras. A Kodak, I believe. It tucks right into your vest. Isn't that clever?"

"Y-yes."

She didn't appear totally convinced, but she'd come around. Eventually.

"I don't believe I'm suggesting this, given our earlier lack of business," Lady Emma said. "Do you think we should hire additional staff? We now have sufficient funds."

The investigative committee had indeed given us the go-ahead to apply the surplus from the queen's payment to the agency. So, for the moment, we were flush.

"I think so. It'll have to wait until after the holiday season, though. No sense hiring someone before then." We planned to close the agency in mid-December so we could attend Margaret's wedding.

Just as we were getting ready to hang the 'Closed' sign on

the front door, Robert telephoned. Apparently, he and Marlowe had arranged a private celebration at the Savoy later that night. Duly informed, Lady Emma and I, along with Betsy, headed back home so we could bathe and dress.

Since Betsy had put in a full day's work, I could not in good conscience ask her to perform her maid duties. So, I asked Grace to step in for her and told Betsy to take off the rest of the day. Heaven knew she'd earned it.

"Is this it, Miss?" she asked, somewhat crestfallen. "Will I never again perform my maid duties?"

"Wouldn't you rather work as our receptionist? It'll be a step up in the world, and you'll receive an increase in pay."

"I love working in the agency, Miss. It's ever so challenging. The thing is I'd miss our . . ."

"Talks?"

"Yes, Miss."

"No sense in stopping those, is there? I very much like them myself." She didn't appear satisfied with that answer.

"I tell you what. Why don't we ease into it? Grace can take over your duties during the week, and you can handle them on Saturdays. Will that do?"

She flashed a brilliant smile. "Yes, Miss. But what about Sundays?"

"You'll take the day off. You can't work seven days a week."

"What will I do with myself?"

I squeezed her hand. "Whatever you want. Now go on and send Grace to me."

She practically skipped out, so happy was she. It would take a bit of time for her to make the transition from domestic worker to office staff. But she'd get there. Now I just had to figure out how Neville could set up his own automobile repair shop. I would discuss it with Ned. Surely, he'd have some ideas.

Promptly at eight, Lady Emma and I descended the stairs, bathed, powdered, and perfumed. She was wearing a gorgeous rose crepe frock with a rather modest neckline and chiffon sleeves. I'd opted for a slightly more risqué sequined black gown with short cap sleeves. A gold headband adorned with black feathers completed my ensemble.

We walked into the drawing room to find Marlowe and Robert waiting for us. Mother, who'd entertained them before our arrival, took one look at me and her lips pruned. No surprise why. The hem of my frock was mid-thigh, with only fringed beads reaching my knees. But she wouldn't criticize my choice of dress. Not in front of the gentlemen who were exuberant with their compliments to both Lady Emma and me.

Once we retrieved our wraps, we headed down the steps to Marlowe's motorcar. The Savoy was situated not far from Mayfair, so we made the hotel in no time. When we arrived, we were shown to a private room where a string quartet was playing classical music. Dinner was a sumptuous affair— roast beef for the meat course with a side of pan potatoes and apple and celery salad. The savories consisted of oysters au gratin and macaroni and cheese tartlets. For dessert we enjoyed a hazelnut cake with coffee icing. A red Bordeaux and a Cabernet Sauvignon made up our wine pairings, and we topped off the evening with champagne. Needless to say, after imbibing all these spirits, we were feeling more than a bit jolly. Which explained why Marlowe got it into his head to travel to Buckingham Palace so we could toast the king.

Robert tried his best to talk him out of it. Of course, Marlowe being Marlowe, that didn't work. Robert, however, was adamant we travel in a taxicab since neither he nor Marlowe was fit to drive. Once we arrived at the palace and descended from the taxicab, Marlowe poured champagne all around into the four flutes he'd borrowed from the hotel.

Somehow, he managed not to spill a drop. Raising his glass, he declared, "To his Majesty, King George's, good health."

We all dutifully echoed his sentiment. But once that was done, Robert suggested taking the same taxicab back home. Unfortunately, Marlowe wasn't finished with his celebration and insisted on going for a swim.

"A swim? At midnight?" Robert asked.

"Where on earth would you do that?" Lady Emma asked all agog.

Marlowe pointed into the distance. "St. James's Park. It has a lake, don't you know?"

"You can't. You shouldn't," I said. "It'd be an extremely foolhardy thing to do."

"Oh, wouldn't I?" In the next instant, he climbed back into the taxicab. We had no choice but to follow suit.

Once we arrived at the park, Marlowe proceeded to remove his clothes. His shoes, his jacket, his vest, his shirt. I must say the man displayed to advantage very well indeed.

When he went for his trousers, though, Robert put a stop to that, "That's quite enough, Marlowe. You can't strip in front of the ladies. It's just not done."

Swaying on his feet, Marlowe blinked at us. "Quite right. My apologies." He sketched quite an elegant bow, staggered to the Blue Bridge, and tossed himself off.

"Oh, for the love of . . ." Lady Emma exclaimed. "I hope he didn't kill himself."

My feelings exactly.

We waited for Marlowe to come up for air. When he didn't, Robert exclaimed, "Blast it. Now I'm going to have to save the fool." Tossing off his jacket and removing his shoes, he was just about to jump in when Marlowe surfaced close to us. "Tally ho!"

"Come, get out of there, Marlowe, before you catch your death from pneumonia." Lady Emma reached out, meaning to haul him out. But when she got close, he grabbed her hand and pulled her in.

"I'm going to kill you."

"Marry me first, and you can do anything you want with me." And then Marlowe proceeded to kiss her fully on the mouth.

The kiss went on ever so long. When she finally was able to breathe, Lady Emma spouted, "You're impossible." He very much was. Still, it sounded more like an endearment than anything else.

Once Robert managed to drag them both out, I wrapped my fur around Lady Emma while Robert tossed Marlowe's coat over him.

The dunk in the water seemed to have sobered Marlowe. "That water was damn bl-bloody fr-freezing."

"Can we go home now, please?" I pleaded. Lady Emma's lips were rapidly turning blue.

As we climbed back into the taxicab, the driver strongly objected to his seats getting soaked. "You'll ruin my cab, you will."

"We'll reimburse you for your troubles, good man," Robert said, before giving the driver directions to Worthington House.

"But my T-tourer is back at the Sa-savoy," Marlowe protested through chattering teeth.

"You can fetch it in the morning," Robert stated, "when you've sobered up."

Once we arrived at Worthington House, Robert left a snoring Marlowe in the taxicab under the gimlet eye of the driver who kept muttering "Bloody nobs," among other less flattering things.

When Carlton opened the door to let us in, his gaze grew wide. "Miss Worthington. Lady Emma."

"We had a mishap, Carlton. Please don't tell Mother."

"Of course, Miss."

I knew I could count on him. Unlike other members of our staff, who shall remain nameless, he didn't snitch.

"You'll be all right?" Robert asked, a look of concern on his face.

"As soon as I get Lady Emma dried off and in bed."

"See you tonight."

"What?"

"The celebration supper your mother is holding."

"Oh, yes. I forgot." When he started to turn away, I pulled him back and kissed him. "Thank you, Robert. I truly enjoyed our evening."

His lips crooked into a smile. "Even after the way it ended?"

I had to laugh. "Who knew Marlowe was that insane?"

Lady Emma sneezed, interrupting our goodbyes.

"I better get her settled."

"Yes. Goodnight." And this time he left for good.

I sighed. It was not the way I'd wished to end the evening. But I consoled myself with the thought we'd have another opportunity to properly celebrate tonight.

CHAPTER THIRTY-SIX

ALL'S WELL THAT ENDS WELL

*T*HAT NIGHT, we held a more sedate festivity. All the usual celebrants were there—Father and Mother, Ned and Lady Lily, Hollingsworth and Lady Melissande, Marlowe and Lady Emma, Mister Clapham, Robert and me. We'd debated inviting the Duke of Andover but thought it best to keep the guest list to those directly involved in the investigation. That way we could freely discuss the aftermath without having to watch our tongues. Besides, Mother was already planning to issue a dinner invitation to the duke and the princess in the next week or so.

The wine flowed freely during supper. The food was divine—turbot with Hollandaise sauce for the fish course, filet mignons Lili, served with asparagus cups entremets, for the entree, and a delicious raspberry meringue for dessert. At the end of the meal, rather than remain behind to enjoy their port and cigars, the gentlemen accompanied the ladies to the drawing room.

Along the way, I watched two guests peel off from the group. "Lady Emma and Marlowe. They've wandered off," I whispered to Robert.

"Did they? I didn't notice."

The innocent air about him did not fool me for a second. "You notice everything, Inspector."

"Not this time. I was too busy gazing at you."

"Ummm. Flattery will get you" —I sighed— "anything you desire."

From the corner of my eye, I noticed Ned and Lady Lily making their exit as well. I nodded toward their rapidly disappearing escape down the hall. "Unless I miss my guess, they're headed toward the music room."

It wasn't until we arrived at the drawing room, that Father noticed something amiss. "By Jove, where did everybody go?"

"We're here," I protested.

Mister Clapham chortled. Mother, however, did not find it a laughing matter. "We can't have Lady Lily and Lady Emma disappearing into the house in the company of gentlemen. Their reputations could be ruined."

"No one present is going to say a word about it, Mother," I said.

"You're right, but it's just not done," Mother had always been a stickler for propriety. "Why don't you and Robert search for them?"

We took our time wandering about the house to give the miscreants a while to enjoy themselves. But after ten minutes, I headed in a likely direction.

"Where are we going?" Robert asked.

"The library. Marlowe and Lady Emma are probably there. She loves the place."

We weren't quiet when we arrived, but Marlowe and Lady Emma were so enthralled with each other, they didn't hear us come in. As a result, we ended up being a witness to their love play.

"When did I give you permission, sir, to take such liberties with me?" Lady Emma declared, sounding not a bit offended.

"You didn't like it?" Marlowe asked, not the least regret in his voice.

"I'm not exactly sure." She sighed. "Do it again."

"We shouldn't be listening," Robert whispered to me.

"No, we should not." I didn't move, however, until he pulled me back toward the door. We announced our second arrival by stomping our feet and rattling the doorknob. By the time we made our entrance, Lady Emma and Marlowe were a distance apart. He, seated on a settee. She, thumbing through the library shelves.

"Oh, hello!" Lady Emma said retrieving an ancient looking tome. "Marlowe and I were discussing—"

Approaching, I took the book from her hand and read the title. *"A Vindication of the Rights of Woman: with Strictures on Political and Moral Subjects."* I gazed at Marlowe. "Planning on some light reading tonight, milord?"

He flashed a devilish grin. "Absolutely."

"Margaret would approve. I'll be sure to mention it to her so she can quiz you at a later date."

His complexion paled. "You wouldn't. She shouldn't."

"On the contrary, milord, I will and so will she."

He had the grace to appear chagrined.

"Now, I suggest you rejoin the company."

After the four of us exited the library, we took a different path from theirs, which, of course, Lady Emma noticed. "You're not coming?"

"Lady Lily and Ned are also missing. We've been charged with finding them."

Sharing a private smile with Marlowe, she linked her arm with his and headed off.

"What are the odds they'll make it back to the drawing room?" I asked.

"They'll get there . . . eventually."

As I expected, we found Sebastian's sister and my brother in the music room doing nothing more scandalous than holding hands. They simply wanted a private moment together. I should have known. Ned would never take advantage of Lady Lily.

We arrived at the drawing room to find Marlowe and Lady Emma comfortably settled on a blue settee, very close to each other.

Mother said nothing about the miscreants. She would never embarrass her guests. While the tea and coffee made rounds, the conversation easily flowed. The subject was, of course, the investigation.

"What I don't understand," Lady Melissande said, "is how the murderer made his escape."

"He jumped from one of the ramparts into the river," Lady Emma stated. "The Tower is located on the Thames."

"Somebody would have seen him," Ned said. "Guards are stationed along the ramparts."

"Could he have swum away?" Lady Lily asked.

"How?" I asked. "The place gets locked up at night."

"Through the Traitor's Gate?" she guessed.

"No one could escape that way," Hollingsworth said. "It's secured with an iron bar."

"He could have swum underneath it," she next suggested.

Was that even possible? "How deep into the water does the Traitor's Gate go?" I asked.

"Far enough," Robert answered.

"I think it was simpler than that," Hollingsworth said. "I

think he simply hid until it was safe and then made his way out."

"But they searched the place," Lady Melissande rightfully pointed out.

"There are plenty of places you can hide in the Tower," Mother affirmed.

"I suppose we'll never know." I turned to Robert. "Do you have a theory?"

He cracked a smile. "I think he turned into a raven and flew away."

Ravens guarded the Tower of London.

"Oh, Robert, you are so droll," Mother said.

His joke held a secret, one he couldn't discuss. I was sure of it. But that was a puzzle to solve on another day. "With Margaret's wedding approaching and enough inquiries at the agency to keep us quite busy," I said, "let's hope another murder doesn't crop up."

Holding my hand to his lips, Robert kissed it. "Now that is something on which we can agree."

* * *

READY FOR SOME HOLIDAY CHEER, a wedding, and a murder? Then check out the adventures of Kitty, Inspector Crawford, family and friends in **A Murder of Christmas Past**, Book 5 in The Kitty Worthington Mysteries. Available from Amazon.

A Christmas wedding in an English castle. Tree trimming, carol singing, figgy pudding. What could be more wonderful than that? Until a dead body turns up and spoils all the fun.

England 1923. No sooner does Kitty Worthington arrive at Wynchcombe Castle for her sister's holiday nuptials than she makes a gruesome discovery—the remains of a woman who perished long ago. Her death was not natural; she suffered a violent end. And there's a mysterious connection to the Wynchcombe family that must be explained.

With the ceremony rapidly approaching, Kitty and her merry band of sleuths—comprised of her assistant, lords, ladies, Scotland Yard's finest detective, Inspector Crawford, and Sir Winston, the family's beloved basset hound—jump into the fray to solve the murder. For if they don't, her sister's wedding may not only be ruined but might not take place at all.

A Murder of Christmas Past, Book 5 in The Kitty Worthington Mysteries, is another frolicking, historical cozy mystery filled with wily suspects, a sly villain, and an intrepid heroine sure to win your heart. For lovers of Agatha Christie and Downton Abbey alike. https://readerlinks.com/ l/2724897

* * *

HAVE you read the first Kitty Worthington Mystery? **Murder on the Golden Arrow**, Book 1 in the Kitty Worthington Mysteries, is available on Amazon and Kindle Unlimited

WHAT'S **a bright young woman to do when her brother becomes the main suspect in a murder? Why, solve the case of course.**

England. 1923. After a year away at finishing school where she learned etiquette, deportment, and the difference between a salad fork and a fish one, Kitty Worthington is eager to return home. But minutes after she and her brother Ned board the Golden Arrow, the unthinkable happens. A woman with a mysterious connection to her brother is poisoned, and the murderer can only be someone aboard the train.

When Scotland Yard hones on Ned as the main suspect, Kitty sets out to investigate. Not an easy thing to do while juggling the demands of her debut season and a mother intent on finding a suitable, aristocratic husband for her.

With the aid of her maid, two noble beaus, and a flatulent

basset hound named Sir Winston, Kitty treads a fearless path through the glamorous world of high society and London's dark underbelly to find the murderer. For if she fails, the insufferable Inspector Crawford will most surely hang a noose around her brother's neck.

A frolicking historical cozy mystery filled with dodgy suspects, a dastardly villain, and an intrepid heroine sure to win your heart. Available on Amazon and Kindle Unlimited readerlinks.com/l/2101140

Made in United States
North Haven, CT
18 February 2023

32814081R00159